The Last Week of May

Roisin Meaney was born in Listowel, County Kerry and has lived in the US, Canada, Africa and Europe. She is the author of two previously published novels *The Daisy Picker* and *Putting Out The Stars* and a children's book *Don`t Even Think About It*. Roisin is currently based in Limerick where she also teaches part-time.

ROISIN MEANEY

The Last Week of May

HODDER
HEADLINE
IRELAND

Copyright © 2007 Roisin Meaney

First published in 2007 by Hodder Headline Ireland

The right of Roisin Meaney to be identified as the Author of the Work
has been asserted by her in accordance with the Copyright, Designs and
Patents Act 1988.

1

All rights reserved. No part of this publication may be reproduced,
stored in a retrieval system, or transmitted, in any form or by any means
without the prior written permission of the publisher, nor be otherwise
circulated in any form of binding or cover other than that in which it is
published and without a similar condition being imposed on the
subsequent purchaser.

All characters in this publication are fictitious and any resemblance to
real persons, living or dead, is purely coincidental.

A CIP catalogue record for this title is available from the British
Library.

ISBN 978 0340 93286 5

Typeset in Sabon MT by Hodder Headline Ireland
Printed and bound in Great Britain by Clays Ltd, St Ives plc

Hodder Headline Ireland's policy is to use papers that are natural, renew-
able and recyclable products and made from wood grown in sustainable
forests. The logging and manufacturing processes are expected to con-
form to the environmental regulations of the country of origin.

Hodder Headline Ireland
8 Castlecourt Centre
Castleknock
Dublin 15, Ireland

www.hhireland.ie

A division of Hachette Livre UK Ltd, 338 Euston Road,
London NW1 3BH

For Betty, my reading buddy

Acknowledgements

Thanks to Faith, my ever supportive agent. Thanks to my editor Ciara Doorley and all the nice people at Hodder Headline Ireland. Thanks to my family for their unwavering certainty that one day I'll be rich and famous. Thanks to the team at Annaghmakerrig for allowing me in, and feeding me so well. Thanks to you for buying this book. (You did buy it, didn't you? If you borrowed it, please give it back and get your own copy – I've a mortgage to pay.)

What This Is

This is a Monday-to-Sunday story, tucked between the second-last Monday and the last Sunday of an unremarkable Irish June, dotted with quick, sharp rain and washed with pale lemony sunlight, as June stories so often are.

Twenty or so people travel through this beginning-of-summer tale, although the baby hardly counts, and a few of the others drift around the edges of the days, wandering in too briefly to make much of a difference – except, perhaps, to poor Bernard. But that will come later, and maybe, after all, Bernard's story will end happily. Let's hope so.

At the centre of this tale sits thirty-three-year-old May O'Callaghan. Put-upon daughter of Philip, beloved niece of Hilda, best friend of Rebecca, neighbour of Bernard and Shaun, employer of Pam – don't worry, you'll be meeting them all very soon now – and object of desire, if her damaged heart only knew it, for Paddy. As she weaves her way through the lives of the people who share this week with her, she is unaware yet that between Monday and Sunday she will make three significant discoveries, and bring about one ending.

This, then, is the story of the last week of June, and the last week of May.

Monday

Rain at first in all areas, brightening slowly in the west and spreading eastward as the day progresses. Chances of more heavy showers overnight. Highs of 14 to 16 degrees.

May

A tractor, that's what it reminded her of. The same irritating, gravelly splutter, *ack-acking* its way roughly into her sleep. She opened an eye and saw 4:18 on the clock radio. Waste of time, putting a glass of water on his locker every night. He never touched it, preferred to cough her awake some time between midnight and daylight.

She'd learned to ignore it, to put up with being woken at least once every night. *It's like having a baby in the house.* The thought leapt out at her before she could smother it, and she felt the familiar lurch of sorrow before she pushed it away and began to think about the week ahead.

Gardening at Paul and Francesca's this morning, just two doors down, if the rain eased up – she could hear it pattering steadily on the roof. No mowing, that would have to wait for a drier day, but the poppies were finished, they needed to be cut away, and the big flower bed under the bay window could do with weeding, which May always enjoyed, even in the wet. She liked the smell of the damp earth, the lovely pungent robustness of it. And the weeds would come up easier from the softened soil. So satisfying, teasing them out.

A window-cleaning job across town this afternoon, up the road from Marjorie's house. She might drop by on her way home, take a chance that her old babysitter would be in from work. Marjorie always seemed so happy to have someone to talk to, and eager for any bit of news May brought. Probably because her teenage daughter provided precious little company – any time May met her, Jude was sullen and uncommunicative. Poor Marjorie.

Painting for Carmel Gannon tomorrow, and again on Friday – good to have a new customer. Nice of Pam, May's home help, to recommend May to her friend.

Lots of work to keep her going. Three years on, May was still amazed at the way things had worked out, once she'd made the decision to quit her job at Dr Taylor's. Not that she hadn't enjoyed it there, answering the phone and making appointments, and doing the post and filing, and generally making sure that things ran smoothly in the busy little surgery.

But it was at Dr Taylor's that she'd met Gerry; it was where it had all begun. And when it was over, after he'd taken everything they'd had together and smashed it to pieces and walked away, after May had picked herself up and somehow survived, she found she couldn't bear the thought of working there any more.

Her decision hadn't gone down too well. Dr Taylor didn't want her to leave, had done his best to persuade her to stay, but May was adamant, and in the end he'd had no choice but to let her go with an extra week's wages and a very nice set of Galway Crystal wine glasses that his wife had probably picked out.

Of course, May's father had had plenty to say. 'You're giving up a permanent job, just after buying a house? Are you out of your mind? How will you pay for it?'

And, as usual, Aideen was more understanding, but even she had trouble with her daughter's decision.

'What if you don't find another job for a while, May love? How will you make the repayments? We'll help you out, of course, but . . .'

'It's OK, Ma – honest.' May smiled. 'I've been living very cheaply for ages, I've got loads saved up.' No need to point out that the savings had been intended for the wedding and honeymoon. No need to bring all that up again. 'I'll be fine, really I will. And I'll get a job in no time, wait and see.'

And May knew well that Aideen saw right through her, saw exactly how terrified May was that it would all go horribly wrong, that she'd have to sell the house and look for someplace else to rent – or even move back home for a while, and put up with Philip's grumbling again. The thought often kept May awake, in her new bed in her newly painted house.

And then one day, while she was prowling through the jobs section in the *Kilpatrick Post*, after three letters of application she'd sent off for secretarial jobs had been ignored, she'd read *Cleaner wanted*, and further down, *Gardener required for light gardening*, and in the next column, *Housepainter needed*, and over the page, *Window cleaner wanted*.

And May had thought, *But I can do all those jobs*.

She cleaned her own house, didn't she? Windows and all. So she could clean anyone else's too. And gardening would certainly be no problem. Since she'd been old enough to grab on to Hilda's finger, May had toddled along beside her aunt as they explored her spacious back garden, as Hilda had pointed with her free hand and said, 'That's called sweet pea, Maisie. Smell it, it's nice, isn't it? And see all those little orange ones over there? They're nasturtiums. They're very easy to grow, and look how they can climb right over the wall. And see these big tall ones here? They're lupins. They're like Rapunzel's tower, aren't they?'

May had nodded, and put out a plump baby hand to pat the flowers, and Hilda hadn't told her not to touch them. And every time Aideen took May to visit Hilda, May would insist on a walk around the garden, until Hilda presented her, on her fifth birthday, with a packet of mixed flower seeds that they sowed together in a long dark blue planter.

It sat on the windowsill in May's bedroom until the little green shoots were strong enough to be planted out in the strip Philip had dug for them at the bottom of the mossy lawn behind the house. And when the flowers appeared, one by one, May dragged a kitchen chair over the bumpy grass and sat beside them and read to them from her English book, telling them about Ann and Ben and their dog Polly that was always getting into trouble. *No, Polly, no*, she'd read. *Bad dog, Polly*.

And every so often, she'd glance up at the flowers and marvel again at the magic that could take the little hard brown things – which looked just like the bits of dirt Mammy would sweep up and *whoosh* into the fire – and transform them into these brightly coloured, delicately scented beauties.

All her life May had adored gardening. She'd learned what she could from Hilda and then taught herself whatever else she needed as she went along. She went from flowers to shrubs, and for her tenth birthday she asked for two dwarf apple trees, because their garden wasn't big enough for the real things. She treated the lawn, got rid of the moss and coaxed it back to a healthy greenness, scattered it with camomile and stretched out on it face down whenever a sunny day came along, inhaling the sweet, herby smell.

And painting? May could paint. Hadn't she just painted her new house from top to bottom? Her bedroom in a rich cream, the cramped bathroom in the palest duck egg blue, the rest in lavenders and whites and soft yellows and shell pinks, all the colours she loved to see in a garden.

So May decided to answer all the ads for jobs she

thought she could do. She picked up her pen and wrote five separate replies, and then, just to be on the safe side, she wrote an ad of her own:

Gardening, house painting, window and house cleaning, any other odd jobs considered. Friendly and reliable service, reasonable rates.

And before she had time to wonder if she really wanted to be this kind of jack-of-all-trades, she was gardening for Paul and Francesca every Monday, and she'd lined up three houses to paint and two other gardens to overhaul.

Over the following few weeks, she got several enquiries from people who'd heard about her through friends. And then a woman phoned to ask her if she walked dogs, and a man wanted to know if she cleared rubbish from sheds, and another was looking for someone to come and do his ironing.

Within six weeks she was turning people down, or telling them that she was completely tied up, that she'd have to get back to them.

She was also earning more than she'd been getting at Dr Taylor's.

Her hours were longer, with the dog-walking in the evenings, and sometimes the jobs were tough — scrubbing years of neglect from a house, shifting the clutter from a dusty attic and hauling it down to a skip, sanding innumerable coats of paint from intricate wrought-iron gates — but May didn't regret her decision to leave Dr Taylor's for an instant.

She loved the freedom of being her own boss, of deciding which jobs to take on and which to let go. She enjoyed meeting new people, and working in a different place every day. And once it became clear to her that she wasn't going to starve, or have to sell the house, she learned to enjoy the uncertainty of not knowing what the next week was going to bring. She invested in a set of expensive paintbrushes, a folding ladder she could carry on the bike and a supply of window-cleaning solution.

She settled on a few regular customers – Paul and Francesca on Monday morning, and window cleaning across town in the afternoon. Wednesday mornings, after what almost amounted to a row, were spent in Rebecca's house.

'You don't need a cleaner – there's just you and Brian.' May knew exactly why her best friend was asking her to come and clean. 'I realise you're trying to help, but—'

Rebecca stood her ground. 'Help, my foot. My house is like a tip, as you well know. Have you ever seen me clean? And Brian, bless him, wouldn't know one end of a Hoover from the other. If you don't come, someone else will have to, or the dirt will take over.'

May folded her arms. 'How come you never talked about getting a cleaner before? How come you suddenly need one now, just when I'm looking for business?'

Rebecca sighed. 'Because in my job I'm suspicious of everyone, so I wouldn't dream of letting a stranger into my house, poking around in my drawers.

You, on the other hand, know all my dirty little secrets, so you're the perfect cleaner. Come on, three hours a week at whatever you charge – and I promise to sack you if you leave one bit of fluff behind.'

So eventually May agreed, and Wednesday mornings were spent in Rebecca's house, tidying up what May always suspected was the mess that Rebecca carefully created every Tuesday evening.

And on Thursday mornings, she went to Paddy O'Brien's. For the past few months, she'd been going to the home of a man she had yet to meet. A man who drank decaffeinated coffee and kept a bowl stocked with kiwi fruit and plums beside the stack of cookery books on his kitchen worktop, and who was some kind of carpenter, judging by the jumble of tools and stack of planks by the back door, and who used nice apple-scented handwash in his bathroom.

The first perfume May owned was a bottle she'd found sitting under the Christmas tree when she was eleven. It was called Orchard and it came in an apple-shaped glass bottle, and she pulled out the stopper and dabbed the bright green liquid on her wrist and sniffed. To this day, the scent of apples reminded her of Christmas.

Before long, between them, her regular jobs were paying most of the bills. And the rest of the time May slotted in the casual jobs, the one-offs that kept arriving. The phone calls that started, 'You don't know me, but you painted my friend's house a while ago . . . '

She smiled in the darkness. Not a bad old life, really. Then she turned over and tried to get back to sleep.

Paddy

Before he opened his eyes, while his thoughts were still scrambling into focus behind his closed lids, she tumbled into his head. Every morning she arrived, always with the same sweet, smiling mouth that he ached to taste. He wondered how she knew, how she could sense that first moment when he was drifting out of sleep, before he became aware of the solid *tek-tek* of his watch on the wobbly little table by the bed, the warm, cottony smell of the pillow against his cheek, the dampish creases in the sheet under his body.

And even as all these things started to take up their positions in his head, May began to fade away, her face disappearing bit by bit, Cheshire-cat-like – her blue-green eyes, gone, her butterscotch hair, vanished, her adorable laughing mouth, all gone – till he had nothing left but the blackness under his still-closed lids.

Did she ever think about him? Did she wonder, like he did, if they'd meet that day? Or did he never pass through her thoughts at all, in the way she so often passed through his?

They could meet any time, in a place the size of Kilpatrick. He'd often see her cycling past him on her blue bike, hair flying. Or crouched over a flowerbed, or walking behind a lawnmower – or, once, up on a ladder, stretching to reach the top corner of a window with her chamois.

Funnily enough, the only morning he knew they

wouldn't meet was the day she came here, to work in his own garden from nine till twelve. For the past eight months she'd been transforming the rectangle of wilderness behind the house into a real garden, with shrubs and flowerbeds and a little gravel path that curved from the patio down to a raised rockery in one corner.

She was gradually hiding the ugly block wall at the back of the garden behind climbers he couldn't name – he hadn't a clue about gardening – and something she'd planted near the back door smelled wonderful in the evenings. He gradually became aware of butterflies around a purple flowering shrub, and bees had started humming recently in the bush he thought might be lavender.

Most of the shrubs she'd planted were producing some sort of colour now – golden yellows and bright oranges, delicate pinks and deep scarlets. He'd taken to going out there in the evenings, just leaning against the back wall of the house and sniffing the scented air. He should get a few deck-chairs – or maybe he'd make a wooden garden seat.

He wondered what May thought of the bird table he'd put out on the lawn last week. He was happy with how it had turned out, glad now that he'd taken so much time over it. But he kept forgetting to put anything on it – he didn't imagine the birds would appreciate a nicely put together table without a crumb of food.

May never helped herself to anything from his fridge, never even made herself a cup of tea, despite the note he'd left for her on her first morning.

He reached out and tilted the face of his watch towards him. He never set an alarm, didn't own anything that was designed to jolt him out of sleep. Winter or summer, he woke a few minutes before or after half past five. Today it was after: twenty-five to six on a wet, grey June morning. Time to get up.

He pushed back the sheet and blankets and swung his legs out, put his feet down to touch the knobbly rug his sister had made eleven years ago as part of a craft project in her teacher-training college. It was amateurishly put together – handwork of any kind didn't come naturally to Iseult. The red and pink and purple stripes travelled uncertainly along its length – now cucumber fat, now pencil thin – and threads from one section meandered carelessly through other colours and trailed from the edges in a can't-be-bothered kind of a way. The scarlet fringes at each end were cut crookedly, like the messy scribbled fringe on a pre-schooler's self-portrait.

But Paddy liked it. He appreciated its charming awkwardness, didn't mind its imperfections. And Iseult, whom he loved, had made it. She'd sat in the tiny, damp apartment they'd shared then in Limerick, cursing as she struggled to pull the big blunt needle through the rough fabric and stopping every now and again to rub her face rapidly, 'Bloody stuff makes me itch like crazy.' And then she'd bend over the half-born rug again, spread in a careless splotch of colours across her lap.

Paddy yawned as he pulled the grey T-shirt over his head and dropped it on to the bed. He hooked his thumbs into the waistband of his shorts, shoved them down over his hips and let them drop to the floor. Then he padded to the bathroom, pulled the cord of the electric shower and switched on the water.

He stood under the warm flow, letting it drench and flatten his hair, feeling it course over his chest and stomach, run down his legs. As he reached for the shower gel, he thought he heard a muffled shout. He paused, tube in hand, and tilted his head out of the water.

More shouting, a single long scream, the screech of brakes and a *rat-tat-tat* explosion of what could only be machine-gun fire. Too dramatic to be coming from anywhere but Mr Kennedy's television on the other side of the wall.

Paddy squirted a glob of gel onto his palm and worked up a rich lather that he massaged into his neck and shoulders, under his arms, across his chest, down his stomach, between his thighs.

May O'Callaghan. The hot water flowed. The bathroom began to fill with a gentle, pine-scented steam.

Philip

He grasped the wooden handle and jerked it up and down again. The ridiculous little bell went *ting-teling-teling* in his hand. How could anyone hear that?

'May?'

Where was his breakfast? She shouldn't keep him waiting, not at his age. Not when he'd already been awake for what seemed like hours. 'May?'

He coughed irritably and pulled himself up in the bed with an effort. These pillows were too flat – how was he supposed to get comfortable with no support? He punched at them awkwardly with his elbow.

The door opened and May appeared with a tray. 'Good morning – did you sleep?'

Always the same question, always managing to make it sound as if she was interested in the answer. He grunted and looked pointedly at the tray.

'There you go.' She laid it on the duvet. 'Are your pillows all right?' She went to rearrange them, but he waved an impatient hand at her.

'They're fine.' A boiled egg again. He hoped it wasn't as hard as the last one. And the toast cut up into those silly little strips, as if he was a youngster. Still, he'd offer it up, say nothing.

She poured tea from the little pot. 'It's wet today.'

As if he couldn't hear the rain, as if he was deaf as well as old and useless. He lifted the knife and sliced the top off his egg. A thin yellow finger dribbled out – good. He looked at the tray, and then back up at May. 'Salt?' She'd forgotten again. Such a small thing to remember, and she kept forgetting it. With an effort he kept his face neutral, managed not to sigh.

'Sorry.'

He listened to her rapid footsteps on the stairs, remembered, with a pang, the breakfasts Aideen used to cook for him. Creamy porridge with a spoon of blackcurrant jam sitting on top. Two fat sausages on Sunday that he sliced lengthways and arranged with a dollop of tomato sauce on top of a thick slice of her homemade brown bread, still warm from the oven.

Or kippers the odd time, deliciously salty, with a couple of grilled tomato halves to keep them company on the plate.

Potato cakes when she had leftover spuds from the night before. Fried to a goldeny brown, knob of butter on top, shake of salt, dip of mustard. His mouth watered at the memory.

He looked down at the little white egg sitting primly in its china eggcup, and the sigh slid out of him loudly. Plenty loud enough for May, just walking back in, to hear.

May

She put the last of the breakfast things away, shook out the damp tea towel and hung it over the cooker rail. She glanced out the big window above the sink, scanning the garden as usual, but of course Lonesome George wouldn't be out in the rain. Was it brightening up? The sky was still pretty grey, but the rain seemed to be easing off a bit.

Didn't matter anyway, she had everything she needed for any kind of weather. She took her yellow oilskin from its hook on the back door and put it on top of the rucksack that held her green wellies and waterproof leggings, her gardening gloves, her hand spade and fork, her secateurs and her blue foam kneeling-pad.

She buttered two slices of bread and separated them with a slice of thick ham and a gloop of mayonnaise. Ridiculous not to come home for lunch, only two houses away, but one meal a day sitting across from his dour old face was more than enough. Much easier to eat a sandwich on her way across town.

Her eyelids felt gritty as they slid over her eyes. You'd think he'd ask her, once in a while, how she'd slept. The glass of water on his locker, still full this morning, as usual. Not caring about having her running up and down the stairs for his bloody salt, not caring that it was bad for his blood pressure. Served him right if—

No, she shouldn't think like that; Ma wouldn't approve. She felt the familiar dart of sorrow when she remembered her mother, buried eighteen months ago now. She lifted her hand and fingered the tiny opalescent shell that hung on its thin gold chain around her neck. Somehow, it always seemed to comfort her. Such a pretty thing, so delicate. She wished, for the umpteenth time, she knew who'd given it to her.

She heard the key turn in the front door. Pam, dead on time, as usual. 'Hi, I'm in here.'

Pam's head appeared around the kitchen door. 'Morning, May. Horrible weather.' She took off her bone-dry jacket and hung it on the back of a chair. 'Make sure you're well wrapped up.'

May smiled. 'Since we're not all as lucky as you with your chauffeur.' Every morning Pam's husband, Jack, dropped her at May's on his way to work.

'That's right.' Pam rummaged in her bag. 'I brought that salmon recipe I was telling you about – you can have a look at it when you get home, see what you think.'

'Great, thanks.' May was half reluctantly planning a birthday dinner on Sunday night for Philip. Not that he deserved, or probably wanted, any kind of celebration, but she couldn't let his eightieth go by unnoticed. A small dinner, just the family – and Rebecca, who usually invited herself along to these things – and May's aunt Hilda, if she was free. Hilda was one of the few people who had always got on well with her brother-in-law.

Pam would be there too, of course, because she was going to cook the dinner. May could do a lot of things, but cooking wasn't one of them.

She lifted her rucksack. 'Right, I'm off. Good luck with the grouch.'

Pam smiled. 'We'll be fine. Talk to you tomorrow.'

Bernard

He bent and dropped a kiss on Shaun's head – such silky hair – and ran the back of his hand briefly along the stubbly line of Shaun's jaw. 'Don't kill yourself today – easy on the word count now.'

'Ha ha.' Shaun added chopped banana to his bowl and reached for a satsuma. 'And don't you forget the Parmesan.' He pronounced it pahr-me-*zhahn*, which secretly amused Bernard.

As he walked down the garden path, Bernard spotted May coming out through the gate next door. 'Well, Miss O'Callaghan, what mischief are you up to today then?'

'Gardening this morning, cleaning windows this afternoon – nothing too mischievous.' May looked towards the sky. 'You know, I think the rain's easing off. How's Shaun keeping?'

'Same as ever. Talented, selfish and beautiful – and still in love with me, thank heavens. And Lonesome George says hello.'

May smiled. 'Does he?'

'Misses you like mad, of course.' Bernard checked his watch. 'Right, must fly – talk to you later. Drop around this evening for a glass of wine, if you're doing nothing – apart from walking your animals, of course. Half-eightish?'

'I might just do that, thanks, Bernard.' Another little break from Philip; she could use all the breaks she was offered. And her neighbours were good company, poking gentle fun at Philip's contrariness, teasing May about the good-looking postman she had such a crush on, who would be *so* perfect for her, according to Shaun.

She watched the white van as it drove away, and then she turned towards the next house.

Francesca

'Come on, sweetie, get your lunchbox. Can you reach?'

Paul smiled as Lucia stood on tiptoe to grab the yellow plastic box from the counter. 'Hey, you're getting tall.'

From behind her newspaper, Francesca thought, *Taking after her father.* She lowered the paper and said, 'Kiss.'

Lucia pressed a sticky mouth to her cheek, and Francesca hugged her raincoated shoulders. 'Have fun, baby. See you later. Keep your coat on till you get into school.'

'OK, *ciao*, Mamma.'

Paul bent and brushed Francesca's lips lightly with his. 'See you about six, OK?'

Francesca lifted the paper again. 'OK.' She heard their voices outside, heard the slam of two car doors. As soon as the engine started up, she dropped the paper and walked to the percolator and refilled her cup. Then she sat back at the table and took out her slim brown cigarettes, lit one and watched as the new au pair began to load the dishwasher.

'*Rinse* first, remember?'

Paul

He drove slowly out of the driveway, wipers flicking. As the car turned on to the road, he pointed. 'Look, sweetie, there's May. Give her a wave.'

Lucia lifted a hand, and May, just turning into the driveway, blew a kiss and hitched her rucksack a bit higher on her shoulders, catching the little clasp on the thin gold chain around her neck and causing it to come undone.

As Paul's car disappeared around the corner, the open necklace slithered slowly and silently over the folds of her loose grey sweatshirt, down past her faded and paint-spattered jeans, and landed, with a minuscule plop, in the shallow puddle that had formed in a dip in the path, just outside Paul and Francesca's house . . .

. . . And when Paul dropped Lucia into her Junior Infant classroom fifteen minutes later, he took her damp raincoat and travelled gingerly through the clatter of twenty-seven other four-year-olds and the scattering of their parents to hang it on the hook that was named after Lucia. Well aware that he was being followed. *Come to Daddy.*

As he looped the coat on the hook, Carmel said 'Good morning' in a bright, Junior Infant teacher voice.

He turned, smiling. 'Morning, Miss Gannon. How are you?' Out of the corner of his eye, he could see a few of the mothers grouped near the door, looking towards them. Wondering what he and the nice teacher were talking about. Or maybe wishing he was talking to them instead. He pulled the kinks out of the purple plastic sleeves of Lucia's coat.

'Never better.' Carmel lowered her voice, kept the same bright smile on her face. 'Can you make it?'

'Mm-hmm, Thursday's fine. Four o'clock OK?' A loud wail broke out above the general buzz. Carmel swung around quickly – 'Hey, what's going on there?' – and threaded her way through the muddle of little people in the direction of the wailing, leaving Paul to assume that four o'clock would be just fine.

He made a point of stumbling against the most attractive of the mothers on his way out, pushing against her breast with his arm for just an instant. Feeling the slight yielding as he pressed. 'I'm *terribly* sorry – *do* forgive me.'

He felt their eyes on him as he walked out.

May

She walked around to the back of the house and waved at the dark-haired girl working at the sink just inside the kitchen window – must be the new au pair. A second later the door opened and Francesca appeared, looking as elegant as ever in a richly coloured robe and deep scarlet slippers. Smoke curled upwards from the thin brown cigarette she held in her left hand. The scent of coffee wafted out. 'May, you're working today, in all the rain?'

May smiled. 'I'll do a bit of weeding and see how I go. I think it's easing off.' She felt so awkward next to Francesca's feminine stylishness. Yellow oilskins weren't exactly the height of glamour.

Francesca lifted her shoulders. 'You like some coffee before you begin?'

'No thanks.' Imagine her sitting next to Francesca, looking like some bulky yellow clown. 'I think I'll just make a start.'

. . . And half an hour later, as the rain finally stopped, she heard the latch of the gate behind her, lifted her face from the half-weeded flowerbed and turned around.

And there he was, walking up the garden path, a bundle of envelopes in his hand.

She smiled. 'Good morning.' Her heart thumping suddenly – how foolish, at thirty-three. Like some sixteen-year-old with a first crush. She hoped Shaun wasn't watching from an upstairs window next door; she'd hear all about it tonight if he was.

'Morning.' He smiled back at her, blushing slightly. 'Nice mucky work you have there.'

May thought, *I must look a fright.* 'I don't mind it.' Her hair sticking up all over the place probably, since she'd thrown back the hood.

'Good for you. Nothing like getting a bit mucky now and then.' He pushed the letters through the slot. 'You have this place looking well.'

She watched him walk away. Such pale blond hair, almost white, it was. And brown eyes, with dark eyebrows – it should have looked wrong, but it didn't.

Probably had a wife waiting for him at home, like most men her age.

You have this place looking well. She wondered what his garden looked like.

Pam

She added a knob of butter to the bowl of sliced, steaming carrots and watched as it slithered sideways, leaving a yellowy trail behind it. She put two floury potatoes onto the side plate, then went to the hall door and called, 'Mr O'Callaghan? Lunch is on the table.'

As she lifted the second lamb chop from the grill and added it to his plate, she heard Philip shuffle out slowly from the sitting room. She arranged a smile on her face as he reached the kitchen. 'There you are. It's turned out nice now.' She put the plate on the table and held out the chair for Philip.

He dropped his stick and fumbled for the back. Pam stood behind him as he inched his way down, but she didn't touch him. She waited a few seconds, until he'd scraped his chair nearer to the table, and then said, 'Everything alright now?'

He grunted, and she bent to pick up the stick and balance it against a nearby chair. She checked the table again swiftly: salt, gravy, butter, glass of water. 'I'll go and tidy upstairs so, if you've got everything.'

He speared one of the potatoes with his fork, but just as he began to peel it, it collapsed and splatted onto the side plate in a floury mass. '*Blast.*'

Pam turned to the saucepan – 'I have more here' – but he said, 'No, no, don't *fuss*, I don't need another one,' and began to poke out the steaming fragments and add them one by one to his plate. 'You shouldn't cook extra – that's just waste.' He spooned carrots onto his plate and lifted the gravy boat, not looking up at her.

'I thought May might like to fry up a few for her tea.' When he didn't respond, when he speared the corner of a chop and a few carrot discs and brought them to his mouth and began to chew noisily, Pam turned and walked through the hall and up the stairs.

God, he was so *cranky* all the time. How did May

put up with him? At least Pam got to go home at three o'clock, and a lot of the time she didn't have to deal with him – thankfully, he stayed well out of her way when she was cleaning and getting his lunch ready.

She opened his bedroom door and caught her breath when the stale air hit her. She left the door wide open and yanked up the window – just as well the rain had stopped. She threw back the duvet and top sheet and lifted out his hot water bottle, still warm from May's last fill-up. The bed smelled musty, and faintly of urine.

Breathing through her mouth, she pulled the bottom sheet straight and swiped away the little bits of grit that had lodged at the end of the bed. She plumped up the three pillows and pulled the top sheet and duvet back up. She shook out his pyjamas – why didn't he let her change them more often than once a week? – and folded them loosely before tucking them under the pillows. She tidied the top of the locker, ran her duster over the surfaces, took the glass of water and the hot water bottle to the bathroom and emptied them. Then she went to get the Hoover from the landing.

Watch it, now. She used her unfamiliar left hand to heft it awkwardly over to his room, cradling the handle in her right. It wasn't that it hurt, exactly; it was just a bit stiff. Tomorrow she wouldn't even notice it.

And it wasn't as if Jack had meant to hurt her, of course he hadn't. He just got a bit carried away, got the wrong end of the stick, that was all. Look how sorry he'd been after, when the bruises had come up so quickly. You wouldn't think just grabbing her like that could cause such bruises. He'd taken her arm so gently then, bent and kissed each round mark. So sweet, he could be really sweet sometimes.

He loved her a bit too much, that was all.

And thinking about it now, Pam could understand why he'd been so upset, could see how it must have appeared to him, a good-looking man driving his wife home from the shops, laughing and joking with her as he carried her bags right up to her front door. It wasn't even as if they were that heavy – she could easily have carried them herself.

Calling 'See you, Pam', for everyone to hear as he walked back down the path and drove off. That would be bound to upset any husband, wouldn't it?

Jack didn't listen when she said, 'But that's Shaun. He lives next door to May, he's gay.' He didn't listen to any of that, just gripped her arm so tightly, with that intense look on his face, and then she said quietly, 'Jack, please, you're hurting me.'

His grip didn't loosen. He searched her face. 'How well do you know him?'

She shook her head carefully. 'Hardly at all. I see him occasionally coming out of next door when I'm at May's, that's all.'

'So how do you know he's a poof?' His face was full of suspicion.

She looked blankly at him. 'What?' Her fingers were aching with the pressure. 'Please, Jack—'

'How come you know he's a *homo*' – his mouth

twisted as he said the word – 'if you only see him coming out of the house next door? He doesn't walk like a poof.'

Pam winced. 'Please, love . . . May must have mentioned it some time, I don't remember . . .' No way could she tell him about the chats over the fence with Shaun when she brought the rubbish out to the bin or the clothes to the line. No way would Jack like that.

'So you must have asked her. You liked the look of him and you asked her about him.' He shook her arm sharply and she bit her lip. 'Right?'

'Please, Jack, please . . . you're getting upset over nothing—'

'Nothing? My wife is joking and laughing with someone who looks like Brad Pitt, and that's nothing?'

If anyone else had compared Shaun to Brad Pitt, Pam would have laughed. 'Jack, Shaun is *gay*, I swear. He lives with his partner, Bernard. I met him in the supermarket and he offered me a lift because it looked like rain—'

Jack had glanced out the window 'Looks fine to me.' But at last he dropped her arm, and she pulled up her sleeve and saw the red marks his fingers had left, touched one gingerly and felt the tenderness there.

It had come to this, then, like she'd been afraid it would. Like she'd known it probably would, some time.

Jack watched her without changing his expression. 'I don't want you taking lifts from men, right?'

And Pam looked back at him and knew that there was only one answer he wanted, so she gave it to him. 'OK, I won't.'

No lifts from men. No low-cut tops or dresses. No nights out or visits to pubs with her girlfriends. No make-up unless she was out with him. The list was growing.

She walked away from him then, went through to the designer kitchen he'd bought her last summer. And by the time the ham and egg flan was nearly ready to be taken from the Stanley range, there was a row of greyish circles on her arm, and Jack had changed completely.

He came into the kitchen with a gin and tonic, which he handed to her with a tentative smile. 'I'm sorry, darling, I know I get carried away sometimes – I'm just so afraid I'll lose you.' He opened the big stainless-steel-fronted fridge, took out a can of Guinness and poured it into one of the crystal tumblers they'd picked up in the January sales.

He watched her over the top as he waited for the head to settle. 'You OK?'

When Pam didn't answer, he put his glass on the worktop and reached for her hand, saying 'Ssh' when she winced and tried to pull away. He inched up her sleeve gently, shaking his head when he saw the line of bruises. 'God, I'm so sorry.' He put his lips to her arm, stroking the inside of her wrist with his thumb as he kissed each circle. Then he lifted his head and Pam saw tears in his eyes. 'I'm a monster. Can you forgive me?'

'Yes,' she said again, like so many earlier yeses. Yes, I forgive you for insisting we leave the restaurant on the night of our anniversary because you thought I was looking at a man across the room. I forgive you for locking me out of my own home when I was late coming back from seeing a film with Carmel. I forgive you for throwing a beer bottle at me when I argued with you about wearing lipstick. I forgive you for burning a top I loved because you thought it looked sluttish.

Yes, I forgive you for branding me with your fingers. I forgive you. I forgive you.

Pam pulled the Hoover back to its place on the landing and went downstairs to clean up after Philip's lunch, remembering, with dread, what she had to buy on the way home.

May

Marjorie looked so tired and worn today – those dark shadows under her eyes. You'd never believe she was only forty-seven.

May remembered the stories Marjorie used to tell her and the boys when she babysat for them, straight out of her head just like that, about singing pigs and purple elephants. The songs she used to make up at the drop of a hat, the dances and games she invented for them.

So full of life she'd been back then, when she and Aideen had met in the hill-walking club, just around the time Aideen was looking for some help with four-year-old May and two-year-old Cathal, now that William was on the way too.

And Marjorie had been one of the first people to phone May when May was setting up on her own. 'I met your mam in the street and she told me what you were up to, May, and I was wondering if you could help me do a bit of a spring-clean sometime – just a few hours, if the two of us did it together.'

So May had arranged to call around on Marjorie's next day off. The little house across town had been a shock, terribly neglected and shabby. May tried not to let her dismay show as Marjorie led her through the small, cramped rooms, the dark, narrow hall. An unpleasant heaviness hung over the place, as if the windows were seldom opened, and May smelled old socks, and onions.

Marjorie's embarrassment was sadly obvious. 'I'm afraid I've let it go a bit, May. It's badly in need of a good scrub out, and I never seem to get around to it. But I think if we get through the worst of it today, I'll find it easier to keep it looking nice.'

It was as if she lived on her own. Not a mention of anyone else in the house, until they came to a closed upstairs door.

'That's Jude's room – she wouldn't want us going in, so we can ignore it.' Marjorie spoke in a whisper, and May wondered, as she followed Marjorie across the landing, why there was no sign of her daughter helping out with the housework.

After three hours of sweeping and polishing and scrubbing, the little house looked and smelled consider-ably better. Floors and windows shone, the kitchen presses had been washed out and reorganised, the cracked old bath gleamed – even Marjorie's battered furniture, which May had wiped down and polished, looked slightly less shabby.

And in all the three hours, there was no sound from the closed bedroom door, and no sign of Marjorie's daughter.

Over tea, which Marjorie insisted on making, May discovered that Jude hadn't managed to hold down a job since she'd left school after the Junior Cert, more than two years ago now. 'I worry about her, May – she's got so little ambition. She spends most of the day in bed – I don't see her till it's nearly teatime – and then at night she goes out with her pal Kathleen and God knows who else, usually till all hours.'

Listening to her, seeing her face so pinched with worry, May felt desperately sorry for Marjorie, and totally helpless. What could she possibly do? What could she offer Marjorie? She'd happily come and clean on a regular basis, even just for an hour or two at a time, but she sensed that money was tight, and she felt Marjorie would be embarrassed if she were to offer to work for nothing, or even at a reduced rate.

But she could visit – and she could listen. Maybe that would help Marjorie, just to have someone to spill out her worries to. So since that first visit, May had taken to dropping in on Marjorie once or twice a month, and the welcome was always warm.

Jude was often at home when May called around, but the two rarely met – Jude's bedroom door at the top of the stairs stayed firmly shut, sometimes with thumping music coming from behind it.

And with every visit, May heard a little more of Marjorie's story, sitting across the rickety, Formica-covered kitchen table from the woman who'd sung her to sleep after a nightmare, or taught her 'My Bonnie Lies Over the Ocean'.

Marjorie Grace had babysat the O'Callaghan children for eight years, from when she was eighteen until shortly after she met Tony O'Dea, the man she was to marry two years later, pregnant with his child. The man who was to run off, when Jude was just eight months old, with the takings from the nightclub where he worked as a bouncer, and a woman he'd met there. Marjorie was left penniless and unemployed – Tony had insisted she give up work to raise Jude and look after him – but within weeks of his leaving, she'd found a job in the big supermarket near her house, where she still worked, six days a week, to support herself and Jude.

When May spoke to her mother about Marjorie, Aideen admitted that she already knew the whole story. 'I've heard bits and pieces down through the years . . . I didn't feel it was my place to be talking about it.'

May nodded. 'Poor Marjorie, she's had it tough. And her daughter seems like a right waste of space.'

'I've heard talk about her – she seems to be hanging around with a rough crowd. It must be a terrible worry to Marjorie.'

When May's mother died, Marjorie called around to the house. She brought a bag of oranges and apples, and she cradled May's head and rocked her like she used to when May was eight, and crying from a fight with one of the boys.

Today she looked tired, and more worn out than usual, and May wished again there was something more she could do for her.

'Well now.' Marjorie lifted the pot and topped up their two mugs. 'Any nice gentleman callers since last week?'

May lifted her mug and smiled. *Nice mucky work you have there.* No, she wouldn't mention the postman. 'Not a single one. I'm thinking of entering a convent, if they'll have me.'

Marjorie pushed the plate of biscuits closer to May. 'Not a bit of it. You're much too pretty. Those men must want their eyes examined.'

The kitchen door opened and Jude's head appeared. 'When's dinner?' She looked at her mother, completely ignoring May. A gold stud sat on the side of her nose, and her lips were deep purple. Her brown hair looked as if it could do with a wash.

Marjorie looked mildly at her. 'About half an hour, love. Come and have a cuppa with us.'

But Jude had already disappeared. 'No, thanks.' The door slammed, and her feet thumped back up the stairs. Marjorie lifted her shoulders at May, who decided that maybe there were worse things than sharing your house with a crotchety old man.

*

Francesca

She waited until the laptop screen went black before pulling it down to meet the keyboard and clicking it closed. Then she lifted the pile of pages beside the computer and bounced them gently into a neat bundle. A movement outside the window caught her eye, and she watched Bernard opening next door's gate, coming home to his pretty boyfriend with a handful of orange blooms Francesca couldn't identify.

She laid the bundle of pages back on the table and crossed the room to her yoga mat, to replenish the spirit that the day had taken out of her. She opened the buttons of her deep purple cashmere cardigan and peeled it from her arms and dropped it onto the striped futon. She unzipped her red wool skirt and shimmied it down over her hips till it fell from her body. She stepped out of the misshapen pyramid it made and picked it up and placed it beside the cardigan. Then she eased off her black pumps, rolled down her stockings and removed the rest of her underwear, and settled herself full length on the mat. Funny how the simple act of taking off all your clothes could be so liberating.

Francesca Tuttoro closed her eyes and began to breathe deeply, thinking of the hot Italian sun, the scents of basil and jasmine, the soft *lap-lap* of the Adriatic on her skin, the sensation of warm sand between her toes. Slowly she raised her arms above her head, slowly she stretched out fully, feeding air deep into her lungs, feeling the delicious pull on fingers, arms, shoulders, ribs, abdomen, pelvis, thighs, ankles, toes, the bones and muscles awakening along the length of her body.

She held the stretch and breathed deeply, slowly, three times. Then she relaxed, bending her knees as she rolled onto her side and moved gracefully to her feet to begin her sequence of Sun Salutations.

Forty-five minutes later, freshly showered and scented and wrapped in a silk kimono of swirling greens and pinks, Francesca walked into the kitchen. Lucia coloured a picture at the table and Marietta chopped onions, sniffing gently. A bunch of thyme lay on the worktop, next to some chicken pieces, and garlic sizzled softly on a pan.

When she saw Francesca, Lucia dropped her marker and picked up something that dangled on a chain and held it out. 'Look, Mamma, what I found.'

Francesca put her palm under the little seashell and lifted it up to examine it. 'Pretty.' No bigger than a toddler's fingernail, a delicate curl of translucent, pink-tinted mother-of-pearl, no flaw in its tiny shape unless you counted the minute circle through which the slender chain passed. 'Where did you find it?'

Lucia pointed towards the front of the house. 'Outside there, in a puggle. Can I keep it?'

Francesca lifted one shoulder. 'I suppose you can, since we don't know who lost it.'

'Thanks, Mamma.' Lucia clapped her hands together. 'I'll give it to Miss Gannon as a present.'

Francesca turned to hide a frown. Miss Gannon this, Miss Gannon that. Lucia's teacher could do no wrong, it seemed. *Miss Gannon says to brush your teeth up and down. Miss Gannon says brown bread is better than white bread. Miss Gannon draws brilliant pictures on the board. Miss Gannon can say the alphabet backwards, really fast. Miss Gannon is funny when she tells stories.*

And every day, some fresh news item. *Miss Gannon was cross with Robbie when he scribbled on his book. Miss Gannon got her hair cut, and there's gold bits in it. Miss Gannon has no children in her house, so we're her pretend children. Miss Gannon brought buns for us that she cooked by herself, with yellow and orange sprinkles on top.*

It was mostly Paul who brought Lucia to school, on his way to work, but Francesca had met Carmel a few times during the year. Unremarkable face, cropped auburn hair with badly done copper highlights – and a boy's body underneath, no trace of womanly curves. Flat chest, skinny hips, no behind.

Francesca was proud of her own full, heavy breasts, her voluptuous hips. She liked the way the rounded cheeks of her behind pushed against her skirts and bounced gently as she walked. She enjoyed the feel of men's eyes on her ripe body, liked to see them wandering down from her face to the smooth curves and satin lace that rose from the open top buttons of her cardigan, knew that they watched her rear view as she moved away.

Francesca assumed Lucia's teacher was unmarried – otherwise why refer to her as Miss? With such a boy's body, she might well be a lesbian. It wasn't something you asked your daughter's teacher – and anyway, Carmel Gannon didn't interest Francesca in the least. She wasn't someone Francesca felt an inclination to get to know. Let Paul handle that end of things; he seemed happy enough to be the one dropping Lucia to school, and he was surely not the only man who showed up in the Junior Infant classroom in these enlightened times.

Francesca felt a tug on her sleeve. 'Look Mamma, this is the boy who cried wolf, see, and that's all his sheeps . . .'

Francesca bent her head over Lucia's picture, and Marietta sprinkled thyme onto the chicken and vegetables in the casserole, and it was all this – Francesca's dark, shiny hair spilling on to the table, her smooth, bangled arm encircling Lucia's shoulders as Lucia chattered and pointed to her picture, Marietta straightening up from the stove, the tantalising smell of herbs and fried garlic, the warm kitchen – this was what greeted Paul as he walked through the door a few minutes later.

Paul

And in the second before Francesca lifted her head and noticed him, before Lucia scrambled down from her chair and went flying towards him, he wondered why all that was not enough.

May

'*Damn.*' It couldn't be gone. It was tangled up somewhere in her clothes – it had to be. May pulled off her sweatshirt and shook it out, felt her way carefully down each sleeve. She searched the carpet on her hands and knees, her face inches from the floor. Then she took off her white T-shirt and shook it. It couldn't be gone. She unzipped her jeans, pulled them off, shook everything out again. Carmel's front-door key fell out of her jeans pocket and landed on the carpet with a tiny thump.

May sat on the floor with her clothes spread out around her. It was really gone, she'd really lost it. How could she have lost it? It couldn't be lost.

She walked on her knees over to the dressing-table, pulled out the bottom drawer, felt under the jumpers and brought out an envelope. Ordinary-looking, white, with her name, just the first one, written on the front.

May, it said. Although the first time she'd looked at it, she thought it said *Mai*, because the leg of the *y* was lighter than the rest, as if the flow of ink had been interrupted whenever the person – who? – had written her name.

There it had been, sitting on the hall floor just inside the front door, waiting for her when she'd got home from work one cold day in February. She'd almost stepped on it, nearly put her boot right down on top of it. She'd bent and picked it up, and turned it over and read *Mai*.

And inside the bulky envelope, instead of a letter or a note, she'd found a little wad of bubble wrap, and inside that a bundle of tissue paper, held together with Sellotape. Very light, hardly weighing anything. Was it empty? Was it some kind of a joke, someone sending her a folded bit of tissue? But then she felt a bump in the tissue, a little unevenness. There *was* something there. She tore off the Sellotape and unwrapped the tissue slowly, lifting the wafer-thin layers apart in her palm until, right in the middle, she uncovered the shell.

Tiny. Perfect. Threaded on a fine gold chain. A beautiful delicate pearl-pink shell on a chain – and that was all. Nothing to tell who'd sent it. No message of any kind, no words except her name on the envelope. *May. Mai.*

And no stamp. Whoever had given it to her must have come here in person. Must have walked up the path and lifted the letterbox flap and slipped the envelope through.

She liked 'Mai', liked the exotic look of it.

It couldn't be a birthday present – that was still nearly a month away. And anyway, Cathal or William would have sent a card or a letter with it, they'd never give her something anonymously like this. Not that May suspected that either of her brothers, or their wives, would have chosen the shell for her. Their presents for May were usually more practical, like something for the garden – a wheelbarrow, a planter, a piece of trellis – or for the house after she'd bought it.

The year she'd failed the driving test for the third

time, given up and bought a second-hand bike, Cathal got her a cycling helmet and a puncture-repair kit for her birthday. Last year, William sent her a voucher for the local paint shop.

And for her last birthday, the first that her mother hadn't been there for, her father had given her money. It had always been Aideen who'd chosen May's presents from her parents – the green apple perfume had come from Aideen, that long-ago Christmas. And every Christmas that May could remember, the label that read '*To darling May, with all our love*' had been in her mother's rounded handwriting.

If Aideen were still alive, *she* might have given May the necklace. It was the kind of gift that someone who truly loved you would pick out for you.

But Aideen had died of cancer a year and a half ago, and there was nobody else May could think of who might have sent her this beautiful necklace in the middle of February, for no reason at all.

It wasn't until a few days later, when she was checking the calendar for something entirely different, that May realised the necklace had arrived on 14 February. Valentine's Day.

When May showed it to her best friend, Rebecca demanded to know why nothing like that ever happened to her. 'I get two Valentine cards in my life, one from my mother and the other from the bastard, ten days before he runs off. The price is still on the back, and he spells my name wrong, with one c. Very romantic.'

Rebecca Donegan had got pregnant seventeen years ago, aged sixteen and a half. A week after she told Declan Geoghegan, her boyfriend of six months – her three-doors-down neighbour forever – he packed his bags and took the next plane to England. When Rebecca realised he was gone, she knocked on his parents' door and told them why, and his mother called her a liar and slammed the door in her face.

Four months later, just after Rebecca had sat the Leaving Cert, she was visited at home by a subdued Patsy Geoghegan, who said that Declan had finally admitted that he was the father, and that she and her husband wanted to be a part of their grandchild's life, and could Rebecca please forgive them?

She could. When Brian was born eight weeks after that, small, pink-skinned and perfectly bald, he was doted on by his four grandparents. 'I hardly get a look in,' Rebecca complained to May, 'except when it's time for bed, and then I'm the one walking the floor all night.'

May had no sympathy. 'You can't blame them. He's the first grandchild on both sides – they always get spoiled rotten.'

Rebecca grinned. 'You're as bad as them. You hog him all the time too. I should never have made you godmother.'

But she survived the sleepless nights, and she saw enough of Brian to make sure that he was as healthy and unspoilt as she could make him, and as soon as he started school she went on to train for a job that delighted her father and terrified her mother.

Rebecca had been May's best friend for almost thirty years, since they'd met in the Junior Infant class of Kilpatrick's convent school. She was big-boned and plain, with awkwardly assembled features in a freckly face, and thin, fair hair that refused to either straighten or curl, and overlapping teeth that had never been corrected. Declan had been Rebecca's first boyfriend, and had only been followed by two since then, neither of whom had stayed around once they'd heard about Brian.

But Rebecca Donegan was a survivor. Whatever unkindness Fate chose to send her way, she somehow managed to look beyond it, to find her way around it and move on. She reminded May of those children's soft plastic skittles, with rounded, weighted bottoms that allowed them to bounce back upright each time a ball knocked them sideways.

Rebecca was a bouncer-back – ignoring the school bullies who pointed to her teeth and changed Becky to Bucky, getting through her pregnancy with only one tearful episode on May's shoulder the week after Declan disappeared, coping with months of his mother crossing the road whenever she saw Rebecca walking towards her.

And when May was the one in trouble, Rebecca was there. When May failed the third driving test, Rebecca called around with two bottles of cabernet sauvignon, and halfway through the second they calculated how much money May would save in each car-free year. And the following day, when the hangovers had eased, they went shopping for a second-hand bike.

When May sobbed that she'd never, ever look at another man after Gerry Scanlon, Rebecca was there to hold her hand and agree that all men were bastards. When May's mother Aideen died, Rebecca was everywhere, taking phone calls, cutting sandwiches, running to the shop for more milk.

And, of course, she was there for the good times too – and genuinely charmed when May showed her the necklace. 'You must have some idea who sent it, though.' She held up the chain and watched the tiny shell twirling slowly. 'You'd know if someone had an eye on you.'

But May had shaken her head. 'I honestly have no idea. And you'd know if I knew anyway – you have a way of worming things out of people.'

'So they tell me.' Rebecca nodded. 'But this is just gorgeous – we have to find out who sent it. Show me that envelope again, and I'll use my excellent powers of deduction.'

She peered at the three letters, at the tailing-off of the *y*'s leg. 'Someone who uses a cheap biro.'

May laughed. 'Well done – that's a big help.' She took the chain back from Rebecca and held the shell carefully between forefinger and thumb. 'Someone with a cheap biro and excellent taste.'

It was beautiful – and now it was gone. It must have slipped off her neck some time during the day. But she'd find it. It might even have turned up already some-where. She'd call around to Paul's in the morning on her way to Carmel's – no need to go bothering them now – and she'd drop by the house where she'd cleaned the windows, and then Marjorie's, on her way home tomorrow afternoon.

She lifted her dressing-gown off its hook, slipped her arms into the sleeves and went off to have a shower.

Paddy

He tipped the can and drained the last of the Guinness into his tilted glass, watching the creamy brown swirl as it gradually settled and darkened. He relished this time after the main part of the day was over, dinner still to come, the stout in his empty stomach causing a faint but pleasant buzz.

He took the prawns from the fridge and brought them to the cooker; k.d. lang's voice floated from his CD player, almost managing to muffle the sound of Mr Kennedy's TV, which floated in as usual from next door. No gunfire tonight, no screams, just calm voices. A nature programme, maybe, or one of the more serious quiz shows.

May had looked like a little girl today, dwarfed in that too-big oilskin, all rosy-cheeked in the rain, tiny drops on her face.

As he was about to tip the prawns into the wok, he heard a rattle at the front door. 'Only me.'

He turned down the heat and walked through the hall. 'Hang on.'

Iseult's pale brown hair was piled into a messy topknot and tied with what looked to Paddy like a red sock. She wore a long dark green skirt and a blue lacy cardigan over something frilly and pink, and pale green canvas boots. His sister's taste in clothes was certainly original. 'Just checking up on you.' She walked past him and into the kitchen. 'Mmm, what's cooking?'

Paddy turned up the heat and gave a shake to the wok. 'Just a little stir-fry.' He tipped in the prawns and they sizzled loudly. 'Don't suppose you'd care for a glass of wine.'

'Ha ha.' Iseult opened the fridge and looked in. 'Oh, good, there's one open.' She pulled out a half-full bottle. 'How do you put up with that TV blaring all day long?' The cork squeaked as she eased it upwards. 'Does he never turn it off?'

'Occasionally. It doesn't bother me.' Mr Kennedy was almost completely deaf, and long since retired. He smiled vaguely at Paddy whenever they came face to face – as if he recognised him but couldn't quite remember where they'd met – and whenever he spoke, he bellowed, as if Paddy was the deaf one.

Paddy had got used to the almost constant sound of next door's TV – sometimes he was glad of it, glad to be reminded that another human being was just a wall away. He had no idea what Mr Kennedy's first name was.

He opened a press above his head and handed Iseult a wine glass.

'Ta.' She yawned as she poured. 'God, I'm wrecked. Cheers.' She lifted the glass and took a long sip. 'Mmm, that's nice. Remind us how many days till the holidays again?'

'Four.' Paddy smiled as he tipped the little bowl of

sweet-and-sour sauce into the pan, making everything sizzle loudly again. 'Will you last?' He lifted his Guinness and drank.

'Just about. Don't know if I'll do the end-of-term night out on Thursday though – not sure if I'll have the energy.' Iseult groaned as a new thought struck her. 'Oh, God, I've the dentist after school that day too.' She took another sip. 'I hate the dentist.'

Paddy tried to look sympathetic. 'Poor Izzy. A visit to the dentist after such a long, tough day at work.' He lifted the lid on the rice, and took it off the cooker. 'What is it again? Three and a half whole hours?'

'Don't start.' Iseult swirled her wine and watch-ed it trail back down the sides of the glass. 'I'd like to put you into the class for a day. You'd soon go running back to your Mickey Mouse job.' She looked into the gently bubbling wok as Paddy rinsed the rice. 'Mmm – that does smell divine.'

'Want to stay?'

She shook her head. 'Thanks, but I've just put a very nutritious frozen pizza into the oven. You totally put me to shame with your cooking.'

Paddy took his plate from the warming shelf over the oven and tipped rice onto it. 'It's a lot easier than you think.'

'So you keep telling me.' Iseult studied him over the top of her glass. 'When are you going to make some lucky woman very happy? And I'm not talking about in the bedroom, because I have no idea what you're like in there.'

Paddy grinned at her and opened his mouth, and she

added hastily, 'And I have absolutely no desire to know, big brother.'

He spooned some of the prawn mixture onto the rice. He was often tempted to tell Iseult about his feelings for May. He wondered what she'd say.

'Seriously, you're an amazing cook.' Iseult picked a prawn from the wok and munched. 'Yum. And not a bad person, generally. And here you are, thirty-five and all alone. How long has it been since Chloe – a year?' She thought. 'Hey, it's more than that – well over a year and a half. And you're still a total hermit.'

Paddy smiled. 'You're not exactly putting down roots yourself.'

'No, but I'm still young – and I'm out and about a lot more than you. And I have my moments, thanks.' Iseult gulped what was left of her wine, then belched cheerfully as she put the glass into the sink. 'Sign of good manners in the Middle East, or somewhere.'

Paddy took his plate and glass to the table. 'Such a ladylike little sister I was blessed with.'

'And only three doors away too, to keep an eye on big brother. Right, I'm off.' She hugged him and ruffled his hair. 'So unfair that big brother got to be the natural blond in the family. Tell me when you're doing that dinner again, and give me a bit of notice.'

Halfway to the door she turned, as if a thought had struck her. 'Oh, by the way, a few of us are going out for a Chinese on Friday. D'you fancy coming?'

Paddy looked suspiciously at her as he sat down. 'You mean a few women.'

She shrugged. 'Just Trish and Cath, actually. And you know well that Trish thinks you're cute.'

He shook his head, smiling. 'Sorry, got a pressing engagement on Friday. Close the door on your way out.'

After she'd gone, Paddy glanced out the window. The watery sun was going down, the sky striped with pale pink and blue-grey. Might be nicer tomorrow. He picked up his fork.

He loved cooking, loved experimenting with flavours, seeing what combinations worked. He was the one who'd done most of the cooking when he and Chloe were living together. It made sense, with him being home from work earlier than her, but he suspected that he would have done it anyway. Chloe wasn't interested in cooking, couldn't see the point of spending all that time preparing something that disappeared so quickly once it was ready: 'I'd be happy with a microwave, if I was living on my own. Ten minutes max, that's enough cooking for me.'

Paddy had grabbed her, spooned up some homemade tomato soup from the saucepan and held it to her lips.

'You're not living on your own. You're living with me, and you'll eat proper food, not microwaved crap. Now taste that and tell me if it needs more basil.'

'You decide.' She blew on the spoon and sipped. Then she kissed him, and the warm liquid flowed from her mouth into his.

'Hmm.' He swallowed, considered. 'I'm not sure.' He licked her lips. 'Could we try that again?'

And then, four years after they'd met, he'd asked her to marry him, so sure she'd say yes that he'd taken her away for a weekend to Donegal, to a thatched holiday cottage on the coast. They'd gone out to dinner on the first night, but he'd waited until the second, when he dipped fillets of freshly caught mackerel into beaten egg and seasoned flour and fried them on the little cooker, and opened the bottle of good white wine that he'd snuck into the fridge when they'd arrived.

Chloe came back from a trip to the nearest shop with Magnums for dessert, and newspapers to read in bed in the morning, and they sat at the table by the window and Paddy lit a candle and served the fish with roasted potato chunks and baby carrots. And then, over the remains of the dinner and the Magnum wrappers, he took out the little velvet box and asked Chloe if she'd like to marry him.

She looked from his face down to the box. She made no move to pick it up. 'Is that what I think it is?'

Paddy smiled. 'Probably.' When she still didn't touch it, he opened the box and held it out to her. 'It may not be what you want, but we can exchange it. I checked.'

'Ah, Paddy.' Chloe put a hand over her mouth, took it down again. 'You didn't.'

He pulled out the white gold ring with the solitaire diamond and reached for her left hand. 'Stop messing about and put this on, woman. I know it's your size – I measured your silver one.' Why wasn't she smiling?

Chloe drew her hand back, out of his reach. 'Hang on. You're really . . . you're serious? This isn't a joke?'

'A joke? You think this is a joke?' For the first time, he felt a prickle of unease. 'Isn't this what you want?'

She said nothing, just looked at him.

He laid the ring on the table, fear starting to take hold of him. 'Chloe, it's been four years, almost. We can't go on like this forever.'

'Why not?' She reached across, encircled his wrist with her fingers and squeezed. 'I thought we were happy.' She looked at the ring, sitting on the table between them. 'I never— Getting *married* was never part of my plan. I thought you knew that, you must have known that.'

'What do you mean, not part of your plan? How could I know that?' Something icy cold was snaking around inside him. 'Everyone gets married. It's just what happens when you love someone.'

She shook her head rapidly, her grip tightening on his wrist. 'Paddy, I *do* love you, you know that. I just don't want— I can't deal with the whole marriage thing. I never saw myself getting married to anyone. You *know* about my parents, how awful their whole—'

'But you can't let that—'

'Look, aren't we doing OK, the way we are? Aren't you happy just leaving things like this?' She was still holding his wrist. Her fingers were cold.

Outside, the sky was darkening. A sudden burst of wind rattled the window between them. Paddy pulled his hand gently away from Chloe's, picked up the wine bottle and held it over her glass. When she shook her head, he emptied what was left into his.

'God, talk about killing the moment.' Chloe brought both of her hands up to her face and pressed the backs of them to her cheeks. She sighed deeply. 'I'm really sorry, babe.'

Paddy lifted his glass and swallowed quickly. The wine tasted sour. He shook his head. 'Doesn't matter. My mistake. Forget it happened.' He shoved the ring into its box, snapped it closed and dropped it back into his pocket.

Chloe looked at him. 'Really? We're still OK? You can forget about this?'

'Of course.'

And of course he couldn't. He pretended to, for a month or so. They carried on as normal – or what probably looked like normal to everyone who knew them. Carried on living together, sleeping together. Still met their mutual friends every weekend.

But everything had changed. Everything.

One day, five weeks after Donegal, Paddy walked into his boss's office and listened to himself handing in his notice, and that evening he told Chloe he'd decided to move away from Limerick. He was thinking of going to Kilpatrick for a while, where Iseult had got a teaching job a few years earlier. She'd put him up while he thought about what he wanted to do.

Chloe cried, as he'd known she would. She begged him not to go. Told him she loved him, couldn't bear the thought of living without him. Said she was sorry about what had happened in Donegal – was careful not to use the words *marriage* or *proposal* – but that she couldn't change the way she felt. She pleaded with him tearfully to accept her the way she was, to carry on the way things were.

And Paddy listened, and held her while she cried, and felt desolate at the thought of never seeing her again.

As soon as he'd worked his two weeks' notice, he packed his things and moved out of their rented apartment, and back in Kilpatrick he slept on a couch in Iseult's two-bedroom townhouse – her tenant had the second bedroom – while he searched for a new job and a place to live.

And every day it got a bit easier not to pick up the phone and tell Chloe he'd made a terrible mistake.

The job had come first, after three weeks, followed a week later by a miserable house share for four months with two accountants who left dirty dishes in the sink and empty milk cartons in the fridge. By the time a house went up for sale three doors away from Iseult, Paddy had decided to stay put in Kilpatrick. It took two months for the deal to go through.

And he'd been living here alone ever since. Taking care of his heart, nursing it back as best he could. Keeping his distance from the single females that Iseult never stopped trying to pair him up with. Not looking. Not trying to find. Until Iseult, all innocently, had brought May O'Callaghan into his life, just over eight months ago now.

He'd listened with amusement as Iseult outlined her thirty-fifth birthday present to him. 'She's going to what?'

Iseult pointed to the long, narrow rectangle outside Paddy's back door, still untouched five months after he'd moved in, still a mass of straggly weeds and limp, yellowing tufts of what might or might not have been someone's attempt to plant a lawn once upon a time. The only change Paddy had made was to drive two poles into the ground and string a clothes-line between them.

'She's going to get rid of that jungle out the back. I've asked her to clear it away, so you've no excuse for not planting stuff in the spring.'

Paddy laughed. 'Me? Plant stuff? You're joking, right?'

Iseult shrugged. 'Well, then, you'll just have to keep her on, and get her to do it instead. I've paid her for a month, three hours a week, and after that you're on your own.' She looked out the window again. 'Actually, I had no choice – you're a disgrace to the neighbourhood.'

His own gardener – the idea was intriguing. 'So who is this woman?' He imagined a big, mannish creature in a straw hat and sensible rubbery shoes, who could steer a loaded wheelbarrow as easily as other women pushed buggies.

'Her name is May O'Callaghan. I heard about her from Carmel at school. Carmel's friend works as a kind of home help for May, and apparently she's in big demand all around town – May, I mean. She can do pretty much anything, by the sound of it. We were lucky to get her.'

May O'Callaghan: the name rang a bell. 'So when's she starting?'

'She can do Thursday, between nine and twelve. If you give me a key I can pass it on to Carmel.' Paddy's house was the middle one in a terrace of three; May would have to go through it to get to the back garden.

And that was that. The next morning, Paddy discovered where May O'Callaghan lived, and two days later he noticed her for the first time, wheeling a blue bicycle down the path towards her gate. She caught his eye and smiled, and Paddy rapidly revised his mental picture of his birthday present.

She wasn't mannish at all; quite the opposite. A good six inches shorter than him, with hair the colour of honey, and eyes that looked green from where he stood, and a sweet, cupid's bow mouth. An oversized yellow oilskin hid her figure from him, and well-worn workman's boots looked clumsy on her feet. She reminded him of a little girl dressing up for a school play in her big brother's clothes.

When he got home from work the following Thursday, Paddy found a note propped up against his fruit bowl, written on the back of the one he'd left for her:

Hello Paddy, happy birthday – I hope you enjoy your sister's present, and I hope you know someone with a trailer. May.

He walked through to the garden and discovered that the end section had already been pretty much cleared away, with a stack of filled black plastic bags leaning against his back wall. That must have taken a bit of effort.

And as the weeks went on, Paddy began to discover something strange. With each Thursday that came and went, with each improvement to his garden, with each glimpse of May he chanced to get during the rest of the week – working in someone else's garden, or cycling past him on her blue bike, or walking various dogs past his house in the evenings – he felt something unwind inside him. A kind of easing, a letting go that he couldn't explain. For the first time in almost a year, he felt a flicker of interest when he thought about a woman who wasn't Chloe. May began to wander into his head when he was about to fall asleep or just as he was waking up.

On the morning of her fourth and last day in his garden, Paddy left another note by the fruit bowl:

Hello May, and thanks for all your work so far – you've made a big difference already. I wonder if you'd continue to come once a week, and when the clearing-away has been finished, do whatever you think needs to be done to make my garden presentable? I have no idea about plants, so I'd be happy to give you free rein. Charge me for whatever you spend and I will, of course, pay you your going rate, if you're happy with this arrangement.

It sounded terribly stilted and formal, but it was the best he could do. He scribbled Paddy at the bottom and waited for her reaction.

She wrote:

Hello Paddy, I'm glad you like what I've done so far, although of course it's only the beginning.

Why on earth did that cause his heart to flip?

I'll be happy to keep coming to you on Thursday mornings – there's still a fair bit of tidying up to be done – and hopefully in another few weeks the weather will be softening and we can start to think about plants. We're too late for spring bulbs now, but there's plenty more out there to make your garden nice.

We're too late for spring bulbs now. He hadn't been part of a *we* for a long time. He felt that curious unwinding feeling again, he saw her face in his mind, imagined her bending over the page to write to him, pushing her hair out of the way.

And by the time February came around, and the first narrow green shoots had started to push their way through his crumbly new topsoil, and May O'Callaghan had been coming to his house every Thursday for more than three months, he was completely lost.

May

As she was leaving the house, her phone rang. She pulled the front door closed and pressed the answer button as she walked down the path. 'Hello, you.'

'I'm bored. What are you up to?'

May smiled. 'I'm on my way next door for a glass of wine and a half-hour of gossip.'

Rebecca sighed loudly. 'Oh God, I wish I was there – those two have the best scandals. What are you wearing?'

'My blue top with the lace at the sides, and my white skirt.'

'That'll do. What are you up to tomorrow night?'

May thought, pushing Bernard's gate open. 'Going around to your house?'

'Exactly. Remember everything you hear tonight, word for word. Brian says hello, and not to forget his birthday next week.'

'Ma!'

May laughed at Brian's indignant voice in the background. 'Tell him not to worry, I haven't forgotten. What kind of godmother would that make me?' She suddenly remembered. 'Oh, guess what, though – I've lost my little shell necklace.'

'What? Where did you see it last?'

'Not sure – I put it on this morning as usual, and it wasn't until I was changing to go next door just now that I missed it.'

'Damn – can you retrace your steps?'

'First thing tomorrow.' She reached the door and raised her hand to press the bell. 'OK, gotta go. See you about half eight, and hopefully I'll have found it by then.'

As she hung up, Shaun appeared at the door, holding Lonesome George.

'Look who's come to see you, Georgie.'
May smiled and opened her arms.

Pam

And what of Pam Treacy, sitting on the side of her bath at twenty past eleven on a Monday evening in June, crying quietly? What about the white plastic wand balanced on the edge of the basin, its little blue window turned away from her? Wasn't she happy to be pregnant? Hadn't she a comfortable home, and a husband who never stopped telling her how much he loved her, and weren't they earning enough money between them to support at least two or three children, let alone this single one?

What was wrong with her?

Pam wiped her eyes with a wad of toilet paper, shouted, 'Just a minute,' to her husband, who was wondering aloud what was taking her so long, why she wasn't coming to bed.

She ran the cold tap and splashed her face and gathered wand, box and instruction leaflet into the paper bag it had come in, and screwed it all up tight and shoved it down in the bin, way down under the toilet roll cores and wadded tissues and yellowish-brown-tipped cotton buds and curls of dental floss and an empty shampoo bottle.

Then she went to join her husband in bed.

Tuesday

Clear at first, with sunshine over much of Munster and Leinster. A band of low pressure spreading from the north and reaching all areas by nightfall. Highs of 13 to 15 degrees.

Bernard

He climbed into the van just as May came out her hall door, and he waved as he drove away. Poor girl, having to put up with that man ordering her around in her own house – insisting she get rid of her cat as soon as he moved in. Telling May he was terrified of tripping over him, and how would she feel if he broke a hip some fine day?

When May had reported this to Bernard, when she was asking him if he and Shaun would like to take Lonesome George, Bernard had silently thought that it might be no bad thing if Philip O'Callaghan broke a hip – at least then May would get a breather for the few weeks he was in hospital.

Although, knowing her, she'd be in and out to see

him like a yo-yo.

Naturally they'd agreed to take Lonesome George. He and Shaun adored cats, and you couldn't say no to May, she was such a sweetheart. Such a good neighbour, putting out their bin when they were away, turning on their outside lights at night, watering their houseplants. Being so welcoming to Shaun when he'd moved in, not like a couple of the other neighbours, who'd made a point of ignoring him. And May's father, when he'd moved in with May just a couple of months after Shaun's arrival, was one of the worst. Glaring out at them from his bedroom window, deliberately looking the other way on the few occasions they happened to be in their gardens at the same time.

How did May put up with the old bastard's crankiness, day after day? Running around, waiting on him hand and foot. Breakfast in bed every morning while she was trying to get herself out to work. At least she had him and Shaun next door if she needed a moan, or just to get out of his way. They'd had a good laugh last night, made quick work of those pinot grigios.

Pity May was on her own, though. Pity she and that good-looking postman didn't get together, but when Shaun had suggested the night before that she ask him out, May had just laughed and blushed. 'Ah no – I couldn't do that.' Then she reached out and took another sesame-toast triangle from the dish on the table. 'Now, tell me how you did these – I'm going to give Pam the recipe and order her to make them at least once a week.'

And Bernard, watching the colour ebbing from her face, had wondered what had happened to May O'Callaghan to make her so afraid of leaving her heart open to love.

He rounded the last bend and pulled up in front of Flower Power. He turned off the engine, looked out at the shop front and said, 'Oh, *fuck*,' with great feeling. Another visit from the right-wingers of Kilpatrick. Across the metal security grille, in thick black two-foot-high letters, he read GAY BOY and FAGOT and QUEER.

So original, and such impeccable spelling. At least they'd left the bins alone this time. He sighed heavily, got out and slammed the van door shut behind him. He unlocked the grille, pushed it up, then went inside for the bucket and the bottle of bleach.

May

No sign of it, around the back or anywhere in the front garden. She rang the bell and waited, and after a long time the door was opened by the new au pair.

May smiled. 'Hello – I'm May, from two doors down. I do the gardening; I was here yesterday.' The au pair watched May's face carefully as she spoke. 'I just wondered if anyone found a necklace here yesterday?'

The au pair looked puzzled. 'Neck lace?'

With her finger, May traced the path of the chain

around her neck. 'A little shell on a gold chain – I think it may have slipped off while I was here.'

The au pair shook her head. 'Missus not here now, sorry. Missus out.' She began to inch the door closed. 'Sorry. You come later.'

May gave up – the girl obviously hadn't a clue what she was talking about. But if Paul or Francesca had found anything, they'd surely ask her if she owned it, knowing she'd been there yesterday. She'd just have to wait and see.

In the meantime, she'd call by the window cleaning house, and Marjorie's too, this evening. She'd walk over there with Jojo, her Tuesday dog.

You never knew, it might be there, waiting for her. She turned back to the gate, where her blue bike stood.

Carmel

'It's gorgeous.' Iseult fingered the chain. 'Is that real gold?'

'Yeah, it's hallmarked, look.'

Iseult peered at the tiny clasp Carmel held out. 'Wow – that's pretty impressive. Must have cost a bit.'

'I know. Makes a nice change from the bath salts and Quality Street.' Carmel squeezed her teabag against the side of her cup, picked it up by a corner and aimed it at the bin on the far side of the table. It bumped against the cream wall before hitting the floor six inches from the bin. 'Blast.' She made no move to pick it up.

Of course Paul had bought it. How sweet, letting

Lucia give it to her as an end-of-term present. How clever to arrange somehow to have Lucia 'find' it, so there was no danger of Francesca getting suspicious.

Carmel must think of a way to thank him on Thursday afternoon. Her skin tingled at the thought.

Iseult stirred milk into her coffee. 'Isn't it today you're getting the kitchen painted?'

Carmel dragged her thoughts back. 'Yeah – May should be there now. She's doing a lovely kind of deep yellow in the kitchen, and on Friday I'm getting my bedroom done in a pale lilac.'

'Nice.' Iseult lifted her cup. 'She's a real all-rounder, isn't she? May, I mean. You should see what she's doing in my brother's garden, totally putting mine to shame.'

Carmel looked at Iseult in surprise. 'What? I thought you only paid her for a month. That was ages ago.'

'I did.' Iseult nodded. 'But he kept her on himself, once he saw the difference she was making.'

'Oh, right.' Carmel thought. 'Maybe they've hit it off?'

Iseult laughed. 'Paddy and May? Ah no, they haven't even met – he's always gone to work when she's there.'

'I'm surprised you haven't done something about that – aren't you always trying to fix him up?'

'Ah no. May wouldn't be his type at all, I'd say.' Iseult looked thoughtfully at Carmel. 'What about you, though? You should come over to my house some time – I could arrange for him to call around; he wouldn't suspect a thing.'

Outside, a bell clanged. There was a general stirring

in the staffroom as people began to gather cups and move towards the sink.

'Mm . . . yeah – maybe I will, some time.' Carmel lifted her cup and drank, conscious of the colour flooding into her face. She hadn't mentioned Paul to anyone except her friend Pam, couldn't risk it getting out.

She certainly had no intention of telling anyone on the staff – Iseult mightn't be too bad, but Carmel had a fair idea how some of the others, especially the older ones, would take it. They'd totally disapprove of a teacher having an affair with any parent, not to mind one who was attached. They might even feel they had to bring it to the attention of the principal – Carmel shuddered at the thought. No, much safer to say nothing. Wasn't any of their business anyway who she slept with.

Of course, this meant that, as far as Iseult and the rest of the Kilpatrick Junior School staff were concerned, Carmel Gannon was ripe for matching up with any available brothers. If they only knew. She dumped her cup in the sink and followed the others out, smiling, fingering the little shell around her neck.

So what if Paul was attached? They weren't hurting anyone. They were both adults, both knew exactly what they were doing. And if they were careful, they could go on doing it for as long as they wanted.

She walked towards the straggly line of four-year-olds waiting for her in the yard. *Roll on Thursday*. His little teacher-girl would have a few new tricks ready for Paul.

May

Holding the cut finger under the running water, she pulled open the little mirrored door of the press above the sink. As she reached for the plasters, an open blue box in front fell out and scattered its contents into the sink. *Durex*, she read as she pushed the little packets back inside. *20 flavoured latex condoms.*

So Carmel probably wasn't on her own; another happy couple. Seemed like she was surrounded by them these days. Pam and Jack. Brendan and Shaun. Paul and Francesca. She ripped open a plaster packet and wound it around her finger, noticing a silver chain sitting on the edge of Carmel's bath.

The shell necklace slid into her head again. Would it turn up later, when she went looking? Ridiculous how lost she felt without it. She replaced the box of plasters and went back downstairs.

As she finished making her tomato sandwich, being more careful with the knife this time, she looked around the walls of the half-painted room. At the rate she was going, she'd be finished with the whole thing by about three, if the paint lasted. She still had to do the biggest wall, then work her way around the units, and the fridge freezer wasn't built in — she'd have to manoeuvre it out to paint behind it.

After lunch, she dipped her brush back into the paint and began again. The ochre colour Carmel had picked wouldn't have been May's choice — a couple of shades too dark for this north-facing kitchen, with no direct sunlight to soften it. Although it was warm, of course, much warmer than the lemon that she was painting over, and the units were off-white, so—

Her mobile rang, and she balanced the brush on the top of the can, wiped her hands on her jeans and pulled the phone from her pocket. Hilda. Funny, she never phoned by day, always waited until May was off work. Her aunt lived by the sea, forty minutes' drive from Kilpatrick, and she and May spoke often, at least twice a week.

She pressed the answer button. 'Hi, Hilda. Everything OK?'

'May, I'm glad I got you.'

Something had happened – May tensed. 'What is it?'

Hilda spoke quickly. 'Nothing's wrong, dear, there's just something I wanted to let you know, and I didn't want to phone you at home, in case…' Hilda's voice trailed off, and May waited. 'Can you talk now, Maisie? I mean, are you in the middle of something?'

May lowered herself onto the edge of a kitchen chair. 'No, no, I'm painting, but it's fine. What is it, Hilda? You're being very mysterious.'

She heard a sigh at the other end of the line. Then: 'Maisie, it's Terri.'

Terri. Hilda's only daughter, the cousin May hadn't met for more than three years, not since— She shut the thought off, forced herself to concentrate on what Hilda was saying. 'There's no easy way to say this.' Hilda sighed again. 'She's pregnant, Maisie. I'm so sorry.'

May closed her eyes. 'But Hilda, that's wonderful. You're going to have a grandchild.' She twisted the phone cord tightly between her fingers. 'You must be thrilled.' She pressed her eyelids together, so nothing could fall out.

'Maisie love, you don't have to—'

But May rushed in. 'No, Hilda, it's OK, I'm fine. You must stop feeling so guilty about all that. It's in the past and I'm over it, really and truly I am.' She dug the nails of her free hand into her palm, eyes still clamped shut. 'So – when is it due?'

'November.'

November. Five months away. 'Well, congratulations.' And then, because she simply couldn't pretend to be bright and cheerful about it any more, May changed the subject. 'Actually, Hilda, I was going to ring you this evening. It's Dad's birthday on Sunday, his eightieth. And I decided the other day – the boys are going to come to dinner with Gaby and Dolly, nothing fancy, and we'd love you to come too.'

She could sense Hilda's distraction at the other end. Still thinking about it, still feeling guilty about Terri's news. Still trying to come to terms with what her daughter had done to May.

'Cathal and Gaby will have Phil with them – you haven't seen him yet, he's just gorgeous. Do come, Hilda – I know Dad would be delighted to see you too. You could stay the night. I can make up the bed in the spare room. And Rebecca will be there.'

November, she was due. She was pregnant with Gerry's baby.

After she'd hung up – after Hilda had agreed to come to dinner, after they'd settled on a time – May put her phone back into her pocket. And then she stayed sitting on the edge of the chair, in the middle of the half-painted kitchen.

When she was twenty-seven, and beginning to wonder if she'd ever find someone who'd want to stay with her for longer than six months, May O'Callaghan had met Gerry Scanlon. He'd walked into Dr Taylor's waiting room late one afternoon, just after May had shown the last patient into the surgery.

She was tidying the magazines and emptying the wastepaper basket, and planning what she'd cook for dinner. Spaghetti, maybe, with the last of that jar of pesto stirred through it, or she could get some eggs on the way home – or was there still some breaded cod in the freezer? Cooking didn't interest May in the least: the sooner it was over and the less preparation it involved, the better.

She looked up as the door opened and saw a man she didn't recognise. Blue jacket, black jeans. A little taller than her, but not much. Nice reddish-brown hair, almost to his shoulders. The length suited him.

May straightened, still holding the plastic bag she'd just pulled out of the wastepaper basket. 'I'm really sorry, we're about to close.' He didn't look like an emergency. 'Would you like to come back tomorrow instead? I could make an appointment for you now.'

He glanced at his watch. 'It's only a quarter to five,

and there's nobody waiting. The sign outside says afternoon surgery is two to five.'

May was half amused, half annoyed at his persistence. 'Well, the last patient has just gone in, so it's unlikely she'll be out before five.' She hoped that Mrs Danaher wouldn't suddenly reappear and make a liar out of her. But Dr Taylor hardly ever spent less than a quarter of an hour with someone, let alone a talker like Mrs Danaher.

The man still wasn't giving up. 'Why don't I wait a few minutes and see? If she's not out by five to five, I'll give up and come back tomorrow. How's that?'

May could hardly refuse – the sign *did* say five o'clock. 'Fine – but I'll need to take your details, since you haven't been here before.' She went to her desk, took a form from the top drawer and handed it to him. 'Do you need a pen?'

'Thanks.' He took the form and began to fill it in right there, at the desk, just across from her. May grabbed a file from the cabinet behind her desk and pretended to be engrossed in it, but by the time he handed the form back to her she knew his name, (Gerry Scanlon) and his age, (twenty-five, but only a year and nine months younger than her) and that he hadn't a history of congenital heart disease, epilepsy, allergies or diabetes.

And that he smelled of mints. And that he didn't wear a wedding ring. And that his hands were—

'Thank you.' She took the form and glanced at the

clock. It was almost five to five – looked like he was going to have to come back.

'I think I know you.' He was studying her, frowning slightly. 'Are you Cathal O'Callaghan's sister?'

'I am. Are you a friend of his?' Cathal hadn't lived in Kilpatrick for six years, since he'd gone to college in Galway and ended up working there after he graduated. He and his girlfriend Gaby had just bought an old farmhouse in Oranmore, badly in need of renovating. When he had seen it, May and Cathal's father hoped loudly that Cathal had been paid to take it.

'We were in school together. I haven't seen him for years – what's he doing now?'

And May was still telling him by the time five o'clock came round, and Mrs Danaher still hadn't reappeared, so she arranged for Gerry Scanlon to come back at ten o'clock the next morning.

That evening May phoned her mother, and in the middle of the conversation she said, as if it had just occurred to her, 'Oh, by the way, I met someone called Gerry Scanlon today. He was in Cathal's class at school – d'you remember him?' Cathal must have brought him home at some stage, if he remembered May.

Aideen thought. 'Can't say the name rings a bell. Gerry Scanlon . . . what does he look like?'

'Reddish hair, not very tall.' May decided not to mention the nice smile, or the lack of a ring. She didn't want her mother getting ideas. 'Average-looking, really. He was asking about Cathal, so I thought . . . '

But the next morning she spent a bit longer than usual getting ready for work. Stroked on the eyeliner she didn't normally wear by day. Chose the red shirt that one of her flatmates always admired on her.

He walked in at ten to ten. The waiting room was empty except for one pale teenager, who jiggled a foot in time to the tinny sounds that escaped from his headphones and coughed harshly every so often.

Gerry Scanlon walked up to May's desk. 'Do I have to sign in or say a password or something?'

May smiled. She wondered what he was going to the doctor for – he looked perfectly healthy. 'Just take a seat.'

'Can I not stay and talk to you?' He glanced across at the oblivious teen. 'Doesn't look like the conversation would be very stimulating over there.'

May tried not to look pleased. 'If you want to.' She indicated a nearby chair. 'Pull that up, and I'll try to be stimulating.'

He grinned. 'You know, I remembered something about you last night. I remember one day a few of us were out in your back garden, kicking a ball around, and you came charging out and gave out stink to us for damaging the flowers or something.'

May gave a delighted laugh – he'd been thinking about her last night. 'Did I really? I don't remember, but I was always big into gardening, so it doesn't surprise me.' She tried to picture herself stalking out to them, full of indignation. She must have been a right little miss. 'Sorry about that.'

He smiled back at her. 'I think you're forgiven by now.'

Dr Taylor's door opened just then, and Gerry stood up as the patient who came out approached May's desk. 'I'll disappear while you do your thing.'

He took a chair by the window and looked out, but as soon as May had taken the patient's cheque and Dr Taylor had put his head out and called the teenager into his surgery, Gerry came back to the desk.

He had a habit of pushing a hand through his hair, which promptly fell straight back onto his forehead. Such a rich, auburn colour. She wondered what it smelled like.

By the time the coughing teenager came out, May had agreed to go for a drink with Gerry Scanlon after work. Within six weeks, she'd stayed the night three times in the small apartment he rented above a butcher's shop in the middle of Kilpatrick.

She'd lie awake beside him, listening to the slamming of car doors and the footsteps of passers-by – much noisier than the flat she shared with two others on a side street. Seeing how the clothes they'd thrown over a chair, or let fall onto the floor, looked orange in the light that filtered from the street through the cheap curtains. Following the beam of a car's headlights as it travelled the length of the far wall.

His hair smelled of coconut, and his eyes were grey, and he'd pull her plait gently until she tilted her head back, and then he'd press his mouth against her throat. And she'd close her eyes and thread her fingers through his shiny hair.

After six months, she sent her flatmates out to the pub and brought Gerry and her parents together for dinner, and he called Philip 'sir', which went down very well. He wore the first suit May had seen on him, and he brought a pot of yellow pansies for Aideen, and a bottle of wine to go with the tuna casserole that May had spent the whole afternoon getting ready. The recipe had said *preparation twenty minutes, cooking thirty minutes*. May figured the book was aimed at people who could actually cook, who knew what sweating onions meant, and how to make breadcrumbs without grating their fingers and having to start all over again.

Sometimes he called for May after work, if he finished early – he did shifts in the research department of the big dairy plant outside Kilpatrick – and he drove them to the sea at weekends, and they walked along the cliff edge, and sometimes they gathered bags of seaweed on the beach for May's parents' garden, which she still tended, and they visited May's aunt Hilda now and again.

Once, May filled Gerry's bath with hot water and threw in a handful of seaweed, then stepped in after it, but when he joined her, Gerry found the weaving fronds off-putting – 'They're like bloody sea serpents' – and he waited for her in bed instead.

When they got engaged, two years and three months after Gerry's first visit to Dr Taylor's – to have a mole on his chest checked out – after they'd called to tell both sets of parents, May insisted that they drive to Hilda's house. 'I have to tell her in person.'

And when they arrived at Hilda's, her twenty-two-year-old daughter Terri was there, just home from three years of college in Dublin. And they congratulated May and Gerry, and he made some joke about his and Terri's names rhyming, and on the way home, May wondered aloud about asking Terri to be one of her bridesmaids.

Nothing happened right away. Things went on as normal between them for another few months. They settled on a date for the wedding, 15 September, and May booked the hotel, and went to talk to Father Murphy about the ceremony, and began to look in the estate agent's window at the houses for sale.

And whenever they visited Hilda now, Terri was there. She'd got a job in one of the local craft shops, to save for the trip around the world she was planning in the autumn. 'If I don't do it soon, I might never have the chance again.' She was back living at home with her mother, putting as much money aside as she could.

And she didn't have a boyfriend.

When did it first occur to May that she was the one doing all the running around for the wedding? When did she begin to notice that Gerry kept finding excuses not to go and look at the houses for sale she found? 'Go on your own or bring one of your pals along – you'll have a better idea than me, anyway, what you want.'

What *you* want, not what *we* want.

Aideen didn't seem to think it was a problem. 'Men aren't usually good at that kind of thing,' she told May. 'It's normal for him not to get involved. I wouldn't worry.'

Then he stopped calling for May after work, saying they were busy at the plant, that he had to stay later than usual. Sometimes he didn't answer when she spoke to him, looked blankly at her when she waved a hand to get his attention.

Rebecca put it down to pre-wedding nerves. 'Who says only brides feel jittery? He should be allowed to feel nervous too. He'll be fine on the day, wait and see.'

May told herself that Rebecca and her mother were right – there was nothing to worry about.

And then, two weeks before the wedding, he came to pick her up from work, like he used to. May smiled at him when he walked through the door. 'Hey, I wasn't expecting you. I'm about ready.' She finished tidying the magazines and pulled the plastic liner out of the bin.

'Take your time.' He stood at the door, fiddling with the car keys. 'I thought we'd go for a drive.'

'Great.' May finished up, gathered her things together, called goodbye to Dr Taylor and followed him outside to the car. It was drizzling steadily, that warm August kind of rain.

Gerry took the road out of town and pulled into a lay-by as soon as they'd left Kilpatrick behind them. As May was opening her mouth to ask why they'd stopped there, on the side of the road, he turned to her and said, 'There's something you have to know.'

And as the cars raced by, making Gerry's car shudder slightly, as the rain dribbled down the windscreen, he told May that he'd fallen in love with her cousin Terri, and that he was going to go off with her around the world in two weeks' time. And that he was very, very sorry, and that he hated hurting May like this, but that he didn't know what else he could do.

And May said nothing, just looked ahead of her, noticed how the rain on the windscreen made the trees and the road and the telegraph poles all wavy, and she wondered what it would feel like to be out in all that waviness. So she opened the door and stepped out, and began to walk back to town, holding up her head so she could feel the wetness on her face.

She heard the passenger door being pulled closed behind her, and the engine starting up, and she waited for Gerry to turn the car around and pull up beside her, and she got ready to tell him that she'd rather walk, thank you. But he didn't turn around, he just drove off in the same direction.

Towards Hilda's house, where Terri lived.

Poor Hilda took it almost as hard as May. The following day she turned up on May's doorstep in tears. Put her arms around May and cried on her shoulder, begged May to believe she had known nothing, nothing at all, until last night when Terri had told her.

'I can't believe she could do it to you, Maisie,' Hilda wept. 'I just can't believe she could do a thing like that. And him too – it's just unbelievable.'

And May, still numb, felt the sobs running through Hilda's body and wondered why she wasn't crying too.

When she felt able to face the world again, and taking Rebecca with her for moral support, May brought her engagement ring back to Clint's jewellers, to Fergus at Clint's who played golf with Philip every second Thursday, and who was very understanding, and gave May almost as much as Gerry had spent on it eight months previously.

The money helped with the deposit for the last house she'd looked at, which was still on the market, and she moved in six weeks before her thirtieth birthday.

A week later, Hilda came to visit.

'I have something for you, a kind of housewarming present.' She held a shoebox in her hands, with a few ragged holes punched in its sides.

'Come in, and ignore the mess.' May led the way through the jumble of still-unopened boxes in the hall to the small concrete-floored kitchen at the back of the house. 'Hang on till I fill the kettle.'

She was so glad that she and Hilda had survived, that Terri hadn't destroyed that relationship too. May assumed they were still away – Terri's name, naturally, never came up in conversation, and May, naturally, never asked about her. Although now and again there was a funny kind of awkwardness between her and Hilda. How could there not be?

Hilda put the box on the table and opened the lid, and May peered in at the ball of ginger fur that sat looking up at her.

'Oh Hilda, a kitten.' She put the kettle on the table, lifted out the ginger fur and held him up, six inches from her face. He gazed back at her, then mewed loudly, and surprisingly deeply. 'Oh, he's gorgeous.' May rubbed her cheek against him, and he mewed again.

They poured milk into a yoghurt carton lid from May's recycling bag and he stuck his face in it, spluttering until he got the hang of it, lifting up his head when he'd finished to show off his milky moustache. Tumbling sideways when he tried to balance on three paws to lick himself clean.

May named him Lonesome George, after a turtle she'd read about once, the last of its kind on a beach somewhere. He took possession of the house very quickly, ignoring the basket May bought him at the charity shop, sleeping curled up in a corner of her dark red couch or tucked into one of her slippers.

He chased his tail and ate May's ferns, and sharpened his tiny claws on the kitchen chair legs, and left a light layer of ginger fur everywhere he went. When he got big enough to jump onto the sitting room windowsill, he sat there, watching the goings-on outside, making a funny guttural sound in his throat whenever a bird perched on the telegraph wire above the garden wall.

If May stretched out on the couch, he settled himself on her stomach, eyes closed, purring happily, lifting his head to fix his green eyes on her if she coughed or sneezed. May would stroke his soft fur and feel the hot weight of him, and wonder if she'd ever be brave enough to fall in love again.

The year after May moved into her house, two things happened. Her mother was diagnosed with lung cancer in February, and Gerry and Terri, living together in London since they'd stopped travelling, got married there quietly in November.

Of course Aideen's death early in June, just four months after the diagnosis, was worse, much more devastating. May was heartbroken at the loss of a mother who'd always loved her so completely, who'd stood between Philip and his children all her life, softening his effect on them.

But when Hilda told her the other news, as gently as she could, May burst into loud sobs that sent Lonesome George scuttling away from her into the kitchen and caused Hilda to begin apologising, in tears too, all over again.

And now they were having a baby. At least May hadn't disgraced herself by bawling this time.

She got up from the chair, dipped the paintbrush into the pot, and stroked it across Carmel's kitchen wall.

Life went on. She wondered if it would look like him.

Shaun

He swiped the shortbread crumbs from the counter into his hand and brought them to the bin. Then he topped up his mug with what was left in the cafetière and brought it out the back. Shame to waste the sun when it made one of its rare appearances – he'd sit and read what he'd written this morning, see if it still sounded OK.

He took the plastic cover off one of the four teak-framed green canvas chairs that he and Bernard had bought together shortly after Shaun had moved in – their first significant joint purchase – and breathed in the fresh, clean air as he settled back.

So nice here when the rain held off. Hardly any humidity, and no bugs to speak of. Not like at home, where you couldn't put your nose outside the door in summer without getting it practically bitten off, where you had to shower three times a day just to keep from stinking. Where the roaches were never far away to gross you out. Could be a bit warmer here sometimes of course, but what the hey?

He couldn't imagine ever moving back to Boston, or anywhere in the States. Ireland suited him – the weather, the food that wasn't stuffed with added this and fortified that, the easygoing friendliness of most of the people.

Most, not all. Not the idiots who regularly sprayed Bernard's shop front with their cans, who'd tried to force the lock of the security grille a few weeks ago. Who emptied the bins outside the window whenever they felt like it, strewing the dead flower-heads and screwed-up tissue right across the street. But, then, there were idiots everywhere, even here in Kilpatrick.

The Irish police weren't much help – but you couldn't really blame them: they were so woefully under-resourced. I mean, whoever heard of unarmed cops? They just said that Bernard would have to catch them at it, or get some kind of foolproof evidence so arrests could be made.

What did they expect? That he and Bernard would stake the place out, sit across the street in a car until the freaks showed up? And then what? Ask them to say cheese and take their photos? Challenge them to a duel? Shaun couldn't imagine any kind of physical confrontation, knew he wouldn't be capable of lifting a hand to anyone, not if his life depended on it.

And even if he could, he'd fight like a girl, for sure – he and Bernard both. They'd be useless against any kind of street life, even the Kilpatrick species, who probably wouldn't stand a chance against some of those big city drugs gangs.

So Bernard had come up with his master plan.

'I'm getting two CCTV cameras outside the shop.'

Shaun had raised his eyebrows. 'You are? What's that gonna set you back?'

Bernard made a face. 'A lot. But it'll be worth it if we can get those morons to stop.'

'You think it'll put them off, having a camera outside? Can't they just wear hoods or something?'

Bernard shrugged. 'Why would anyone pay to have CCTV then? Look, Kilpatrick's not exactly a metropolis. The police have got to have some idea who's doing this stuff, even if they don't see fit to share it with us, right?'

Shaun considered. 'Maybe . . . I guess so.'

'So any kind of evidence, even if their faces can't be seen clearly, should be enough to go on. The clothes, the size of them, whatever.'

Shaun hoped he was right. Anyway, the cameras

were going up this week some time. Hopefully, that would put an end to the shit.

He turned to the pages in his lap and began to read. This week, he was back to food. There was always something more to say about the difference between what was piled on the shelves of an average Irish supermarket and what you could pick up in a Boston deli.

As one of our great common denominators [he'd written in an earlier article], *it's pretty amazing how radically different food is over here. We speak the same language – more or less; we watch the same movies. All that separates us is a body of water – admittedly a pretty humungous one. But apart from the fast-food joints, which are depressingly similar here to ones you'll find in Boston, or anywhere in the States for that matter, the food in Ireland is so not the same.*

There was only one shop in Kilpatrick that sold bagels, prepacked in sixes and usually well past their best by the time Shaun got to the last one. No one had heard of sourdough bread. Half-and-half was another unknown: if you wanted a blend of milk and cream – and what else could you possibly put in your coffee? – you had to buy the two separately and mix them yourself.

Don't get me wrong [he'd written, not wanting to alienate Boston's considerable Irish population]

There's plenty of good stuff here, like joints of mmm-mmm salty bacon that's boiled and sliced thickly for dinner; potatoes that, I'm sorry, beat Idaho's hands down (they call them balls of flour, if you can believe it); home-baked goods in the weekly market – apple tarts, fruit cakes, soda bread – that wouldn't know a preservative if it came up and bit them in the ass. All good wholesome stuff, if a little pricier than I've been used to. But all very, very different from what I've eaten up to now.

His two-thousand-word column, 'Stars, Stripes and Shamrocks', was syndicated to half a dozen papers on the east coast, and the three hours or so a week he spent on it nicely covered his living expenses here. It detailed the everyday experiences of an American living in a medium-sized town in the west of Ireland at the start of the second millennium, and covered everything from supermarket shopping to house hunting, from pub culture to politics to topics of conversation and speech patterns of the area.

Shaun had been writing the column for the past eleven months, since he'd first arrived in Kilpatrick, since he'd persuaded his editor at the *Boston Telegraph* – his soon-to-be-ex-editor – that what he really needed to make the *Telegraph* complete was a weekly column from Shaun about living in Ireland. 'Look, I'm going anyway – you don't even have to pay my fare. Why not give it six months, see how it goes down?' And the editor had agreed, after a lot of grumbling about how he didn't see why one of his best reporters should suddenly up sticks and head to some hick town no one had ever heard of in Ireland. What was all *that* about?

Shaun might have told him what it was all about, but he didn't figure it to be any of the other man's business. He hadn't introduced Bernard to any of the work crowd, not because they didn't know Shaun was gay – they all knew, some had personal experience of it – but because he wasn't entirely sure that what he was planning wasn't the height of idiocy.

Throwing away his $65,000 a year job with the *Telegraph* to go and set up house three thousand miles away with a man he barely knew, a man ten years older than himself? On paper, it didn't exactly sound like a viable idea.

Bernard thought it was very viable. 'You can write your novel. Don't tell me one of the *Telegraph*'s chief writers hasn't dreamed of producing the next great American novel.'

Shaun grinned. 'Hey, you're a mind-reader too?' He *had* often wondered idly about trying his hand at a book – but that was as far as he'd got.

'I'm whatever you want me to be.' Bernard laced his fingers through Shaun's. 'You'll have all the peace and quiet you need in Kilpatrick, and I'll be at your beck and call – and hey, you can help out in the shop if you want something to do in between the chapters.'

But Shaun didn't fancy working in a flower shop – far too clichéd for a gay couple – so he'd signed on the dotted line with the editor, packed his bags and followed Bernard to Kilpatrick, telling himself he could always come home if it didn't work out. He'd be taken back full-time tomorrow, Shaun was sure, even if the editor made out to be mad at him now for leaving.

And so far, so good. After a shaky first few weeks, when the lack of movie theatres and gay bars and gyms – and, Jesus, some decent *olives*, for crying out loud – was getting to him, when he was on the point of admitting that he'd made a colossal mistake and hopping on the next flight west, things began to turn around slowly.

A deli opened beside Flower Power, run by second-generation Italians and carrying halfway decent olives, and some damn good prosciutto. He'd taken Bernard's bike out from the shed one dry day, and discovered, somewhere during the four-and-a-half-hour round trip to the coast, that it definitely beat lifting weights in a sweaty gym.

He was learning to cope with a choice of just two or three movies a month in Kilpatrick's single cinema – all commercial box-office stuff – but he could still order his DVDs online, even in a little west-of-Ireland town.

Bernard had weathered the outbursts of those first few weeks, gently persuaded Shaun to give it another while, just until the end of the month. Weren't they good together?

They were. Amazingly, they seemed to have beaten

the odds – setting up house after a three-week fling, for Chrissakes – and now, eleven months on, Shaun was doing just fine, thank you. He got his two thousand words out of the way every Monday, e-mailed them on Tuesday, and used the rest of the week to work on *Up to No Good*, his story of an American con artist working the hotels and bed-and-breakfasts of Ireland. So far he'd written eighty thousand words – he figured another couple of months would finish his first draft. He should start looking up agents soon, calling in some favours back home.

He finished reading through the pages of his article. They'd do. For a bit of variety this week he'd included a couple of recipes he'd found in a *Tastes of Ireland* cookbook in the Kilpatrick library, colcannon and tea brack. He wondered if any of the readers would try them out in their air-conditioned American kitchens.

He heard a door opening and turned. Pam walked out from the kitchen next door with a white plastic basket full of damp clothes under one arm.

Shaun dropped the pages on the table and covered them with his coffee mug. 'Hey.'

Pam turned and smiled. 'Hi, Shaun.' She looked tired, darkish shadows under her eyes. She lifted a pillowcase from the basket and began to peg it on the line. 'Thanks for the lift the other day.'

'No problem. That's a great top.' Pink, with blurry splashes of green and blue flowers. Buttoned up to the neck, long-sleeved. 'You should undo a coupla buttons, though – you look like a flowery nun.'

Pam laughed as she bent to pull a shirt from the basket. 'Watch it – I'll tell Bernard you're trying to get me to show a bit of flesh.'

As she raised her arm to peg the shirt up, her sleeve rode back a little. Shaun saw two small black circles just above her wrist. Looked like tiny bruises. He pointed. 'You hurt your arm there?'

Pam pulled the sleeve down quickly, her smile fading. 'It's nothing – I'm always bumping into things.' She looked up at the sky. 'You think this weather will hold?'

Shaun shrugged. 'Hard to know in this place. Rain one minute, sun the next. Didn't hear a forecast.' He watched as she pegged out the last towel. 'Hopefully you'll get those to dry for you.'

Pam nodded, picked up the empty basket. 'Well, I'd better go in and get the lunch on for Mr O'Callaghan.'

Shaun made a face. 'Better not be late for that. See ya.'

What a job, at that old bastard's beck and call. Shaun wondered what kind of work Pam's husband did.

Then he wondered what kind of husband Pam had.

What sort of bump left you with two little circular bruises, right next to each other? Exactly as if someone had grabbed hold of her, hard.

She'd sure changed the subject fast, too, when he asked her about them.

Then he smiled and shook his head. Funny how you begin to see dramas everywhere when you're writing a novel. He picked up his mug and his pages and walked back inside.

Philip

He waited until the noise of the Hoover stopped downstairs, then got out of bed and began to undo the buttons on his pyjama top. Fiddly things, buttons; he hated them. Why couldn't they put stud fasteners in pyjamas? Much easier to manage. His fingers fumbled his way down, over the raised mound of his belly. Scrawny old man with a pot belly, that was what he'd become.

When had it happened? Surely when Aideen was alive he hadn't felt old like this, and that was only a year and a half ago. Eighteen months exactly last Thursday week. He and May had taken a taxi to the graveyard and put the bunch of flowers that May had bought at the homo's shop on her grave, and then they'd said a decade of the rosary together, like they always did on Aideen's monthly anniversaries.

He still forgot, sometimes, that she was gone – and then the horrible shock of it, when he remembered. She shouldn't have gone so quickly, that was the trouble. Oh, he knew some people would think it wasn't quick at all – some people didn't get four minutes, let alone four months. But of course he wasn't thinking like that in the beginning, when he'd yelled at Dr Taylor that he was wrong, that he must be wrong. That she just had a virus – *Give her something, man. Write out a bloody prescription, damn it.*

And Aideen had sat there, white-faced, and for once

hadn't tried to stop him, and Dr Taylor *had* written out a prescription, for painkillers and sleeping tablets, and Philip had gone on refusing to believe that anything was wrong for at least a month, like the pig-headed idiot he'd always been. Waiting for Aideen to get out of bed as soon as she was over whatever bug she had, and make his dinner, like she'd always done.

And in the end she *had* gone quickly, in the middle of a horrible night, lashing rain, wind battering the bedroom window. May and the boys and Hilda standing around the bed with him, not knowing what to say to each other. His two daughters-in-law trying to find things to do downstairs in the kitchen, making tea nobody wanted, putting things away in the wrong places.

And him, finally having to accept that Aideen was really leaving him, that this was one thing he couldn't control, no matter how much he cursed and swore at a bloody heartless God. Sitting up all night in the chair by her bed after she'd gone, covering her cold hand with his. Shouting at May to leave him *be*, for God's sake – and then wishing, as soon as she'd tiptoed from the room, that he hadn't.

He poked the second arm into his cardigan and pulled it up over his shoulders. More bloody buttons – he'd get one with a zip next time, if there was a next time. He shuffled to the window as he fumbled the buttons closed, looking down at Pam hanging out the clothes now, talking to someone – Philip turned and saw the other homo, the American one, sitting in his fancy chair, with his fancy coffee.

He was glad Aideen wasn't around to see this, him having to live next door to a couple of homos. Anything went now, nothing taboo any more. He was expected to smile and say hello when he met them, act as if there was nothing wrong with two grown men – he made a disgusted sound – living together, no doubt sharing a bedroom. Sickening. There was Pam now, chatting away to that one, and he'd heard May too, all pally whenever she met either of them. Well, he'd die screaming before he'd acknowledge that pair of sinners.

He sat on the side of the bed and pushed first one foot, then the other, into the Hush Puppies that May had bought him for Christmas. They were comfortable enough, but the colour was all wrong – he hated that horrible sandy shade. She should have got brown or black, she knew they were the colours he always went for in shoes. But at least these ones had no bloody laces for him to trip over.

He stood, stumbling a little. Where was his stick?

Old. He felt old, and it terrified him.

His birthday was coming up at the end of the week – he hoped to God May wouldn't make a fuss. She hadn't mentioned it . . . Maybe it had slipped her mind. He'd never been one for a fuss, Aideen had always understood that.

He reached for the stick, which was leaning against the wall, and made his way carefully from the bedroom. The smell of onions met him halfway down the stairs. Didn't that woman know onions gave him gas?

He sighed heavily as he made his slow, careful way through the hall and into the sitting room, where the *Irish Independent*, brought every morning by Pam, was waiting on the little table by his chair.

Hilda

She sank onto the garden seat and lifted her face to feel the gentle heat, enjoying the unaccustomed stretch in her neck. She should do exercises sometimes, keep the bones and muscles from seizing up, now that she was getting on. Seventy-three next birthday, could you credit it? Two years older than Aideen. Just the two of them, after their mother's miscarriages.

Hilda herself had only managed one baby. Terri, her big surprise after eleven years of marriage. Her first baby at forty-seven, the miracle she and Jim had prayed so hard for. Her replacement for Jim, she often thought, whose car had skidded into a ditch three months after Terri was born.

What a horrible, nightmarish time that had been. Even all these years later, Hilda couldn't think about it for long. Aideen had been wonderful then, coming over as often as she could, bringing eight-year-old May to watch the baby, leaving the boys at home with Marjorie, the babysitter, while the two women sat over cooling cups of tea in the kitchen, Hilda raging and weeping and mourning, and Aideen rocking her and whispering, 'You poor thing,' and 'I know, I know, darling.'

Enough. Hilda ran her fingers over the letter in her lap,

felt the crinkle of the two pages. She'd been surprised to see Terri's writing on the envelope – why would she be writing when they spoke on the phone every weekend? It seemed an extravagance to Hilda, a phone call from London so often, but Terri insisted that they could afford it, that it was much cheaper from England.

Stifling the tiny concern she felt – why wouldn't Terri write for a change? – Hilda had torn open the envelope and quickly scanned Terri's sloped writing, and *wonderful* and *pregnant* and *thrilled* and *November* had jumped out at her. And then she'd begun again at the beginning, and forced herself to slow down.

> *I wanted to write, because I didn't want to spring it on you over the phone. I wanted you to have plenty of time to digest it before I called you. Gerry and I are absolutely thrilled; I hope you will be too.*

When you get used to the idea of me having a baby with the man I stole from May, she might have added. If the day ever comes that you can forgive me for that.

Hilda sighed, turned her face up to the sun again. How had it happened? What unkind Fate had decreed that her only daughter should be the cause of such heartache for the next dearest person in Hilda's life? Hadn't losing Jim been cruel enough?

Hilda had been married three years when May was born to Aideen and Philip. She'd held her tiny niece in her arms and wondered when it would be her turn.

She'd driven the forty minutes to babysit as often as she could, greedy for the powdery smell of May, impatient to gather the warm weight of her against her chest, to feel the tiny, rapid breaths on her neck.

She's my rehearsal, Hilda would think. *I'll learn from her, and when my babies come along, I'll be ready.* And then Cathal had come along, and William – but for Aideen, not for Hilda.

And mixed with the pain of that, the almost physical ache she'd feel as she watched her sister feeding her babies, pulling tiny socks onto their adorably chubby feet, wiping dribble tenderly from their chins – mixed with that sadness was the consolation of the bond that Hilda was forming with her little niece. With Maisie.

They were close. Everyone noticed how close May was to her aunt, growing up. She and Hilda would spend hours in the garden, weeding and planting, mowing and clipping. Every summer, from the time she was five, May would be sent to Hilda and Jim's for her week-long 'holidays', stomping with her little suitcase up the stairs to what came to be known as 'Maisie's room'.

When Hilda discovered, unbelievably, that she was pregnant, her first thought was *How will May take it*? May was seven, going on eight, used to being the adored niece, comfortable in the undivided glow of Hilda's attention whenever she visited. Would this news alarm her? Would it change the way things were between the two of them?

But May was delighted when Aideen told her. The thought of a baby to look after at Hilda's charmed her. 'It'd better be a girl, though,' she told her mother. 'We've enough boys, haven't we?' And Aideen had solemnly agreed that they had more than enough boys.

Terri had obliged by turning out to be a girl, and May fussed around her tiny new cousin as much as she was allowed. She passed on her old dolls and tea-sets, and read to the baby from the same books that she'd read to her flowers a few years before.

'Look,' she'd say, pointing to the picture. 'See him? He's a boy. Look, here's his name, see it? It says Ben. B-E-N is how you spell it. Say Ben,' she'd command, and Terri would yawn and wave her miniature fists, and Aideen and Hilda would look on, trying not to laugh.

And then Jim was killed, and May watched over Terri while Hilda concentrated on not falling apart. And the years went by, and the cousins gradually drifted into their own lives and only met now and again – Philip and Aideen's silver anniversary, Cathal's science project award ceremony, Hilda's surprise sixtieth birthday party organised by Aideen, Terri's performance in the local dramatic society's production of *A View from the Bridge*.

And when she was nineteen, Terri went away to study languages in Trinity. And three years later she came home and met Gerry Scanlon, who had just got engaged to May.

The registry office wedding in London had been awkward. They had tried, Hilda had tried, and Gerry's parents, to make the best of it. They'd gone to a lovely hotel for dinner afterwards, and Gerry's father had made a short speech and welcomed Terri into the family, and toasted the newlyweds. And Terri had looked pretty in a pink trouser suit, and it was obvious that Gerry adored her, and that he was making a big effort to be charming to Hilda.

And of course Hilda hoped they'd be happy, of course she did.

But Maisie . . . wailing in anguish when Hilda had told her, shaking her head and trying to apologise to Hilda, completely unable to stop the sobs that had burst out of her when she heard. But Maisie . . .

And now this news. Hilda knew she should phone Terri, knew her daughter would be waiting to hear from her. Writing was the coward's way out – surely she could manage a phone call.

But what if he answered? What if he waited for her to congratulate him, when Hilda knew she couldn't, just couldn't? Not yet, anyway.

She picked up her biro and opened the writing pad that sat on the cast-iron table in front of her. She began *My darling Terri*, then paused, one hand resting on a corner of the page to stop the little breeze lifting it.

Then she wrote, *I have just got your letter, and of course I'm delighted with your news. Congratulations to you both.*

She stopped. It sounded so stilted. She couldn't bring herself to use his name. He was going to be the father of her grandchild.

She lifted the pen again and wrote, *I would love to see you, if you could get away. Or maybe I could come over for a few days.*

And every word hurt.

Francesca

The hairdresser held up the mirror behind Francesca's head, and Francesca looked at the back of her newly trimmed hair and nodded politely, wondering if anyone ever did anything else. Did some people take a look and say, *Oh no, that's not what I wanted, that's not what I asked you for at all?* Hardly. What could be done, after the scissors had got rid of it?

'Thank you.' She took the soft, wide brush that the hairdresser offered her, then swept it across her face and around her neck. She waited as the hairdresser pulled apart the Velcro fastening at the back of the shapeless flowery robe, and she stretched out her hands to allow it to be taken off her.

Leaning forward, she checked her face in the mirror, brushed a few stray hairs from her cheek, ran a red gloss over her lips, sprayed her wrists and cleavage with Chanel No. 5.

In the street she turned left. As she approached her neighbour's flower shop, three doors down, she noticed the trails of water that ran across the path to a gathering of suds in the gutter. Washing his window earlier, she assumed. Bernard was behind the counter, talking to a customer. Francesca slowed her pace as she walked past, searching for lilies among the filled buckets on the wooden display unit outside but seeing none.

She turned into the deli beside Flower Power, picked up a basket from the stack inside the door. Horrendously expensive place, but what choice did you have in Kilpatrick if you wanted the kind of food Francesca did?

She chose some organic lemons and two jars of roasted red peppers, and chunks of *biscotti* and some pickled artichoke hearts, coffee, olives and fresh pasta. At the counter she asked for half a pound of bufallo mozzarella, and a wedge of frittata, some mortadella and a slice of gorgonzola. Knowing, as she paid, as she rummaged in her purse for change, that the handsome young shop assistant was staring openly at her breasts. Just for fun, she leaned forward slightly as she put the money on the counter, allowing her blouse to fall open a little more, and treating him to a better view of her rose-coloured lacy bra.

In the café down the street she ordered an espresso, conscious again of eyes following her as she walked towards a table in the corner. People watched her, and she didn't mind.

Two years, six months, she thought as she sipped the deliciously bitter dark coffee. Lucia a two-year-old toddler, babbling to Francesca every day in baby Italian, brown from running around almost naked in the big sunny garden of Francesca's family home in Perola. Screaming on Francesca's lap as they'd flown with Paul, two years and six months ago, from Rome's Ciampino airport to Shannon, Ireland.

Had Lucia sensed, in the way that very young children can sometimes sense, that everything was going to be different now? That Paul's assignment to set up the company's Irish operation meant they were leaving behind the blues and oranges and violet pinks of Italy for the grey and green of Kilpatrick?

Paul had grown up in a tiny village ten miles from Kilpatrick. It had been his suggestion to base the new branch of the Italian computer company just outside the town, in the vacant space beside the dairy plant. Lower ground rent, he'd said. Cheaper employment than in Dublin. Within commuting distance of Galway, with all its computer graduates, and Shannon Airport, for the Ryanair flight to Ciampino. His Italian bosses had agreed, on condition that Paul, as the local, move back and oversee operations.

He'd been so anxious when Francesca and Lucia had arrived with him in Ireland, so eager for them to be happy in their new surroundings, hunting around, using his old contacts to find an agency that was looking for Italian translators, setting up interviews for Francesca. He'd been so good with Lucia too – arranging for a nanny, the present au pair's forerunner, to come and live with them so that Francesca would have time to work on her translations.

And to be fair, moving to Ireland had been what Francesca wanted too. It had seemed like the answer to her prayers, a place where she could lick her still-too-raw wounds and forget, or at least learn to live with, the heartache of the past. She needed to go away, to be someplace where everything didn't torture her with reminders of the past. She needed to leave until she felt strong enough to come back. To be happy, once again, in Perola.

Because that had been the plan when they'd left. A year, eighteen months at the most, to make sure everything was sorted and in place, and then they could go back to live in Italy for good.

And even when things hadn't quite gone according to plan – when Paul complained of deliveries being delayed, or not happening at all; of employees getting better offers and leaving, or turning out not to have the qualifications they'd claimed on their CVs; of customers insisting on lower prices to match Far Eastern competitors – Francesca had still trusted that one day, maybe a bit longer than they'd thought, but some day, they'd go back to Perola.

And the longer they stayed in Ireland, the further away Perola seemed, and the more foolish Francesca's hopes. Now Lucia had started school, and was refusing to speak Italian with Francesca because all her friends spoke English. And the two holidays Francesca and Lucia had spent in Perola – Paul had been too busy to accompany them, he hadn't been back to Italy at all, apart from one conference in Rome in March – had only emphasised Francesca's piercing homesickness.

But should she still be feeling so lonely when she had Paul? Surely her longing for Italy shouldn't be so strong, when she had a good man here in Ireland, who provided for her and Lucia, who saw to their every need?

She finished her espresso and picked up her bag. Maybe this summer she and Lucia could go home for a month instead of the two weeks she'd booked. Paul might be able to get some time off – but even if he couldn't, he'd manage without them. Marietta would be there to cook for him, her meals were just about approaching a tolerable standard – not that Francesca was letting her near any of the food that she'd just spent a fortune on. She'd check out the Ryanair website when she got home. She walked rapidly past the other tables, oblivious, for once, of the stares.

Carmel

As she opened the classroom door that led straight out into the school yard, the first drops of rain began to fall. Typical. Carmel made herself smile at the gaggle of parents and minders who stood waiting – 'Hello there, everyone' – and then she began to sort out the children behind her.

'James, come on, Mammy's here. Robbie, please pick up your lunchbox. Mags, Daddy's waiting. Here, let me do up your coat, and don't be cross with Robbie any more – he's very sorry, aren't you, Robbie? Hurry up there, Joe – are you still drinking your milk? Ah, come on now. Hoods up, everyone. It's raining, it's pouring, the old man is snoring.'

And all the time she talked, she kept half an eye on Lucia, running over to the new au pair – Marianna? Marietta? Looked young, could hardly be more than nineteen or twenty. Sleeping under Paul's roof, maybe in the next room. Lying in bed at night, maybe imagining him with her, instead of beside that tarty-looking wife of his.

Carmel watched the au pair fiddling with the buttons of Lucia's coat. Not pretty, not at all. Dumpy, with dull black hair and a wide, flat nose. And that cheap, quilted jacket, and those awful shoes.

Carmel fingered the little shell around her neck. Nothing to worry about there then, not his type at all. She had a last check in the yard to make sure everyone was accounted for, then closed the door on the steadily worsening rain.

As she leaned back against the glass, as she heard the rattle of the drops on the windows, she dipped again into the first time they'd met. Three or four days into the new school year, when Carmel was still surrounded by tears and tantrums every morning, when she could hardly string a sentence together at the end of each manic day, Paul had arrived into the classroom with Lucia by the hand.

It was his height she noticed first, towering over the other parents, at least a foot taller than Carmel herself. She nodded at him briefly over the heads of her charges, and went back to trying to separate Fergus and Robbie, who were each claiming custody of a red crayon.

'You've got your hands full.' She looked up and there he was, smiling. 'Just wanted to introduce myself – Paul

Ryan. I brought Lucia in.' He stuck out a hand. Carmel took it, and smelled something spicy, and noticed the well-cut suit. 'Carmel Gannon, unfortunate teacher.' She held his gaze, conscious of the rising babble of indignation behind her. His hand was cool, his grip nicely firm. He must be around forty, maybe more. Carmel's current boyfriend was twenty-two. Obliging enough in bed, but nothing much to say for himself out of it.

Paul dropped her hand, and she saw his eyes flicker over her body – just for an instant – before he turned towards the door.

It was enough. The boyfriend didn't last beyond the weekend, and within two weeks he'd been replaced in Carmel's bed by Paul Ryan.

Who was to say who'd made the running? They'd both recognised something in the other, that was all. The rest was easy. Carmel had never had any trouble with the rest.

She pulled herself away from the door and began to bring some order back to the chaotic classroom. The days were crawling towards Thursday. She could hardly wait.

Francesca

'Mamma!' Lucia slipped her hand out of Marietta's and ran down the wet street, her hood slipping backwards bit by bit.

'Wait, Lucia.' Marietta plodded heavily after her, hair slapping against her uncovered head.

Francesca was just coming out of a café, pushing

open her umbrella. She stopped and turned, then crouched slightly, her free arm extended to grab Lucia as the little girl reached her.

'*Ciao*, baby. Are you wet?' She pulled Lucia's hood over her head, then jerked up her umbrella. 'You must put up your hood in the rain, OK?'

The au pair reached them in time to hear the note of impatience in Francesca's voice. 'Hood is up before, but it fall off just now when she run.'

Francesca held the umbrella over Lucia and herself as she scanned the road, not looking in Marietta's direction. 'I see.' She lifted a hand, and a passing taxi pulled up immediately, sloshing through a little puddle as it stopped.

Francesca ushered Lucia towards it – 'In you get, baby' – then turned back to Marietta and smiled, her eyes darting briefly to Marietta's drenched hair. 'Will you be an angel and collect the dry cleaning for me? You remember where it is, don't you? Just down to the end of this street and around to the left.' She passed Marietta the still-open umbrella. 'Here, this will keep you dry.' Then she rummaged in her bag and pulled out a green ticket and a twenty-euro note. 'That should cover it.'

As the taxi pulled away, she turned to Lucia. 'Now, tell me all about your day, *cara*.'

Neither of them watched Marietta as she turned back in the direction of the dry cleaner's, umbrella held above her already drenched body, ticket and money clutched damply in her trembling hand.

May

She stamped irritably through the puddles, not caring that her jeans were wet now almost to the knees. And, of course, she would have to choose tonight to leave her hair down, when anyone could see it was going to rain again. Serve her right to have it swinging in rats' tails around her shoulders now. Take hours to dry it when she got home – she'd have to ring Rebecca and cancel.

Great. A great end to a shitty day.

Of course she'd run out of paint at Carmel's, with just a bit of a wall to go. Which meant she'd have to call by the hardware shop between this and Friday, buy a whole new can of that awful colour just for the last bit.

And her father had complained about Pam again at dinner. 'I've said to her about the onions – loads of times. She does it on purpose.'

It was all May could do not to pick up his plate of sausages and throw it at him. Better still, break it over his head and make him clean it up. Him and his onions.

Her hand went to her throat automatically, and felt nothing. Stupidly, her eyes filled with tears. It was only a necklace – she didn't even know who'd sent it to her. She brushed away the tears angrily.

So ignorant, Jude had been earlier. No, her mother was working late tonight. No, she hadn't said anything about a necklace. Yeah, she'd ask her when she got in. A pink shell on a gold chain, right. Barely a minute's worth of conversation on the doorstep, Jude chewing something and not looking above May's chin. Closing the door before May had fully turned away. Ignorant.

Nobody at home at the window-cleaning house, no sign of the necklace anywhere on the ground outside.

She pulled on Jojo's leash as the dog lagged behind, sniffing at something. 'Come *on*, hurry up.'

How could Terri be pregnant? It wasn't fair. It should have been May picking out tiny clothes, choosing names, ticking days off on a calendar. *It should have been me.* More tears came, and she didn't bother to wipe them away, just let them roll down her face along with the rain. *He loved me, I know he did. If she'd only left us alone—*

She splashed angrily into another puddle and, out of nowhere, a man's voice said, 'Hey, watch it.'

May lifted her head and the voice became black boots, a pair of faded jeans, a leather jacket with a turned-up collar and a wet blond head, almost as wet as May's own. He looked different out of his uniform. His lashes glistened with rain. He was smiling as he drew level with her. 'I'm wet enough without you drenching me too.'

'Sorry.' She found herself smiling back, her black mood lifting. 'I didn't think I'd meet anyone out tonight.' *Please don't let him notice the tears. Please let him think it's all rain.*

'I know – we must both need our heads examined.' Jojo sniffed at his leg, and he put a hand down to stroke the dog's wet head. 'Hey, buddy, I think you need to take this young lady home now. We don't want her getting pneumonia, do we?' Drops were forming on the ends of his hair. May smelled wet leather.

He straightened up, then lifted a hand. 'Take care, May.' And he was off, striding quickly past her, disappearing around the next corner as she pulled Jojo's leash in the opposite direction.

It was the first time he'd called her May. She hadn't a clue what his name was. Her skin was tingling. God, she must look like a drowned rat. Every time she'd seen him lately, she'd been like something the cat dragged in.

We don't want her getting pneumonia.

The night was still young. If she hurried home, she could still make it to Rebecca's.

Carmel

She added a bottle of burgundy to her basket and checked her list. Chocolate digestives for the staffroom – her turn – duck pâté and crackers that were most definitely not for the staffroom. And wine, of course. And cheese, she had to get the Brie he'd commented on last time.

Oh, and maybe some dark chocolate, for afterwards.

She was so happy with her newly painted kitchen walls, so glad she'd gone with her instinct and chosen that ochre instead of the caramel shade Pam preferred. Pity it wasn't quite finished, but May had done a nice job all the same, nice and neat.

She wondered if Paul would like it – or even notice it. Men were often so unobservant and, of course, his mind would be on other things when he called round on Thursday . . .

At the checkout, she rummaged in her bag for a fifty-cent piece, reluctant to break another tenner, and then, after she'd paid, she realised that she'd forgotten to bring a bag so she had to break the tenner after all to pay for a plastic one, and the cashier wasn't too happy, by the look of her.

And maybe it was because there were three or four behind Carmel in the queue, or because her mind was on Thursday, and what would happen after the Brie and burgundy, or because she was anxious to get home and put her feet up, maybe it was because of all these things that she didn't notice her present slipping from her neck and landing in a little pink and gold heap on the floor at the checkout.

And by the time the third next customer had spotted it and handed it to Marjorie O'Dea at the cash register, by the time Marjorie had taken it and put it for safe keeping on the shelf underneath, beside her handbag, by that time, Carmel's car had long since disappeared from the supermarket car park.

It wasn't until she was undressing, much later that night, that Carmel missed the necklace. She threw on a dressing-gown and searched the room, then the stairs, and the sitting room where she'd been reading the paper, and finally the car, with her flashlight. 'Fuck, fuck, *fuck*.'

Where had she noticed it last? She remembered Iseult admiring it, in the staffroom . . . Jesus, it could be anywhere – the classroom, the staffroom, the school yard, anywhere.

Fuck. Paul would look for it in the morning when he brought Lucia in and she wouldn't be wearing it.

The supermarket – could it have fallen off there? She'd phone first thing in the morning – what time did it open? If they had it there, she could collect it on her way to work. If not, she'd just have to search everywhere she could think of in school. She'd get the kids to search the class, turn it into a game. *Fuck.*

Suddenly she remembered that she was meeting Pam after work – good, she'd need a drink by then for sure. She pulled off her dressing-gown and yanked back the duvet.

Of course, that was long after Marjorie O'Dea got home from her late shift at the supermarket, and opened her bag and said to Jude, her eighteen-year-old unemployed daughter, 'Look what I found for you at work today.'

Jude

And remembering the cleaning woman calling around earlier, when Ma was still at work, and thinking, *So she didn't lose it here after all – weird that Ma still found it, though*, Jude put out her hand and said, 'Hey, nice one.'

Paddy

He wheeled his bin through the house, over the trail of spread-out newspapers, and positioned it at the edge of the path, ready for the morning's collection. Mr Kennedy's bin already stood there, branded with a shaky TK in thick, black letters. Tom? Timothy?

He went back inside, shaking the drops off his hair. The Horslips CD had finished so he pushed the eject button. Half past ten on a wet Tuesday night.

He wondered what Chloe was doing this evening. Collecting some of that rain, maybe. She used to wash her hair in rain water, and let it dry naturally. It was always wonderfully soft, and it smelled of the minty shampoo she used.

Funny, he hadn't thought about Chloe in months. He wondered why she'd popped into his head again this evening.

May's hair was longer than Chloe's, and thicker. And when the sun shone on it, it was the colour of butterscotch, and sometimes she wore it twisted into a thick plait and other times it fell around her shoulders.

He lifted an Eric Clapton CD from its case, slid it into the drive and pressed play. He went back to the sofa and picked up the newspaper with its half-finished crossword.

He'd like to put his hands into May's hair. To grab fistfuls of it and lift it up and bury his face in it.

I'm standin' at the crossroads, sang Eric Clapton.

Tryin' to read the signs, to tell me which way I should go to find the answer.

You and me both, pal, thought Paddy.

Rebecca

'Ah no, it can't be gone.' She poured tea into both cups.

'It can be. It is.' May added milk. 'It's definitely gone.' She lifted the cup to her lips and sipped the pale brown liquid.

'But when did you see it last?'

'I told you, when I put it on yesterday morning. And I didn't miss it till I was going to bed.'

'It might still turn up.' Rebecca blew on her tea, then sipped. 'Have you retraced your steps?'

May nodded. 'Pretty much. There's no sign.' She drank again. 'Hey, you haven't forgotten about Sunday, have you? The big birthday celebration.'

'God, no.' Rebecca dipped a biscuit into her tea. 'Remember I'm working though, so I won't be there till at least six.'

'Fine.' May let a beat go by, and then she said, 'Guess who I bumped into earlier.'

The biscuit stopped in mid-air, dripping tea. 'Who?'

'Guess.'

Rebecca considered. 'You're going as red as a beetroot so it's got to be our favourite postman. He wasn't doing night duty, was he?'

May laughed. 'Just out walking in the rain, like

myself.' She hesitated. 'He called me May, the first time he's used my name.'

'Well.' Rebecca munched her biscuit. 'A giant leap for mankind, I'd call that.'

May picked up her cup. 'I know you think it's ridiculous—'

'I do.'

'—and I know I should do something about it, but I just can't. Let's wait and see, OK?'

Rebecca started to speak, then stopped. She dipped her biscuit into her cup again. 'May, it's been how long now? Three years? Longer?'

'I know, I know. . . '

'Life goes on – *blast* –' as a soggy chunk, halfway to her mouth, plopped back into the tea.

'I know it does, it's just. . . ' May watched her fish it out, then said, as if she'd only just thought of it, 'Oh, and there's news about Gerry.'

Wednesday

Dry, settled weather throughout most of the country, with the best of the sunshine in the west, and a mild, dry night. Highs of 18 to 22 degrees.

Philip

It came clattering into his head, yanking him roughly out of sleep. Blasted bin men, roaring around at this ungodly hour, rattling and banging. Making more noise than they needed to, Philip was sure, just to make certain they left no one asleep. A game to them, that's all it was.

They'd never heard the bins being collected in the old house, up the narrow cul-de-sac the lorry couldn't negotiate. They'd all wheel their bins to the end of the road every Tuesday evening, and the lorry would be far enough away not to bother them in the morning. Different story here – it passed right by May's house, like a bloody juggernaut.

He turned over, knowing that sleep would not find him again. He'd been such a sound sleeper when he was younger – Aideen had been convinced that he was just pretending not to hear the babies when they cried at night. Now the slightest thing woke him, and once that happened, he could forget about getting back to sleep.

And his feet were freezing, as usual. The middle of summer, practically – not that you'd know it from the weather – and his toes were like bloody ice.

He sighed heavily. So many crosses to bear. What day was it? Hard to remember when you weren't going out to work, when there was nothing to structure your week any more. Not that his civil service job had been what you'd call stimulating, but at least he hadn't had to wait till he saw the paper to be sure what day it was.

Then he remembered: bin day. Wednesday.

The lorry drove on, its din receding, and he cocked an ear for the sound of rain on the roof or against the window. It had been so wet last night. May had come home like a drowned rat from walking that dog, out without a hat or umbrella. And then turned around when her hair was only half dry and cycled over to Rebecca's. As if they didn't talk enough on the phone, those two. May'd get a cold now probably, be laid up for days. Be lucky if it didn't turn into pneumonia.

But he could hear no patter on the roof this morning – it must have stopped during the night. Probably still be damp, though.

His daughter's lifestyle, her various jobs, confused him. What was wrong with having just one job like everyone else? Why did she have to become this kind of daft menial worker, cleaning and painting people's houses, pulling up their weeds, washing their windows and walking their dogs? No way to make a living for a woman – and she couldn't actually enjoy it, could she?

According to May, she could. When Philip had moved in with her first, and made some reference to her lack of normal work, wondering aloud whether she was ever going to get another job like she'd had at Dr Taylor's, May had just laughed and assured him that she loved what she was doing now, that she made more money this way, and met more people, than if she was stuck in some office. Ridiculous, it had sounded to Philip.

And then, some months ago, May mentioned that she had a new job. Some man, whose garden she was going to be overhauling every Thursday morning for a month. 'I'm his birthday present from his sister,' May explained. 'She's paid me to clear his garden for four weeks. She says he's useless at it, hasn't looked at it since he bought the house months ago.'

It sounded daft to Philip, paying May to be somebody's birthday present. 'And what does he have to say about it?'

'He's delighted – apparently. I haven't met him yet.'

There was no more mention of it, and Philip had forgotten about the whole thing, until one day, much later, May had said something about her Thursday morning gardening job.

Philip stared at her. 'Not the one you were doing for someone's birthday – you're not still at that? I thought you were only doing it for a few weeks.'

May nodded. 'That was the arrangement at the start. But when the month was up he left a note for me, asking me to keep coming. Now he pays me himself.' She smiled. 'Iseult, his sister, was hoping that would happen.'

'What age man would he be?' Philip pictured someone elderly — a widower, maybe, like himself, finding the garden beyond him now.

May thought. 'Around my own age I'd say, early thirties or thereabouts. I know Iseult is younger than him, and she's about thirty.'

Philip frowned, digesting this. So a young man was paying May to come to his house every week. He began to wonder if it was entirely respectable. 'What's he like, this man?'

May smiled again. 'I've no idea — I've never met him. He's always out at work when I go around there. He's some kind of a carpenter.'

At least he had a trade. And never there when she went around — so nothing underhanded about the arrangement, Philip supposed. Strange, though, to be working for months for someone you'd never met. Going to his house, working in his garden every week, taking his money and never coming face to face with him.

Philip was sorry May had never married. She'd have made someone a good wife, even if her cooking wasn't a patch on her mother's. But she'd been unlucky there, hooking up with that unsavoury character who'd ended up marrying Hilda's girl. Shame about that. He'd felt so bad for May when all that had happened.

He'd watched her cry in her mother's arms and he'd kept his distance, completely at a loss as to what to say, or not say – men were so useless when it came to things like that. Or at least, *he* was. He'd never been one to talk about his feelings, never felt comfortable when people got personal like that. He was better at doing than talking – he'd have taken a punch at that man, no bother, for what he'd done to May.

But Aideen wouldn't let him talk like that, even if it was just to her. 'Whether we like it or not, he's chosen Terri,' she'd say, 'and Terri is family – see how good Hilda's always been to May. So we have to put that behind us, and concentrate on May.'

And so Philip had helped out with the deposit on May's house, because it was the only thing he could think of to do. The January day she'd moved in, he and Rebecca had ferried boxes and suitcases in their cars from the apartment May had shared with two others to the house across town.

When everything had been moved, Philip assembled May's new bed in the room she'd chosen while Rebecca got a fire going in the sitting room, because the previous owners had left the boiler empty of oil.

May swept floors and unpacked the most immediately needed boxes while Aideen wrestled with the camping gas stove in the kitchen, and then the four of them had sat on canvas chairs around the fire – the red sofa had yet to be bought – and toasted the new beginning with mugs of tea and plates of sausages and beans.

'Like camping,' May said, although they'd never gone in for camping holidays as a family. In the firelight she looked excited, and happier than she'd been for weeks, and Philip hoped that settling into the house would keep her too busy to brood over her recent trouble.

He wouldn't have chosen the house for himself — those narrow stairs, and none of the walls straight, you could see that clearly. Three bedrooms, but the third one was tiny — you'd hardly fit a child in there. And no bath, just a shower, in the bathroom. Why call it a bathroom if it didn't have a bath? It might be fine for May, but not for him. He'd never been one for a shower, nasty, uncivilised things. Dangerous, too, for a man his age, standing on that slippery floor.

Just as well he couldn't see into the future. Just as well no one had taken him aside that evening and told him his wife had less than two years of life left, and that he would become increasingly less able to live alone after she was gone.

Just as well he'd had no idea then how soon he'd have to take May up on her offer to move into the house he wouldn't have taken a present of the first time he saw it. He'd kept insisting he could go to a nursing home — although the thought secretly terrified him — but May was having none of it. 'Of course you'll come to me. Haven't I lots of room? We won't be in each other's way at all.'

Lots of room — in this poky little house that would never feel like home to him. But here he was, nothing but a burden to May, and the knowledge infuriated him.

He turned towards the window and saw light seeping through the curtains. Was the sun shining? It looked like it. Although yesterday had started off fine too – probably be lashing by lunchtime.

He needed the toilet. He pushed the duvet down, struggled into a sitting position and heaved himself out of bed to begin another wretched day.

Pam

She took the saucepan off the cooker and spooned the two brown eggs out of the water, into the waiting eggcups.

Jack walked into the kitchen as she was slicing bread. He dropped into his chair and put up a hand to stroke the arm that was holding the loaf. 'You sleep OK? Thought you were tossing a bit.'

Pam looked down at him; he could do with a haircut. 'No, I slept fine. Looks like it's going to be a good day.' The sun was pouring in the window, catching the breadknife and making it gleam. He watched as she took two slices from the toaster and fed another two in.

'Thanks, sweetie.' He spread butter onto his slice and cut it into triangles. Then he topped his egg, sprinkled salt on it and dipped a corner of toast in. He caught her eye as he took a bite, and winked at her. Pam smiled back at him, lifted the pot and poured tea for the two of them.

He spooned out some more egg. 'Any plans for after work?'

After a heartbeat of silence, Pam said, 'Actually, I'm meeting Carmel for coffee and a chat so I'm not sure if I'll be home before you.' She added milk to her tea, keeping her eyes on the thin white stream.

He nodded, munching. 'OK.' When he'd swallowed, he said, 'Where's good for coffee in town, these days?' He spooned sugar into his cup and stirred.

Pam looked at him, her hand still on the jug. 'I don't know yet – we're meeting at the supermarket, and then we'll choose a place.' She cut butter from the block and began to spread it over her toast.

'Tesco?' He was still stirring his tea. Twice as much sugar would have been well dissolved by now. 'Tesco, you're meeting at?'

Pam nodded. The toaster popped and she got up quickly, walked over, took the new slices from it and put them both on his plate. 'I'll probably be home before you, but just in case.'

He bit into his toast and chewed without responding for a minute. Then he said, 'As long as you're going to Tesco, can you get me some shaving foam? I'm nearly out.'

'Of course.' She had taken the top off her egg, but she hadn't begun to eat it. Now she cut her toast in half, took a tiny bite and put it down again.

He noticed. 'Why aren't you eating?'

Pam shook her head. 'Just not hungry.' She picked up her cup and drank. 'It's nothing.' Her hand shook slightly. The kitchen was too quiet.

When he went upstairs to shave, she threw her

breakfast into the bin and stood by the sink, breathing deeply, trying not to be sick. The knot she'd had in her stomach while she was telling him the lie was still there. She could picture his reaction if she'd said she was meeting Carmel in the little bar near the school. Now she'd have to go to Tesco, in the opposite direction, when she left May's house. She'd be late for Carmel, probably. At least ten minutes late.

She hadn't told him about the baby. She was pregnant with their first child, and she hadn't told her husband. She hadn't told him because she was thinking about having an abortion: she was afraid to bring a child into their house.

She leaned against the sink, full of despair, hearing his footsteps on the stairs. What in God's name was she going to do?

May

She sat, chin in hand, half-written shopping list on the table in front of her, watching the dust motes dance in the sunbeam that slanted across the kitchen. Beautiful day, the real start of summer. Lots of gardening over the next few months. She wrote *bird seed* on the list. Not much good putting a beautiful bird table in your garden if there was nothing on it . . .

She doodled a stick figure at the bottom of the list and drew a postman's hat on its head. Rebecca was right: it wasn't fair to expect him to make the first move.

But the thought of her making any kind of move scared May witless. She wrote *whiskey* on the list, and added *gin*. Hilda liked gin. She wrote *tonic* and *lemons*.

Dad was in fair enough form this morning. For once, she'd remembered the salt for his egg. Maybe he'd like cereal tomorrow, as a change. She'd get him something nice, with berries in it. She wrote *cereal*.

She heard the key in the front door and called, 'Good morning,' as she stood up. Time to head off for Rebecca's.

'Morning, May.' Pam appeared, shrugging off her jacket. 'Lovely day, after yesterday.'

'Fabulous. I'm making out the shopping list for Sunday night. I'm going with the salmon, it sounds great. What veg do you think would be good with it?'

Cycling to Rebecca's, May thought, *Pam looked pale this morning. Hope she's not finding the going too tough with Dad.* She didn't know what she'd do if Pam left. Getting out of the house every day was her lifeline, and Pam was so dependable and capable.

She hoped that good-looking husband of hers realised how lucky he was.

Bernard

Lucia's mother had just left the shop with a dozen lilies. Bernard was thinking how well the elegant cream flowers suited the equally stylish Francesca when the phone rang. He gave an apologetic smile to a woman who was coming in – 'I'll be right with you' – and picked up the receiver. 'Flower Power, how may I help you?'

'Is that the flower fairy?' The voice was muffled, high-pitched, hard to make out.

Bernard must have misheard. 'Pardon me?'

'I said, is that the fucking flower fairy?' Not so muffled now, the words over-emphasised, deliberately slow, the way you might speak to a person who wasn't too bright. Every syllable all too insultingly clear. Some odd, gasping noise in the background – laughter?

Bernard felt something cold uncurl inside him. He turned away from the customer and said quietly, 'Who is this, please?' He could feel a pulse banging in his throat. His face was clammy.

'It's the fairy killer' – in a singsong chant now – 'coming to get you' – like a child might recite a skipping rhyme – 'you fucking *queer.*'

The last word was spat out with such menace that it sounded nothing like a child's rhyme any more. 'You *faggot*, you—'

Bernard took the receiver away from his ear and pressed the disconnect button, then switched off the phone. Then he turned back to his customer, praying that his legs would support him.

After she'd left – had she noticed anything wrong? – he hung the *back in five minutes* sign on the door, turned the key and went to the rear of the shop where he sank onto the battered old couch, letting his head fall forward into his hands. Who was doing this? Why was he being targeted? There had been so much malice in the voice – whoever it was must despise him.

Bernard shuddered, hands cradling his head, pulse beating steadily in his skull.

Six years he'd been running the flower shop, since his parents had decided to take early retirement, and there'd never been a problem until about two months ago. He knew a lot of the people who came in – he'd been working in the shop off and on since his teens – and, having grown up in Kilpatrick, he was also acquainted with a few of the people in the town who wouldn't dream of buying his flowers, but nobody had ever bothered him like this before.

In the last few years, Kilpatrick had seen a lot of change. Since the motorway had been extended to just a few miles outside the town, it had become a relatively easy commute to Galway, and a few big new housing estates had sprung up on the outskirts to meet the sudden demand.

Was it someone who'd recently come to live in Kilpatrick, who'd heard about the gay florist and decided to have some fun with him?

Bernard had never been openly gay in his hometown. He'd told his parents in his twenties, and they'd taken it badly, especially his mother, but eventually they'd come to terms with it, sort of. He did wonder sometimes if their decision to retire early and leave the shop to him had anything to do with his revelation. Now he only saw them about once a month, when he was invited home – without Shaun – for dinner. They'd politely refused to visit him since Shaun's arrival, and he respected their sensitivities.

Bernard had always tried to make it as easy as he could for them. While he was living at home, he'd gone to Galway and found what he wanted there. And even when he'd moved into his own house, he'd been as discreet as possible if anyone stayed the night. Until Shaun, whose arrival had changed everything.

It still made him smile, how he and Shaun had met in Boston. How he'd sat in the restaurant, trying not to make it obvious that he was *feasting* on Shaun, easily the best-looking man he'd ever laid eyes on, with those perfect eyes, that lazy smile, that hair, those cheekbones. God, some people had everything.

Shaun was with two others, one male, one female, gradually revealing themselves to be a couple as Bernard pretended not to watch. So the hunk was on his own. Forking up his pasta, Bernard saw the waiter eyeing Shaun as he served them what looked like a round of blue drinks. There was a lot of laughter going on at their table. Shaun, of course, had perfect teeth, the perfect dimple. On impulse, Bernard ordered another half-bottle of white wine. What the hell? He was on his holidays.

The party of three were joined ten minutes later by a fourth – an older man, who embraced each of them when he arrived, then sat beside Shaun. Great, thought Bernard. His date. *The grateful sugar-daddy, who'll probably pick up the tab.*

He was right about the daddy bit. Shaun's father was meeting his son and daughter, and his daughter's husband, for dinner. Shaun's father, Bernard was to discover, was perfectly fine about the fact that his only son was gay.

By the time he'd finished the second half-bottle, Bernard was buzzing pleasantly. He paid the bill and left what he hoped was a respectable tip, then walked past the table of four he'd been trying not to watch all evening.

Or he would have walked past, if some mad impulse – or that last glass of wine – hadn't made him stop and say, 'Excuse me, I hope you don't mind my butting in, but I was wondering what the blue drinks you were having earlier were. They looked very interesting.' He tried not to focus on Shaun as he talked, tried to look at each of them in turn, with their faces turned up towards his.

'You're Irish.' Shaun smiled up at him with that wonderful face. He wore a green shirt that perfectly matched his eyes.

Bernard smiled back, aiming for a casual grin. Hoping it didn't come out as a ferocious leer. 'I certainly am.'

'Join us.' Shaun was already pulling over a chair from the next table. 'You can have your very own blue drink.' Ignoring Bernard's 'Oh, no, I really. . . ' he turned to the older man – 'Dad? Same again?' – and when his father nodded, he signalled to a passing waiter and ordered four Curacaos and a dirty martini.

Bernard sat, thinking again, *what the hell*? He was in Boston for three weeks, minus the past two days, which he'd spent wandering from art gallery to bargain basement to food hall, wondering why on earth he'd come, already planning to change his ticket home if things didn't start looking up.

They stayed in the restaurant another two hours, except for Shaun's father, who left after a plate of paella. He shook hands with Bernard and told him it was nice to meet him, and to enjoy his stay in Boston. Bernard assured him he would, making a huge effort not to slur his words, acutely aware of the delicious scent of Shaun's aftershave.

In the morning Bernard woke up alone, in his underpants, with a thumping headache and a ferocious thirst. He registered the bland cream walls of his hotel room as he tried to conjure up the sequence of events from the night before.

He had some vague memory of trying to explain the north of Ireland situation to the sister's husband . . . Someone had mentioned *Riverdance* . . . He'd told them about the flower shop – the sister was interested in gardening, wasn't she? Or was it flower arranging?

And how had he got back here? Had there been a taxi ride? Had the driver said something about the Blarney Stone? Or was that someone else, earlier?

He turned his head carefully and saw his clothes on a chair, neatly folded. He lifted the phone and croaked out an order for two bottles of Perrier, eggs and bacon, rye toast and lots of coffee, and as he was padding back gingerly from the bathroom he saw the note, half tucked under his shirt. *Hope we haven't put you off blue drinks for life. Thanks for joining us, it was fun.* The note was signed *Shaun*, and there was a phone number on it. So the beautiful man from last night had been here, in this room. And Bernard had absolutely no memory of it.

He made himself wait three hours, spun out his room service breakfast, the scalding bath, and the hot towel shave in the hotel's barbershop that wasn't a luxury – not with his shaking hands.

When he got together the courage to make the call, Shaun's cheerful voice told him hi, he was sorry he couldn't get to the phone, but to please leave a message. Bernard hesitated, not ready for this. What should he say? Did he dare to suggest another meeting? Was the answering machine Shaun's way of saying that he regretted leaving his number with Bernard?

Then he decided he had nothing to lose – if Shaun didn't get back to him, Bernard would never have to see him again. He'd go home to Kilpatrick in eighteen days, and last night would remain a pleasant memory – what he remembered of it, anyway.

And Shaun *had* left his number.

He'd be casual, leave things open. 'Hi, this is Bernard, from the restaurant last night, just calling to say—'

'Hey.' The phone on the other end was picked up. 'Sorry, I was screening. Lot of nuts out there.'

Bernard smiled. 'So I passed the test?'

He heard a laugh, a delicious chuckle. 'Well, so far anyway. I guess I'll need a bit more time to be sure. How's the head?'

And that had been the start of it. They met after

Shaun finished work at the *Boston Telegraph* and they went for a pizza in a tiny Italian restaurant, then to listen to jazz in some park, and for cold beers in a hot, crowded bar. And after that they'd gone back to Bernard's hotel room.

And that had been the start of it all.

Bernard got up, walked to the phone and switched it back on. Why pander to some sick lunatic who got his kicks from trying to frighten people? He wasn't going to let it bother him. If whoever it was rang again, he'd hang up. He'd tell Shaun about it tonight and they'd have a laugh at the weirdos out there.

And the CCTV cameras should be here by the end of the week. Not that they were any protection against abusive phone calls, but then, what harm could someone on the other end of a phone do to him?

He took down the *back in five minutes* sign, unlocked the door and waited for his lunchtime customers.

Pam

She peeled off her jumper, felt the damp patches under the arms of her T-shirt. So hot today – must be the hottest they'd had so far this year. And it didn't help that she was practically running the half-mile or so between the supermarket and the pub now.

How late was she? She glanced at her watch as she sped along – twenty to four, and she'd be there in five minutes. A quarter of an hour, could be worse, and

Carmel was never on time anyway. Pam was usually the one left waiting whenever they met.

She shifted her bag to the other hand and dug in her jeans pocket and pulled out a lipstick, slowing down slightly as she uncapped it. She'd perfected the art of putting it on without a mirror – just a dab on the lower lip and then press the two together and hopefully it ended up more or less in the right place.

As she put it back into her pocket, she thought, *Look at me, sneaking on my make-up like a thirteen-year-old. Lying about where I'm meeting my friend.*

How had it come to this? What had happened to Jack to turn him into someone she hardly recognised any more? She remembered when they'd first got together: when he'd asked her to dance and she'd thought he was talking to the girl beside her, because why in the world would Jack Treacy, who could have had any girl in the disco – who could probably have had any female under thirty-five in Kilpatrick – why on earth would he be interested in boring old Pam McCormack?

She'd lusted after him secretly for as long as she could remember. He was five years older than her, muscular and dark and long-haired at eighteen, striding through the town in faded jeans and jacket as if he owned it, taking no notice of the shy little strawberry blonde whose thirteen-year-old heart would thump as he passed her. Who had taken swimming lessons in the local outdoor pool the summer he was doing lifeguard – she was fourteen, he was nineteen –

just so she could be near him for two precious hours each week. He would parade along the side of the pool in swimming trunks and sunglasses, and Pam would sneak a look at the broad, tanned chest, the flat stomach, the muscled thighs. The bulge under the trunks.

She fantasised about getting cramp in the middle of the deep end, of nobody noticing her struggles except him. She imagined him diving in and pulling her to safety, then bending over her dripping body as she lay unconscious and putting his mouth gently to hers, breathing life back into her. She'd open her eyes – no unromantic spluttering would occur, of course – and he'd look deep into them and realise suddenly how beautiful she was.

The following September he went off to college in Galway to study computers, and Pam didn't see much of him for several years, apart from the odd sighting when he was home on holidays. She finished school, and had a few boyfriends along the way, then went to Cork to train as a nurse. Afterwards she'd got a permanent job in the same big, busy hospital.

If Jack Treacy ever crossed her mind, maybe in the middle of a quiet night duty shift, she'd wonder idly what had become of her big crush, and then she'd forget about him.

When she was twenty-two, she accepted a job in a new nursing home in Kilpatrick and handed in her notice at the Cork hospital and moved home to live with her newly widowed mother and younger brother on a farm six miles outside Kilpatrick. A week after she'd started work, she was dragged to a disco by the friends she'd left behind, and halfway through the night Jack Treacy strode over and asked her to dance.

His hair was short now, and he'd traded in the head-to-toe denim for a white shirt and chinos, but his eyes were as dark and exciting as she remembered, and his chest filled out the white shirt, and Pam McCormack's twenty-two-year-old heart had beaten just as loudly as it had at thirteen.

'I think I know you.' He had to shout in her ear as they tried to shuffle around the crowded, sweaty dance-floor. 'Your face is familiar.'

Pam almost laughed out loud. 'Really?' she shouted back. 'I don't think we've met.'

So they introduced themselves, and marvelled that they'd both grown up in Kilpatrick and never met until now, and he told her that he was home for the weekend from his job in Galway, and she told him that she'd just moved back from Cork. After a few minutes he steered her off the dance-floor and bought her a beer, and she introduced him to her friends, and he brought his brother over to meet them.

He walked her home and didn't attempt to kiss her, to her great disappointment, but he did ask to see her again, and the next time he said goodnight, after a film and two beers, he bent and touched her lips with his, and his stubble rasped against her cheek and then his tongue eased her mouth open, and she could hardly breathe for wanting him.

She resolved not to fall into bed with him, determined not to be just one more Kilpatrick conquest, although she could barely control herself sometimes. His broad, hard body excited her terribly – she craved the touch of his hands, she dreamed about them together, of her slowly peeling off his clothes . . . far less innocent fantasies than her teenage ones.

She lasted four months. They spent the weekend in his apartment, which overlooked Eyre Square – not that they took in much of the view – and he was well worth the wait. Afterwards Pam lay in his arms, damp with their sweat, and wondered if he'd lose interest now.

He didn't. They married eleven months later, in Kilpatrick's Catholic church. She was twenty-three, he was almost twenty-nine. They rented a house on the Galway side of Kilpatrick, near enough to the nursing home for Pam to walk to work, and Jack commuted to Galway every day.

They decided to wait a while before having children – what hurry were they in? Hadn't they years ahead of them for that? They needed time to themselves – and they were so good together, couldn't get enough of each other.

The thought of his naked body still drove Pam wild. Once she went with him to Galway on her day off to do some shopping, and they arranged to meet for lunch in a hotel. Before he arrived, she booked a room, went upstairs and took off all her clothes. Then she put on her coat, stockings and shoes again and got the lift down to the lobby to wait for him.

When he walked in they went straight to the dining room, and she waited until he asked her why she wasn't taking off her coat. Then she took his hand, brought it under the table and let him find out. By the time they had finished the cold beef salad, she could hardly wait. They almost didn't make it to the room, wouldn't have if an older couple hadn't got into the lift with them.

When had it started? The earliest sign Pam could think of – although at the time she didn't take too much notice – was when he complained about her meeting her girlfriends so often.

Pam was surprised. 'I only see them on Thursday nights, you know that.'

'Still . . . I'm not sure I like you going out with a bunch of girls. Are any of the others married?'

'You know they're not. You've met them all.' Pam smiled, reached over and squeezed his hand. 'Are you afraid they'll lead me astray?'

He didn't respond, and he was cool for the rest of the night. When she changed to go out the following Thursday, he stood in the doorway of their bedroom, watching her. 'You're wearing that?'

'What – this top?' Pam stared at him. 'I thought you loved it.' It was blue with a deep, lace-edged V-neck.

'That's the point.' He didn't smile. 'If I love it, so will other men.'

Pam burst out laughing. 'Listen to you – as if I'm some kind of sex bomb, as if any man who looks at me will want to tear the clothes off me.'

'I did.' He folded his arms.

Pam walked over to him and put her arms around his waist. 'What's wrong? Don't you trust me?'

'It's not you I don't trust, it's other men. I know what they're like.'

'But you know I'd never look at anyone else.' When he didn't reply, she said, 'You do know that, don't you?'

He shrugged.

Pam dropped her hands and picked up her bag. 'This is ridiculous. I'll be home by eleven.'

The following Thursday she wore a less revealing top. Anything to avoid the two-day silence that had followed her last night out. When she was leaving, she stood in front of him.

'Will I do?'

He put a hand on each side of her head and kissed her forehead. 'Sorry. I just get scared sometimes, that one day you'll go and not come back.'

She spread her hands on his chest and leaned against him, loving his vulnerability. 'Never.'

And they were fine, for a while. To show him he had nothing to worry about, she told Carmel that she'd only be meeting her and the others once a fortnight from then on. It was a small sacrifice she was happy to make.

Two and a half years ago, after they'd been married for almost three years, Jack got a job in the new Italian computer company that Paul Ryan was setting up just outside Kilpatrick. He and Pam bought a house in the town, and Pam began to think about children. Now that they were settled, now that they'd put down roots, now that they'd had a few years to themselves, maybe it was time.

Jack wasn't sure. 'This company is so new, who knows how it'll go? I could be out of a job again in no time. Let's wait until it's more secure.'

So Pam had agreed, and kept on taking the Pill. And then, eight months ago, as she was wondering how to bring up the subject again, she spotted an ad in the *Kilpatrick Post*: *Person wanted to care for elderly gentleman in own home, 5 hours per day Monday to Friday. Light housework, simple cooking. Reasonable salary.*

Five hours per day, instead of the eight she did now at the nursing home, more if they were short-staffed. Jack complained if she wasn't home before him, said the house felt empty without her, hated when she had to work weekends. And they could afford for her to be earning less, with his generous salary.

And when she got pregnant, a shorter working day would suit her.

She put it to Jack, who liked the idea of her working fewer hours, but who still resisted the baby part. 'Is it so wrong to want you all to myself? I can't stand the thought of sharing you – am I selfish?'

Yes, she wanted to say, but she didn't know how. Part of her was touched by his devotion – who could object to feeling cherished like that? – but her heart sank at the idea that he might never want children. She loved babies, had always assumed she'd have at least a couple of her own. And she was twenty-seven now, almost twenty-eight.

And then, soon after she'd started working for May's father, Jack began to complain again. Began imagining that she was eyeing up other men whenever they were out together. Questioned her about wherever she'd been, even if it was only down to the butcher's. Wanted to know what the postman had said, why she'd stayed so long at the gate talking to him. Asked her to stop wearing make-up, stop taking lifts. Grabbed her arm and squeezed it so tight—

And then her period hadn't come, even though she was still on the Pill. And the pregnancy test had been positive.

Since then, she hadn't been able to think about anything else.

She saw the pub ahead of her. She pushed open the door and scanned the few occupied tables until she found Carmel, just coming to the end of a glass of something golden.

'I was about to give up on you.' Carmel didn't look too upset.

They'd been friends for twelve years, since they'd both worked as chambermaids one summer in Kilpatrick's second-best hotel. They'd known each other slightly at school before that, but Pam was a year ahead of Carmel, so it wasn't until they were making the beds together every day that they became friendly.

Despite their differences – Pam the much quieter one, Carmel always ready for adventure – they hit it off quickly. Pam, often tongue-tied in social situations, envied Carmel's confidence, her ease around men. She'd never be able to flirt like her friend would, never in a million years.

'Sorry, I had to pick something up, long story.' Pam pointed to Carmel's glass. 'Will you have another of those?'

'I sure will – it's cider. I needed something thirst-quenching in this heat.'

When she brought back the drinks, Carmel looked at Pam's orange juice. 'Are you not drinking?'

'Ah no – too early for me. I haven't got your constitution.' Pam dropped her jumper, jacket and bag and sank into the seat opposite Carmel, flapping the end of her T-shirt. 'Phew, I'm roasting. Jack needed shaving foam, so I had to go to Tesco first.' And then, because she knew Carmel was waiting, she said, 'Go on then, tell me, how's the romance?'

She didn't entirely approve of Carmel's current boyfriend. He was a parent at the school, and quite a bit older. And because he was attached, they could only meet in secret, in the privacy of Carmel's house – apart from one weekend in March, when he and Carmel had flown to Italy.

Pam was convinced it would end in tears, but she hadn't the heart to dampen her friend's enthusiasm – and who was she to judge anyway, with her own far less than perfect marriage? Maybe Carmel was right to grab any bit of fun she could. Pam remembered again, with a pang, the excitement of when she and Jack had first met.

'The romance is great.' Carmel grinned as she picked up her new glass. 'He's bloody fantastic in bed

– and he's coming over on Thursday after school. I can't wait.'

Pam smiled. 'Well, be careful, OK?' The orange juice was wonderfully cold, and thick with pulp.

Carmel laughed. 'Listen to you, all sensible-married-woman. Bet you wish you were me.'

'I do not. What's he look like again?'

'Tall, slim, fair-haired, glasses. Like a sexy professor. And I love that he's older.'

Pam smiled again, took another sip of her juice. She was finally beginning to cool down.

'There's a lot to be said for the older man.' Carmel glanced over her shoulder. 'They know how to please a woman – and not just in bed either.' She grinned. 'My kitchen table's seen a lot of action lately.'

Pam laughed. 'Oh God, it's *The Postman Always Rings Twice*. Doesn't sound too hygienic to me.'

'Look, there you go again, sensible housewife. Speaking of which, how's that hunky husband of yours? Haven't seen him in a while.'

'He's fine. Working hard.' Pam swirled the last of her juice, making the ice cubes rattle. Then she said, in a rush, 'Actually, Car, there's something—'

'Well, speak of the devil – look who just walked in.' Carmel smiled over Pam's shoulder. 'Hello, stranger, what brings you in here?'

'I could ask you two the same thing.'

Pam's head whipped around, and Jack said, 'Hello, love. Wasn't expecting to see you here. Thought you were going for coffee.'

Jude

She walked downstairs to the receptionist's desk, feeling rotten. The left side of her mouth seemed to have grown to twice its usual size, and when she put up a hand to touch it, it was like someone else's horrible dead flesh she was feeling.

And the anaesthetic must be starting to wear off – already she was beginning to get a dart of pain where the dentist had been drilling and poking for the past twenty minutes.

She'd phone Ma, get her to bring home some pills from the supermarket.

She signed the form that the snotty cow behind the desk put in front of her – probably killed her that they had to take medical card holders in their fancy place. When she'd finished writing *Jude O'Dea*, deliberately slowly to keep the bitch waiting, she lifted her head and said, 'Got any painkillers?'

'Hang on.' The receptionist opened a drawer and took out a bubble pack of two pills. 'Panadol OK?'

'Fine.' Jude took the pills and turned to go.

'You can get water over there, if you want to take them now.' The receptionist pointed to a water fountain at the far side of her desk.

Jude kept walking. 'That's OK – I'll take them when I get home.' The longer she hung around, the more chance there was of the bitch noticing that Jude hadn't given her back her fancy pen.

On the bus, she looked out the window and tried to

ignore the steadily growing pain in her jaw. Couldn't go out with Kathleen tonight, that was for sure. Didn't matter, not with Friday to look forward to. She'd watch telly with Ma this evening, pretend she was turning into a good little girl.

Or she could find something else to do. She thought about Friday, and felt a flood of excitement.

She was nearly home when she discovered that the necklace was missing; her hand wandered up absently to fiddle with it, and found nothing. She cursed silently as she searched the floor of the bus around her. Could have fallen off anywhere, could be back at the dentist's – but Jude had no notion of going back to that place for a long time.

She shrugged. Easy come, easy go. Ma would find another before too long. People were always losing things in the supermarket.

Her stop was next. She stood up and walked towards the door of the bus.

Bernard

Shaun chopped fast, the bent fingers of the hand that was holding the carrot moving slowly backwards, out of the way of the knife that was flashing up and down so rapidly.

Bernard was watching the thin, uniform slices materialising on the other side. 'I love the way you chop like a chef.'

Shaun looked at him, knife poised. 'Whaddya mean,

like a chef? I *am* a chef.' He finished the carrot and slid the pieces into the saucepan.

'Of course you are.' Bernard stopped grating the Parmesan. 'Is this enough?'

Shaun glanced at the small pile. 'Sure.' He took a parsnip from the bundle of vegetables and began to peel it. 'So, you have fun today?'

Bernard opened the fridge and took out the container of fresh pasta. 'Not bad, usual kind of things. Except –' he grabbed a corner of the plastic lid and pulled it off '– for one nasty little phone call.' He took a saucepan from under the worktop and ran water into it. 'Our friends, making contact in a new way.'

Shaun stared at him. 'What did they say?'

'Ah, some rubbish about coming to get me.' Bernard turned on the burner under the saucepan, wishing now that he hadn't mentioned it, had just let it go. He opened the fridge again and reached inside for a bottle of wine. 'Nothing too memorable anyway.'

'Jesus.' Shaun shook his head. 'What a sick fuck. Are you OK?'

Bernard twisted a corkscrew into the bottle and levered the cork up slowly. 'I'm fine – although I suppose it did shake me up a bit at the time.' He gave a small, embarrassed laugh. 'Just seems ridiculous now when I say it out loud. Some moron with too much time on his hands.' The cork slid out with a loud pop.

'You shoulda called me. You knew I'd be here.' Shaun shook his head again. 'You call the cops?'

Bernard filled a glass and handed it to him. 'No. Maybe I should have, but I thought they weren't much help with the other stuff.'

'Guess not.' Shaun sipped the wine, 'Mmm, thought that one would be good,' and then began to chop the parsnip into little cubes. 'When's that CCTV comin'?'

Bernard lifted his glass and took a sip. It tasted of chilled, scented gooseberries. 'End of the week, they said. I might give them a call tomorrow to check.' He added salt to the simmering water and eased in the pasta. 'Takes all sorts, doesn't it?'

First thing in the morning, he'd phone and check.

May

She said, 'Oh, I'm sorry to hear that,' and then, after a few seconds, 'No, that's fine, we'll manage,' and then, 'Well, tell her to get well soon, and . . . ' another silence, and then, 'Right, OK Jack, thanks a lot.'

She came back into the kitchen. 'That was Pam's husband.'

Philip looked up. 'Oh?'

May picked up her fork again and stabbed a chunk of potato. 'She won't be coming tomorrow. She's not feeling well.'

'Oh.' He took a drink of milk. 'Right. We'll manage, I suppose.'

May nodded. 'I'll be back here at lunchtime anyway, after Paddy's gardening.' She usually kept Thursday afternoons free for her own jobs. Poor Pam – she'd definitely looked off-colour this morning. May should have said something.

'By the way,' she cut into her fish finger, 'what would you like for your birthday?'

The look of dismay on his face was almost comical. 'Oh, nothing at all. You know I don't want a fuss.' Exactly what she'd known he'd say.

'OK.' She wondered if he'd like the present she'd picked out. It was hard to know what to buy for him. She'd tried with the shoes at Christmas, and she'd known, as soon as he'd taken them out of the box, that he hadn't liked the pale colour. Even though he'd said nothing – and he often wore them – she still knew she'd made a mistake. Maybe this time, though, she'd got it right.

She wondered, too, if she should tell him that she'd invited the family to dinner on Sunday. But she couldn't: he'd immediately order her to cancel the whole thing, and she wasn't having that. It wasn't every day you were eighty, for goodness' sake. She couldn't ignore it.

And surely he'd be pleased when he saw the boys – and Phil, his first grandchild, named after him? They hadn't seen Phil since Christmas, when he was a just-beginning-to-sit-up baby. He must be nearly ready to walk by now.

'So, what'll I get for lunch tomorrow?' She knew before he opened his mouth that he'd tell her it didn't matter, he wasn't fussy. And she knew that she'd get two pork chops, because that was what he really wanted.

Paul

He waited until he heard the water being turned off upstairs. Then he pressed 'phone book', and 'c', and scrolled down past *Cab* and *Callum*, and selected *Car*.

He texted, *All set for 4 pm?* sent it, and waited. After a minute, his phone beeped and he read, *Can't wait. C u in the morning. X*

He smiled and deleted both messages, then replaced the phone in his pocket. He stood up and stretched, collected the bottle of wine from the fridge and two crystal glasses from the cabinet before walking upstairs to join Francesca, inhaling the heady scent of her bath oil as it wafted down the stairs towards him.

Pam

She turned the pillow over to the cold, dry side. Then she pulled her knees tight up to her chest again and wrapped her arms around them. Rocked herself gently in the bed, new tears trickling from her wide-awake eyes.

The baby was gone. Her baby was gone. It was gone.

Almost at the same instant that his palm had struck her face – the same second that his flesh had connected solidly with hers and her head had snapped around with the force – she'd felt the awful lurch in her stomach, and straight after, as her cheek began to sting and throb, the sudden, shocking wetness between her legs.

'Oh—' She doubled over, trying to keep it in, trying not to let it leave her – how could she ever have imagined letting it leave her?

'Oh, Jesus.' Another lurch, another wave of something spurting from her. She sank to her knees, clutched her stomach, bent double, face twisted.

He stood looking down at her, the anger draining slowly out of his face. Then he saw the splotches of dark blood on the beige carpet – 'Oh shit' – and crouched beside her.

'Here, come on.' He put a hand out towards her, and she flinched away from him, still clutching her stomach. 'Come on, Pam, you've got to get up. Come on, hang on to me.'

He put his hands under her arms and half lifted her, and she hadn't the strength to resist him. And all the time, as he helped her upstairs, as she eased off her bloody clothes in the bathroom, as he bundled them awkwardly into the laundry basket, as she wrapped herself into a towel and ran a bath, all the time they didn't speak and she didn't look at him.

When the bath was ready, Pam said, in a voice she didn't recognise, 'Please phone May and tell her I won't be in tomorrow. Her number is in my address book in my bag.' She kept her head turned away from him.

He left the room without a word and she locked the door behind him. A few minutes later, as she lay in the bath, Pam heard his voice downstairs. She closed her eyes and felt her cheek ache in the warmth, listened to the little ripples of the water. Her stomach had stopped cramping; there hadn't been much baby to slip away.

She lay in the hot water, breathed in the warm steam and tried not to think. Then slowly she slid down until her neck, her chin, then her face were under the water. She lay motionless for a few seconds, eyes closed, hearing the muffled drumming in her ears. So peaceful there, under the water. So safe. She wished she could stay.

Jack hadn't joined her in bed. She heard him coming upstairs, a long time after she'd turned out the light, and she tensed as she waited for the door to open. But he'd left her alone – another door had closed quietly a few minutes later.

Her pillow had got too hot again, and she was hungry – she'd been going to make shepherd's pie this evening, had taken the mince out of the freezer this morning before she went to work.

She turned the pillow over and lay in the dark, unblinking. The tears rolled down her face, and she ignored them.

Paddy

He heard a window being flung upwards somewhere behind him, and a second later, 'Is that you down there?'

Without turning, he called back, 'Surprisingly, yes.'

'Hang on.' Sound of closing window. He stood up, went inside and collected another wine glass, then left the front door on the latch before he went back out into the garden.

Iseult, when she appeared, was wrapped in what looked like a dark green tablecloth, looped over her shoulders and tied around her waist with a belt that glittered in the pale moonlight. 'This place looked so inviting, I had to come over.' She carried a chubby, lit candle and an opened box of After Eight. Two fat cushions were trapped under one arm. 'You need some chairs.' She dropped the cushions onto the patio.

'I'm going to make a garden seat.' Paddy poured wine into the second glass and waited while she arranged the cushions and put the candle and chocolates between them. 'Why is there a plastic bag on your head?'

She sat. 'I'm putting in a rinse. Don't let me leave it in for longer than eighteen more minutes.'

'What'll happen? Will it all fall out?' Paddy lowered himself on to the second cushion. The candle flickered briefly, then settled.

'No, it'll go orange or something, which would be much worse. Cheers.' She touched his glass with hers and drank. 'Isn't this nice? Your garden's amazing, and it smells fantastic. I'm dead jealous now.'

Paddy, watching her as she popped an After Eight into her mouth, smiled in the soft light. Much as he loved her, his little sister wouldn't have been his first choice to sit in this wonderful scented garden drinking wine with him by candlelight, but she was a perfectly respectable substitute.

And if he could ever find the nerve to tell May O'Callaghan how he felt about her, maybe she'd be here with him some day.

Thursday

More dry, settled weather spreading from the west to all areas, with extended sunny periods and gentle south-westerly winds. Humid tonight. Highs of 21 to 23 degrees.

Bernard

'Look, you're overreacting, honestly.' He climbed into the van and rolled down the window. 'I love you for being concerned, but really, what can happen in the middle of Kilpatrick in broad daylight?'

Shaun stopped to say, 'Hey,' to the postman who was passing – such striking blond hair, Bernard could see why May was keen – then turned back. 'Nine o'clock in the evening is not exactly broad daylight.'

'It is in Ireland, in the middle of summer, as you well know. Longest day of the year was only a week ago, remember?' Bernard started the engine. 'Look, if it makes you happy, come in around nine, and maybe we'll get a bite to eat in town before we come home, if you can wait that long.'

'Sure – I'll have a late lunch. And you'll call the security firm this morning?'

Bernard smiled. 'Yes, I'll call them. Now I'd better get moving, or there'll be no business to protect.' He leaned over and touched Shaun's hand briefly – they were cautious about how they displayed affection in public. 'Have a good day.'

It *was* sweet of Shaun to worry, but Bernard's anxiety of the previous day had vanished this morning. What could one – or even two – twisted individuals really do to him in the middle of Kilpatrick's busiest street on this hazy summery day? He was willing to bet they had no intention of confronting him face to face. They were cowards, he was sure, only good for daubing a few misspelled words under cover of night, or making silly anonymous phone calls.

All the same, a call to the security firm would take only a minute. And the sledgehammer his father had always kept under the counter, the one Bernard had never thrown out – that was just a sensible precaution. Not that he could imagine using it in a million years.

The security grille was graffiti-free – good, he didn't fancy all that scrubbing again. He unlocked it, opened the shop door and picked up the scatter of post lying on the floor. Usual bills, junk mail – and what was this? He turned the white envelope over. No name or address, no stamp. He glanced over his shoulder, then slid his finger under the flap and pulled out the single folded sheet.

Letters cut out of a newspaper or magazine, like on all the best detective shows. Stuck crookedly onto the page, capitals mixed with lower-case letters. Should have been difficult to read, but it wasn't.

GEt rEadY FagOt.

Just that, just those three words. Bernard crumpled up the page, then thought better of it. He smoothed it out, folded it and replaced it in the envelope.

He walked to the phone and dialled the number that was written on a card he'd stuck to the noticeboard on the wall behind it, and he was told that his CCTV cameras were scheduled to be installed either last thing that afternoon or first thing in the morning.

He hung up and riffled through the phone book, then dialled another number, feeling slightly ridiculous as he explained to the polite voice at the other end what he was calling about. He was told that he should avoid further handling of the anonymous letter, and that he should bring it into the station at his earliest convenience.

He put the envelope under the counter, wondering whether to mention it to Shaun when he saw him later. The sender was surely the same person who'd phoned the day before. And, more than likely, the same one who'd sprayed the graffiti and upended the bins.

So the campaign, if that was what you'd call it, was escalating. Time to get the cameras in place, definitely – and, hopefully, to persuade the guards to take him seriously.

The shop door opened and Bernard's heart jumped before he recognised Mrs Philpot.

Francesca

She lifted the page of the calendar she'd taken from the kitchen wall: 15 July to – she lifted the next page – 12 August, four weeks exactly. She entered the dates on her computer, waited for ryanair.com to tell her that there was availability on those dates, then typed in the necessary information about herself and Lucia. Five minutes later it was settled: they'd fly from Dublin into Rome's Ciampino airport in a little over two weeks' time, and stay a month in Perola with Francesca's parents, who doted on Lucia.

Francesca had brought up the subject with Paul last night, waiting until they were settled in the outsize bath with glasses of cold wine. She sat in front of him, hips cradled between his thighs, leaning back against his chest. The steam smelled of jasmine. A dozen tea-lights burned on a low table nearby.

'Sit up a bit.' Paul lathered his hands with soap and kneaded Francesca's shoulders gently.

'Mmm, that's good.' She sipped from her glass. Then she said, 'Darling, I've been thinking about going to Perola for a little longer this year.'

'Mm-hmm?' His hands moved in slow circles down her spine, his thumbs pressing into her skin, down under the water to the curve of her hips. Francesca breathed more deeply, inhaling the jasmine.

'Yes . . . maybe a little longer this time.' She sipped again, pressed her hips back against his encircling hands. 'Maybe three or four weeks – what would you think of that?'

'Whatever you want, you know that.' He bent and kissed her wet, soapy shoulder. 'But I'll miss you terribly.' His teeth nipped the side of her neck, and Francesca drew in her breath. 'I'll miss this terribly.' Under the water, his warm hands moved around to her abdomen and travelled in more slow, lazy circles up to the curve of her breasts.

Francesca laughed softly, arching her back, pressing herself into his hands. 'Me too, darling.'

And she would. Paul satisfied Francesca, met her body's needs in a way that only one man had managed to do before. She would definitely miss that when they were apart.

But she yearned to get back to Perola – sometimes she almost felt guilty, she hungered for home so much. Soon, they must move back there. A few more months – a year at the very most, surely. She'd bring it up again with Paul when she and Lucia returned.

Now she pressed *print* and waited for the proof, in black and white, that she was going home soon.

Carmel

'Did that necklace turn up?' Iseult was unwrapping a tinfoil package as she spoke.

Carmel shook her head glumly. 'Not a sign of it.

Nobody handed it in at the supermarket, and I turned the classroom upside-down.' She took a spoonful of her yoghurt, and realised why it had been on special offer.

'Too bad.' Iseult spoke through a mouthful of tuna sandwich. 'Hopefully the parents won't notice you're not wearing it.'

'Mmm.' Carmel poured milk into her tea and stirred it. She'd have to tell Paul when he came over – he could hardly blame her for losing it. If only it hadn't been the first real present he'd given her. She sighed, wondering again if he'd noticed she hadn't been wearing it that morning.

'I was over at Paddy's last night. I feel sorry for him, poor thing.' Iseult lifted her mug.

It took Carmel a few seconds to remember who Paddy was. 'Why?'

'Well, there he was, with this fabulous garden that May has created out of absolutely nothing – you should have seen it before – and all he had to share it with was his little sister. It should have been so romantic – wine and candles, the lot – and there he was with me. Pathetic.'

It was obvious she was trying to pair them up again. 'Mmm.' Carmel had no desire to go and sit in somebody's brother's garden, drinking wine and making small talk. Not when she had a much more exciting alternative lined up.

Iseult picked up her sandwich. 'God, I forgot I'm going to the dentist after school – I'll be breathing tuna all over him. Ah, well.' She took another bite. 'Are you going to this thing tonight?'

'What thing?'

Iseult laughed. 'Crikey, what planet are you on? End-of-year drinks, of course.'

'Oh, right.' Carmel had totally forgotten about the staff night out – she'd been far too preoccupied with Paul, and trying to find that bloody necklace. Now she considered. Paul was due at four, and he probably wouldn't be able to stay longer than a couple of hours. By six she'd be on her own again, after he'd gone back to Sophia Loren.

Yes, she might well need to join the rest of the Kilpatrick Junior School staff for a few drinks. Why not? 'I'll probably wander in at some stage. You?'

Iseult shrugged. 'Dunno. The dentist is at four so it'll depend on how that goes. If I'm not numbed up to the nines, I'll probably go along for a while.'

In the yard the bell rang, and there was a collective groan in the staffroom.

Shaun

He moved the cursor to 'shut down computer' and clicked on the mouse. Then he stood up and stretched, his fingers interlocked above his head. He wasn't in the mood to write today, not with that sun beaming in. He'd fix himself a bite to eat, take the bike out, maybe go to the coast. Have a swim, even, if the ocean wasn't too icy.

In the kitchen he made a cheese sandwich with the granary bread they got in the market every Saturday, and ate it standing up, looking out the window at the back garden. He'd cut the grass when he got back, or maybe tomorrow. He turned to look at next door's neat patch of lawn, which May cut once a week in the summer. No sign of Pam today.

He considered calling Bernard, then decided against it. He wouldn't fuss, he'd just go meet him at closing time, like they'd arranged. He remembered how funny 'late opening' had seemed when he'd come here first – a few shops on Kilpatrick's main street staying open till nine o'clock on Thursdays.

In Boston, not even the smallest deli closed till at least ten every night of the week. Funny how accustomed he'd become to the Irish way of doing things, how normal it seemed now to have everything shut up at half five most days. Then he smiled: *half five* instead of *five thirty*. He sure was becoming acclimatised.

He put his plate into the sink and checked his watch: two-ten. A four-and-a-half-hour round trip or thereabouts. If he didn't spend longer than an hour or so on the beach, he'd make it home in plenty of time to get cleaned up and meet Bernard. He went to the shed, whistling, to get the bike out.

Lucia

And here she was in the front garden, in pink shorts and a little orange and blue striped vest top, and a flowery cotton sun hat. Her cheeks were flushed in the heat, and the fringe that poked out from under the hat stuck to her forehead in damp, jagged clumps. Kneeling on the lawn near the flowerbed that May had weeded in the rain on Monday, making daisy chains with Marietta, waving at Shaun when he called, 'Hi, sweetie' as he cycled off on a big black bike.

Marietta going in to get more medicine for her sore throat, telling Lucia to be good, not to go on the road. She'd be back in a minute, OK, baby?

Lucia didn't like when Marietta said 'baby'. She wasn't a baby. Miss Gannon told them they were big now and they had to share and not fight. Mamma called her 'baby' sometimes, but that was OK, because she was Mamma.

Now standing up and walking around the side of the house to the table on the patio, picking up a cracker from the plate and biting into it, just as the big ginger pussy cat came out from under the purple flowers. Going quicker when he saw Lucia.

Nice pussy cat. Lucia loved pussy cats. *Stop, pussy cat.* Running after him, holding out her cracker. *Look, here's a cracker. Stop, you can have some.*

Halfway across the lawn, some cracker got stuck in her neck, hurting her. Coughing. Trying to cough it up, scared of no air. *Marietta. I can't—* But the words got stuck too. *Mamma.*

Pussy cat runned away, under the hedge into the next garden while Lucia fell on the grass. While Lucia's lips began to turn blue. While Lucia stopped making noise.

Iseult

Veronica, the dentist's receptionist, looked up as Iseult came downstairs. 'That didn't take long.'

'No, just one small filling. Didn't even need an injection.' Iseult handed her chart to Veronica. 'You'll probably still make me pay through the nose, though.'

Veronica laughed. 'I'll do the best I can.' She examined the chart and pressed a few buttons on her computer. 'Sixty euro – not too bad this time.'

'Mmm. I've had worse.' Iseult pulled two fifty-euro notes from her wallet and handed them to Veronica. As the receptionist counted out her change, Iseult spotted something sitting on a shelf behind the desk. 'Hey, is that a necklace?'

Veronica turned, following Iseult's gaze. 'Where? Oh, yes, I found it in the waiting room yesterday. I'm leaving it here to see if anyone comes back to claim it.'

Iseult held out her hand. 'Can I have a look? I think I recognise it.'

It was definitely Carmel's shell necklace, Iseult was certain. 'Veronica, I know who owns this.'

'Really? What's her name?'

Iseult shook her head. 'She's not a patient here – at least, I don't think she is – and, anyway, she hasn't been to the dentist this week. But she definitely lost this necklace somewhere earlier in the week. Someone else must have found it and worn it in here.'

Veronica looked doubtfully at the necklace. 'Well, maybe . . . '

'Look, if you prefer I'll send Carmel in, and she can have a look at it herself. But I'm pretty certain it's hers. It's so unusual – and you'd have my number if anyone else came looking for it.'

And because Iseult had been coming to the dentist for years, and because two people arrived at her desk just then, one of whom looked to be in a lot of pain, Veronica agreed to let her take the pretty shell necklace away.

Pam

The clock radio had to be wrong – it couldn't be 3:25. She grabbed her watch and read the dial, then pushed back the duvet and climbed cautiously out of bed. She must have fallen asleep just after he'd left for work – not surprising, after the night she'd had – and now it was the middle of the afternoon, and he'd soon be finishing work and coming home again.

She took her dressing-gown from the back of the door and put it on as hastily as she could, feeling the ache low in her abdomen every time she moved. She should get herself checked out after a miscarriage – even an early one. Maybe in a week or so, after she'd settled back into Cork.

Cork had been decided on, some time during the night. She'd enjoyed it in the hospital, apart from the heavy work schedule, and she still had some friends there. She'd try the nursing homes for work – there were lots of them. Or she could look for a home-help job again, like in May's house.

She felt bad leaving May so abruptly, but there was nothing she could do about that.

In the hall she picked up the phone, dialled his work number and asked the receptionist if she could please speak to Jack Treacy in the accounts department. Yes, it was his wife.

'Hello?' He sounded cautious. Pam hadn't met him that morning, had pretended to be asleep when the bedroom door had opened quietly, had forced herself to breathe evenly until it closed again.

She spoke calmly now, even though her pulse had started to race. 'Can you please bring home some milk and toilet paper?'

'Yeah, sure.' He paused, and Pam waited for him to ask. After a second or two, he said, 'How're you feeling?'

'Horrible. I'm going back to bed now.' She hung up before he could say anything else. That would delay him a bit longer. Even if he left in the next few minutes, she was safe for at least three-quarters of an hour, with the traffic and the stop at the shop.

She dialled the number of a local firm and booked a taxi for four o'clock, going to the bus station. There'd be a bus leaving for somewhere. She went back upstairs and dressed quickly in her low-cut blue top and the jeans he said looked too tight. Then she opened their biggest suitcase and filled it with as many clothes as it would hold. She left the polo-neck jumper he'd brought her home from the January sales, and the long skirt he always admired when she wore it.

She threw shoes and boots into another case, and filled her toilet bag swiftly with toothbrush, dental floss, shampoo, tampons, moisturiser, cleanser, nail-clippers, emery boards and cotton buds.

When everything was packed up, she reached into the back of the wardrobe and took out the little pink vanity case that Carmel had given her for her last birthday, full of the make-up she wasn't allowed to use. Then she sat in front of her dressing table and stroked concealer onto the pinkish stripe that ran down her left cheek. She added foundation and blusher, lipstick and eye liner, eye shadow and mascara. Funny – you never forgot how to do all that.

She dabbed perfume behind her ears, on her wrists and in the hollow between her breasts. Then she packed everything away again and zipped the case shut. She'd have to leave her books for now, and the few CDs she'd bought herself. Her brother could come back for them some time, maybe. Or maybe not – Pam didn't really care.

She brought everything downstairs and left it inside the front door. She had a couple of minutes until the taxi came.

In the sitting room he'd tried to wash the bloodstains off the carpet. They were still there, but much lighter. The room smelled of Dettol.

She walked into the kitchen and looked around. The table was empty, but a cup, a plate and a butter-smeared knife sat on the draining board. There were toast crumbs on the plate. The cup still had the dregs of his breakfast tea in it.

He'd sat at the table and eaten his breakfast as if nothing had happened. He hadn't boiled himself an egg – too much trouble, probably. He'd just about managed to put bread into the toaster.

And he'd left his dirty dishes for her to wash up.

Pam picked up the plate and threw it against the opposite wall. It broke into three pieces and clattered to the ground. She picked up the cup, flung it in the same direction and watched the little shards flying out from the wall, like a mini-explosion. It left behind a small brown splodge that trickled down on to the floor.

She went back out to the hall and checked her reflection in the mirror. She looked like a woman who wouldn't say no if some man, any man, asked her to have sex with him. Suddenly she leaned over and pressed her red mouth to the mirror, then stood back and smiled. He couldn't miss it. Much better than a note.

It wasn't until she opened her bag to see if she'd have to stop at an ATM on the way to the station that she discovered her wallet was empty, her credit and debit cards missing. He'd cleaned her out, left her with nothing, so she couldn't leave him.

Outside, a car horn sounded. Pam picked up the biggest suitcase and opened the front door. If she had to crawl on her hands and knees to get away from him, she would.

*

Paul

' . . . and I don't know what happened, it must have caught in something.' Carmel was coming towards him holding two glasses of red wine. Paul dragged his mind back from picturing her slim, childish body naked – an intriguing change from Francesca's voluptuousness – and tried to concentrate on what she was saying. Something about the chain thing Lucia had found?

'I'm so sorry – I really liked it, and I'm raging that I've managed to lose it so fast –' Carmel handed him one of the glasses and sat in his lap '– and you were so clever, leaving it for Lucia to find like that.' She leaned over and nibbled his ear, like he'd taught her to.

Paul took a sip of wine, felt it course down his throat. Leaving it for Lucia to find? Carmel seemed to think that the chain had come from him, that he had bought it for her. How perfect.

Her tongue was beginning to arouse him pleasantly. He slid his free hand under her top, felt her warm, flat stomach, the ridges of her ribcage, the hardly-there curves of her little-girl breasts, the surprisingly prominent nipples. Felt her breathing quicken as his hand travelled lazily around. Good, she wouldn't take too long to warm up.

'How did you know, though, that she'd decide to give it to me?' she whispered in his ear, traced his mouth with her thumb, rocking slightly in his lap. 'She might have wanted to keep it for herself.'

Paul reached around her hip, pulled her closer. 'You

of all people must know how strong the power of suggestion is with a four-year-old. I simply said it would be a lovely present for you. You know how much she adores you . . . ' he put his lips to her neck ' . . . and she has very good taste.'

Really, this was almost too easy.

Carmel was peeling off her top as his mobile rang. He grimaced, said, 'Sorry, better answer it,' and pulled it from his shirt pocket. Carmel slid from his lap and sat opposite him, watching as he spoke, pulling her top down slowly.

He said, 'What?' and stood up, turning away from Carmel as he listened. After a second he said, 'Is she OK?' then, 'I'm on my way,' and hung up.

He grabbed his car keys and strode towards the door. 'It's Lucia,' he said, over his shoulder. 'She's in hospital.'

'Oh my God – what happened?'

But he was gone, the door slamming behind him. Carmel stood motionless, her hand to her mouth, as she heard his car start and race down the road.

And exactly four minutes later, thinking he'd come back – he was joking, the bastard – she opened the door eagerly, and found Pam standing on her doorstep, all made up, and a taxi with its engine running outside the gate.

*

Jack

He dropped his keys on the phone table, then stood there, listening. Looking up the stairs he called, 'Hello?' Pause. 'Pam?'

No sound. She must have gone back to sleep.

He walked into the empty kitchen and dropped his plastic bag on the table. As he turned to leave, he spotted something white on the blue tiles by the fridge – a piece of paper? No. He crossed over and picked up the shard, then saw the others. A plate, was it? And the question mark of a cup handle, and two thin, spattery lines on the white wall in front of him. He followed them up to the pale brown stain, around eye level.

He pressed his lips together and left the kitchen. As he ran up the stairs he called, 'Pam?' Flung open the bedroom door, looked without surprise now at the empty, unmade bed. Her slippers, always sitting neatly side by side on the mat, were gone. The dressing table looked less cluttered. He looked in her wardrobe – a few skirts, a jumper, everything else gone. Something missing from the top of the wardrobe – the suitcases they'd stacked there.

He flung open the bathroom door. A single toothbrush – his – stood in the beaker beside the tube of toothpaste. Her hairdryer was gone from its hook. He pulled at the little door of the cabinet above the sink. Emptier, much emptier than it should have been. He slammed the door shut, caught his reflection in the mirror. Tense, tight face. Angry white patches at the side of his eyes and around his nose.

He raced downstairs, dialled her mother's number. No, he was told by her brother, they hadn't seen Pam. Was anything wrong? As he hung up without answering the guarded voice – *liar* – his attention was caught by something, some red stain on the mirror opposite him. He walked over and stood, hands on hips, breathing fast, looking at the print of his wife's lips.

He found Carmel in the phone book and dialled her number. She sounded distracted – no, she hadn't seen Pam since yesterday, yes, of course she'd let Jack know if she heard from her, was everything OK? He resisted the urge to say that clearly everything was fucking *not* OK, and told her they'd had a bit of a row, 'you know how it is,' and he was sure Pam would be back soon. He hung up before the stupid bitch could ask any more stupid *fucking* questions.

May's father took a long time to get to the phone, and didn't seem to know who Jack was talking about at first. Eventually he said that May was out shopping, wanted Jack to leave a number. Even when he understood that Jack was Pam's husband, he wasn't much help. 'She's sick today, she's not here.' He sounded irritated that Jack didn't seem aware of the facts.

Jack gritted his teeth. 'I know that – I'm just wondering if she rang earlier. I'm –' he improvised quickly '– I'm delayed at work, and the phone at home is engaged, and I just need to know if she'll be back at work with you tomorrow.'

There was a pause; Jack heard wheezy breathing. Then Philip said, 'Well, I didn't hear anything, and May's out shopping—'

Jack broke in loudly, 'Well, thanks for your help,' and hung up.

He turned back to the mirror then and rubbed a thumb roughly across the lipstick print, leaving a messy red smear on the glass.

She couldn't have gone far, with no money or cards. He'd find her.

Shaun

'Shoot.' He pulled on the back brake and bumped to a stop. Then he bent to examine the front wheel, pressed the tyre and felt no resistance. Flat as a pancake – and no repair kit. He checked his watch: 7:25 and still a good few miles to go. He lifted an arm and wiped the sweat from his forehead with the sleeve of his T-shirt. Jesus, it was muggy now, when he didn't have the breeze the bike created.

He pulled out his phone and pressed the Flower Power number.

Bernard sounded amused. 'So much for my knight in shining armour. Where are you?'

Shaun looked around and saw nothing that wasn't green and leafy. 'The middle of nowhere – so I reckon around a couple of hours from you on foot, which is how I'll have to travel now, by the looks of it.'

'Poor you. At least the weather's OK. I'll come in the car and meet you if you're not there when I get home, right?'

'Sure. Hang on a sec.' Shaun waited until a truck had roared by, and then he said, 'Everything OK with you?'

'Never better.'

'Any sign of the CCTV?'

'Tomorrow, they promised.'

'OK, I guess one more day won't make a difference. Talk to you later.' Shaun slid his phone back into his rucksack and began to wheel the bike along the hard shoulder, groaning as he felt the first prickle of sunburn on the back of his neck. Just what he needed.

May

She unpacked her bags, knowing she was safe from discovery by Philip – the only time he came into the kitchen was when a meal was waiting for him on the table. She put the potatoes into the bottom of the fridge, and the two bottles of white wine in the press beside it, along with the whiskey, gin and tonic.

The birthday cake had been ordered, to be collected on Saturday, and she'd buy the salmon and spinach then too.

She hoped that whatever bug Pam had picked up would be gone by Sunday. The thought of having to put the dinner together by herself was terrifying. Cooking did not come naturally to May O'Callaghan.

Her custard came in a tin, the pastry for her rarely baked apple tarts was from a supermarket freezer, all sauces came out of packets or jars. And she wasn't used to cooking for more than two, so Sunday's dinner for nine would be a challenge she wasn't looking forward to facing on her own.

She might get away with it if she was organised. Dinner would be at six – better not change Philip's routine – so the potatoes, which were going to be cut into wedges, brushed with oil and baked, should go into the oven soon after five. When her visitors arrived, around half five, she'd serve them drinks and leave them chatting with Dad while she got the rest done.

She'd buy the salmon already poached, if Pam wasn't going to be there, and frozen pastry, so it would be just a matter of parcelling everything up together and putting it into the oven – wouldn't it? She must check the recipe again, see if the spinach needed to be cooked first.

And the baby carrots and cauliflower would boil in a few minutes, even she could do that, and make up a packet of cheese sauce. The cake for dessert – no getting ready there. It sounded so straightforward; surely nothing could go wrong.

All the same, she hoped fervently that Pam would be better by Sunday. She'd give a ring later on to see how she was.

Pam's husband had phoned earlier, Philip said, while May was out, but May suspected her father had got the message wrong. He said Jack didn't seem to know whether Pam would be back to work tomorrow, which didn't sound right – surely Jack would know that, living with Pam.

Really, Dad was getting so absent-minded lately.

May pulled her thoughts back to Sunday night. Had she enough drinks? She went through them again – whiskey for Philip and Cathal, gin for Hilda. William's wife Dolly would have wine, and Cathal's wife Gaby too, probably. Maybe she should get another couple of bottles, in case nobody brought some. William wouldn't be drinking, he was driving them all back to Cathal and Gaby's in Oranmore later. She'd better get some mineral water.

There was a small bottle of Bailey's in the press that someone had brought them last Christmas – might be nice in coffee after dinner. But would it have gone off by now? She should have put it in the fridge when they got it.

And there was an almost-full bottle of brandy, must have been sitting there for years, she couldn't even remember where it had come from now. She could offer it around with the coffee too – very fancy.

The whole thing would probably finish up before it got late, with dinner being served so early. Philip wasn't one for staying up at night; May wouldn't put it past him to announce to everyone that he was going to bed around nine.

Not exactly a wild social life May O'Callaghan was enjoying, these days.

She wondered what presents the boys would bring for him. Something safe probably, a new shirt (blue or white) in the collar size he'd worn for the past thirty years. Or a bottle of Powers, or the port he always used to drink at Christmas – but that he hadn't touched since Mam died.

Maybe the three of them should have gone together, got a present between them. It hadn't occurred to May till this minute.

She opened the press over the fridge that normally held just the fire extinguisher and fire blanket that William and Dolly had given her the Christmas after she bought the house, and lifted down the present she'd bought for him to have another look at it. She'd spent a long time thinking about what to get him, and still she hadn't the faintest idea whether he'd love or hate the one she'd finally decided on.

Philip had never been demonstrative, even when May and the boys were small. Mam had always been the one they'd run to with scraped knees or hurt feelings, never Dad. But, to be fair, maybe that was typical in families. Maybe the mother was always the softer parent. Philip had certainly been the one with the temper – one sharp word from him always got their attention.

He'd never, as far as May could remember, laughed with real abandon – the most you'd get out of him was a short bark. She wondered what he'd been like as a young man, when he and Aideen had met at the wedding of her best friend and his cousin. She would love to have seen him then – he must have been happy when the dark-haired young bridesmaid had agreed to go out with him.

May didn't doubt that he'd loved Mam. They'd been together for almost forty years, and despite Philip's quick temper, May couldn't remember a time when he and Aideen had fallen out, not seriously. Somehow Aideen had always known how to handle him, how to soothe his outbursts.

And since she'd died, the change in Philip had been shocking. He'd aged terribly, turned into an old man frighteningly quickly. A tired, cranky old man.

He hadn't wanted to come and live here, in this house, with May. He'd made that quite plain, had gone on terrifying them – almost setting his own house on fire, almost breaking his hip, almost gassing himself to death – for longer than any of them had imagined he could. But finally, even he'd seen that he couldn't manage on his own any more, and May had packed up his things while he was still insisting impatiently that he could go to a nursing home, that May didn't have to do this.

But the thought of him sitting in an armchair with other old men, waiting to die, was awful – even if he was such a misery. 'I'm happy to have you, Dad, really I am,' she'd told him, hoping she sounded more convincing to him than she did to herself, and he'd grumbled, shaken his head and sat glumly in the back of Cathal's car on the way to May's house.

Getting Pam had been his idea. He'd offered gruffly to pay for someone to come in while May was out. 'Take the pressure off you.' He'd looked challengingly at May, and she'd known enough not to offer to split the cost. He could afford it, with the sizeable payout from Aideen's life insurance policy, and his pension – and now, of course, he also had the rent from the family home.

It was not to be sold – he was adamant about that. 'That's your legacy, you and the boys,' he'd insisted, so May had arranged for one of Kilpatrick's estate agents to let it. She hadn't gone around there since she'd been told that it had been taken on a long lease – she avoided the neighbourhood when she walked the dogs, not wanting to see someone else's car in their driveway.

A neighbour of her parents had offered to keep the grass cut, so at least it wasn't going to look like one of those obviously rented houses that nobody—

The phone rang in the hall, and May went to answer it. 'Hello?'

'May, it's Pam.' She spoke quickly. 'I'm sorry I haven't been back to you till now.'

'No, that's fine, I was going to ring you later. Jack was on earlier to Dad, but—'

'He was? When?'

How could Pam not know that? Wasn't she at home with Jack now? 'Er, about an hour ago, I think.' May paused. 'Pam, is everything OK?'

A long silence then, and just as May was about to speak again, Pam said, in a suddenly shaky voice, 'No, May, everything is definitely not OK.'

*

Bernard

He brought the buckets of flowers inside and wheeled the display units in after them. The air was heavy this evening, even with the sun gone down. He turned the sign on the door from *Come in, we're open* to *Sorry, we're closed*. He was glad the long twelve-hour day was over, would have been quite happy to close at six on Thursdays except that everyone around him stayed open late.

He lifted his briefcase from the counter, walked out and pulled the door shut behind him.

He was just putting his key into the lock when he felt a hand on his shoulder.

'Gotcha,' said a voice.

Francesca

She sat on the side of the bed, stroking her daughter's hair. Lucia slept on her stomach, as she always did, her face turned towards her mother, arms flung out on either side. Her breathing was rapid, her cheek flushed lightly. Her mouth was slightly open, showing the tips of small, tidy teeth.

Francesca's lips moved noiselessly, reciting prayers she hadn't known she remembered. Her fingers stroked Lucia's head, curving around the small skull, sliding over the silk of the hair, finding the soft, smooth skin at the back of the neck. Feeling the rapid, precious pulse under Lucia's jaw. *Grazie, grazie.*

Francesca closed her eyes, and immediately she was back in the nightmare – wondering what Marietta was bending over in the garden as she approached the gate . . . then catching her breath and racing up the path, shoving Marietta out of the way, screaming at her to 'Phone 999, quick, phone them, you idiot,' falling desperately to her knees beside Lucia, searching desperately for a pulse as Marietta sobbed into the phone, 'Ambulance, please, quickly.'

Francesca's eyes snapped open. She forced herself back into the present, trying not to think about breathing air into Lucia's mouth, crying and breathing, pushing her hair – their hair – out of the way, pressing on her chest, one-two-three-four, breathing again, her tears streaming down onto Lucia's face, willing her daughter to *breathe, breathe, come on, please breathe* – screaming at the ambulance men, *No, no, make her breathe, you have to* – and the blessed, wonderful sound of Lucia's cough, the miracle of her whimpers, the relief of her croaky *Mamma, Mamma*, and Francesca holding her, carrying her to the ambulance, shouting back at Marietta to *Phone Paul, tell him*, as they sped, siren screaming, towards the hospital, Francesca clutching Lucia's hand as the ambulance man fed her daughter oxygen.

Now she took a deep, shuddering breath. It was over. Lucia was alive, and home again in her own bed. It was over. Grazie. Her cheeks were tight with salt.

She heard a sound behind her and turned to see Paul getting up from the armchair, stretching. 'Back in a sec.'

She watched him leave the room, her hand still stroking Lucia's hair. It could have been so different, if she'd been a few minutes later getting home, if—

The beeps, breaking in on her thoughts, startled her. She looked towards the armchair, where they seemed to be coming from. Paul's phone – must have fallen out of his pocket. Without thinking, she went over, picked it up with her free hand and read 1 new message in the display. She pressed show with her thumb.

Is she OK? x

The sender was *Car*.

Francesca stared at the little screen. Is she OK? Whoever it was meant Lucia, must mean Lucia. Someone from Paul's work – whoever he'd been with when Marietta phoned him, probably.

But why would a work colleague add *x* to the end of a message to him?

She tried to remember anyone called Car, or a name that started with Car. Carol? Carl? Carter, maybe? Nothing rang a bell with her. His PA was Stephanie, and there was a Julie on the front desk.

Then she shrugged – what did it matter who it was? They'd been concerned enough to ask after Lucia: the least Francesca could do was to let them know. She pressed the *return call* button.

It was answered almost before it had begun to ring. A female voice said in a rush, 'Paul, sorry, I know you said never to contact you, but I had to find out – how is she? Is she—'

Francesca pressed the disconnect button and

dropped the phone back onto the chair and sat on the bed again. A minute later Paul walked in. He stood beside her and stroked her arm.

'Want anything? Tea, coffee?' He spoke softly.

Francesca shook her head. Marietta had brought them sandwiches and coffee at some stage, had put the tray on the bedside locker and left without a word, sniffing. Francesca hadn't touched it. 'You go to bed. There's no need for the two of us to stay. I'll sleep here tonight.'

'Sure?' When she nodded, he leaned and kissed her forehead, and touched Lucia's cheek with his palm. 'Sleep tight, see you in the morning.' As he passed the chair, he bent and picked up his phone, slipped it into his pocket.

She waited until he was at the door. 'By the way,' she kept her eyes on his face as he turned, 'were you still at work when Marietta called you?'

Did she imagine the tiny hesitation? 'Actually, no – I was on the way home.' He looked completely innocent. 'Had a bit of a headache so I cancelled a few things and came away earlier than I should.' He smiled. 'Why?'

Francesca shrugged. 'Just wondered how you got to the hospital so quickly, that's all.'

As he left the room she watched him thoughtfully, one hand still stroking Lucia's hair.

Car, she thought. The voice had been familiar.

And much later, lying next to Lucia, curling her

body around her still-sleeping daughter, feeling the airless heat of the bedroom pressing down on her, *Carmel* slid abruptly into her head.

Carmel Gannon, Lucia's teacher – who, it would seem, wasn't a lesbian after all.

Friday

Further hazy sunshine throughout the country during much of the day, with a band of low pressure spreading gradually from the west towards nightfall, bringing with it the risk of thunderstorms and severe gusts, particularly in Munster and Connacht. Highs of 16 to 21 degrees.

Carmel

She hadn't been able to face breakfast, not even the cup of coffee that was normally so essential before the demands of the Junior Infant day. Her insides felt knotted up, all twisted and tied together, so she had to keep taking deep breaths to stop feeling like she was suffocating.

Thank goodness Pam hadn't appeared downstairs before Carmel had left for work – the last thing she needed this morning was to have to concentrate on someone else's problems when she was so eaten up with her own. Not that she hadn't been sympathetic last evening. Of course she had, when Pam had shown up so unexpectedly, stammering out an apology until she realised she wasn't interrupting anything, that Carmel was on her own.

In spite of her disappointment, Carmel had done her best to listen as Pam – who looked pretty fabulous, done up to the nines – explained why she'd appeared so suddenly.

And of course it was terrible to hear what had happened between Pam and Jack – he'd always been so charming to Carmel, almost flirting with her whenever they met. To think he'd actually hit Pam, and she'd miscarried – it was awful, really it was.

But between pouring tea and putting a frozen lasagne into the oven for the two of them, Carmel couldn't help wondering frantically what was going on at the hospital. Had Lucia been in some kind of accident? Was she seriously hurt? Of course it was Lucia Carmel was concerned about – she and Paul weren't important, not when the life of a little child might be hanging in the balance. She was desperate to know what was going on.

But Paul had been adamant that Carmel must never phone him, never even send him a text unless he contacted her first. So she had no way of finding out what the hell was going on, and it was all she could do to concentrate on what poor Pam was telling her.

By the time she'd finally persuaded Pam to go to bed, hours later, Carmel couldn't bear the suspense any longer. One quick text – what were the chances of Francesca reading it? And when her phone had rung immediately afterwards, and she'd seen *Paul* in the display, she'd grabbed it without thinking and shot her mouth off without waiting to make sure it was actually Paul.

And then when it had been cut off, she didn't know what to think, didn't dare try ringing back.

She hadn't slept a wink after that, of course.

Maybe everything was OK – maybe it *had* been him, and maybe Francesca had walked in when he'd rung her, or something. But wouldn't he have rung back later when the coast was clear?

What if it hadn't been him? Carmel imagined Francesca listening to her voice on the phone and shuddered at the thought.

But it was Paul's fault – he should have got back to her to let her know. Surely he could have managed a quick call, or even a text. It wasn't fair to leave her waiting like that – what had he expected her to do?

She lifted her head from her hands and glanced around the quiet classroom. Thank God this was a half-day, only an hour and three-quarters to go. And thank God for the *Madagascar* DVD – the reason why her twenty-seven charges were so quiet now.

Twenty-seven, not twenty-eight. Carmel looked again at Lucia's empty chair, wondered again whether the child was alive or . . . Her empty stomach lurched at the thought. No Lucia, and no word – and Carmel's nerves were so jangled, her eyes stinging from lack of sleep, that she'd shouted at Robbie earlier when he'd torn a page from his reader, yelled at him like a fishwife just as the principal walked in, wouldn't you know?

She put her head in her hands again and closed her eyes, trying to shut out the noise from the DVD.

Francesca

She could have rung the school, of course she could. Told them that Lucia wouldn't be in, explained briefly about yesterday. It was the last day of school anyway, only a half-day, nobody would be too worried – and Lucia had missed only one or two days in the whole school year so far.

But Francesca had no intention of ringing – she was going to the school in person. She was going to knock on the Junior Infant classroom door and look into Carmel Gannon's eyes and see what there was to be seen.

She'd lain awake most of the night beside Lucia, exploring the implications of the three-word text. Paul was having an affair – there was no doubt now in Francesca's head. The only thing she wasn't completely sure of was the identity of the woman. Everything pointed to that teacher, but could it really be her? Could Paul possibly be interested in so unfeminine a creature?

But whoever it was, whoever Car turned out to be, some kind of confrontation was inevitable now. This was not something Francesca was prepared to ignore. The thought of coming face to face with Paul's other woman irritated rather than unnerved her – it was all so . . . *undignified* to be caught in the middle of such a sordid business.

Towards morning, as the first pale rays of sun appeared behind Lucia's cheery bedroom curtains, as she heard Paul moving around, getting ready for work, Francesca thought about the life that she and Paul had built together in this country. She imagined it coming to an end, and realised, with some surprise, that the prospect didn't sadden her at all.

After she heard his car driving off, she got up and made a soft-boiled egg for Lucia's breakfast, ignoring Marietta, who hovered uncertainly in the kitchen. As she sat beside her daughter, cutting narrow fingers of toast for her, Francesca noted with satisfaction the dark rings around the Filipina's eyes. It would have been totally unforgivable if she'd slept.

After breakfast, Francesca told Marietta that she had to go out for an hour. 'Kindly keep a careful eye on Lucia, and do *not* leave her alone again, even for a second.' She spoke crisply, slipping an arm into her lime green linen jacket, sure that this time, Lucia would be safe – the woman would be too afraid to take her eyes off her.

Marietta nodded, hands twisting a dishcloth. 'Of course.'

As Francesca drove through the school gates and parked beside the jumble of staff cars, she could hear various noises coming from the open windows of the different classrooms: the cat's chorus of beginner tin-whistlers, a chant of multiplication tables, a burst of childish laughter.

She turned the rear-view mirror towards her and opened her handbag. Lipstick, eyeliner, mascara. Warpaint: wasn't that what it was called?

Carmel

The sharp knock on the door – two quick, confident raps – startled her. She stood up too fast, had to grab the edge of her desk and wait for the blackness in front of her eyes to disappear. As she walked towards the door she prayed that it wouldn't be—

Francesca

The door opened and Lucia's teacher stood there, white-faced. She looked at Francesca and opened her mouth to speak.

Francesca waited.

'Er – good morning. I was just wondering where Lucia was.' As she spoke, her neck and face filled with an ugly red colour. Most unflattering.

'Yes. We got your text last night.' Francesca looked coolly at Carmel. 'At least, I assume it was you.' Look how flat she was on top – nothing for a man to get hold of. See how terrified she looked. Francesca began to enjoy herself.

Carmel

She gripped the edge of the door and felt the blood still racing towards her face, giving her away. Her legs felt like rubber – she prayed they'd keep supporting her.

Francesca was waiting for an answer, but Carmel said nothing. What was there to say? Behind her, the DVD played on. Some character said, 'Oh no!' and a burst of laughter erupted from the class.

Francesca flicked her hair over her shoulder, and the movement brought a wave of perfume towards Carmel. 'Oh, and by the way, I'm taking my daughter out of this school. I'd rather find a teacher who doesn't fuck around.'

She spoke loudly and clearly. Behind Carmel, a few small heads swung towards the door.

Francesca

She didn't look back, wasn't interested in seeing the silly woman's reaction. Her blood raced, it felt good. She strode down the corridor, swinging her hips, pushing doors open ahead of her. A woman walked towards her, smiling, and Francesca beamed back.

Outside, the air smelled wonderful. She climbed back into her car and drove straight to Paul's company, humming.

Stephanie looked up as Francesca's heels clicked across the parquet flooring to her desk, just outside Paul's office door. 'Oh, hello, Francesca, he's actually—'

Francesca swept past her and walked straight into the office, taking no notice whatsoever of the man sitting opposite Paul, who turned as she came in and eyed her openly from head to toe as she talked.

Francesca spoke clearly, as she had at the classroom door. 'Just to let you know that I've found out about you and your whore at the school, and I'm leaving you and never coming back. You can sleep with whoever you like from now on.'

Halfway out of the room she stopped, as if something had just occurred to her. 'By the way, you do realise I was only using you, don't you? To help me get over Luca.'

And then, simply because she was feeling so wonderful, she turned to the other man and said, loudly enough for Stephanie to hear, 'He's useless in bed. Tries his best, but you can only do so much with a tiny penis.'

Then she swept out, aware of the stunned silence behind her, feeling Stephanie's horrified eyes on her as she sashayed back over the parquet.

So easy, she thought, driving home. *It was so easy, after all.* She thought of Perola in full summer bloom, and her heart sang. She ignored her phone, which rang in her bag all the way home.

The first thing she had to do was change their plane tickets. Then she'd talk to Marietta.

May

'I can't believe it.' How many times had she said that in the past half-hour?

And again Pam nodded and replied, 'I know.' They were sitting in Carmel's spare bedroom, perched on the bed that Pam had slept in the night before. Pam fiddled with a button on the duvet cover, opening it, closing it.

She had just finished telling May everything, right up to arriving on Carmel's doorstep yesterday afternoon with a taxi at the gate waiting to be paid. 'Thank goodness Carmel had cash on her.'

As she listened, May felt her horror turning to shame. To think that Pam had been going through all that trauma and May hadn't had the smallest idea. She'd been wrapped up in her own dramas, which seemed so unimportant now – a cranky father, a lost necklace, a pregnancy that had nothing to do with her – that she hadn't seen what had been going on right under her nose.

And to think that Pam was still trying to protect her husband, calling the bank and saying she'd lost her credit card. Refusing to consider the possibility of reporting Jack to the police. 'I can't report him, May – he's my husband. I just can't.'

May watched her now, twisting the button, round and round. 'So, what are you going to do?'

'I'm going to move back to Cork on Monday.' Pam lifted her head and looked steadily at May. 'I'd be gone already except I hadn't the money last night, and this morning I decided I want to try to meet my mother first, but I'm afraid to go home yet in case—'

In case Jack goes looking for me there. May nodded, as if Pam had said it out loud.

'Conor phoned me last night – my brother – and told me Jack had phoned, asking for me, and just hung up when Conor said I wasn't there. Jack phoned here last night too – Carmel said she hadn't seen me. And he phoned your house, and he keeps trying my phone, but of course I don't . . . ' Pam trailed off. 'I don't know what to tell poor Mam – she'll be devastated.'

'Don't worry about your mother. She'll be fine, once she knows you're OK. You need to think about yourself now.'

Pam bit her lip. 'And, May, I hate leaving you in the lurch like this, you've always been so— '

May shook her head. 'Let that be the least of your worries. I'll find someone else, who won't be half as good as you, no doubt, but we'll manage fine.' Even as she spoke, her heart sank and she wondered how long it would take to find someone else with enough patience to cope with Philip's contrariness.. She'd have to cut back on her own work for a while.

May had met Jack Treacy a few times. The first time was when Pam had applied for the home-help job, and May had phoned to ask her to come and meet them. Jack had driven Pam over, then sat in the car waiting for her, until Pam had mentioned he was out there, and May had insisted that he come in to have tea with them. Dark, good-looking, quite charming. Complimenting May on the house, asking Philip about the book on the table beside him. And after Pam had started working for May and Philip, he dropped her there every morning, occasionally meeting May on her way out to work. Always a friendly word for her, always seemed in good form.

Once he'd called around in the late afternoon to collect an umbrella Pam had forgotten, and he'd chatted with May for a few minutes on the doorstep, politely refusing her offer of tea, saying Pam would have dinner ready for him at home.

Rebecca had arrived at May's just as Jack was leaving that day, and May had introduced them. As soon as he was out of earshot, Rebecca had demanded to know why some women had all the luck. If only they'd known.

After a while May stood up. 'Well, that kitchen won't paint itself; I'd better get started.'

Pam got to her feet too. 'I'll help you. I'm looking for something to do anyway.'

They were about to go downstairs when the doorbell rang.

Pam stiffened and clutched May's arm. 'That could be him.' She looked terrified.

May shook her head. 'Doubt it – he'd know Carmel was at work.' But just to be on the safe side they went back into the bedroom. May crossed to the window and peered out. The porch hid the front door from her, but she could see the road.

'What car does he drive?' She couldn't remember, although she'd seen it often enough.

'Dark blue Mazda 626.'

There it was, three doors down. 'Reg four-two-seven-nine?'

Pam drew in her breath sharply. 'Oh God, it's him.' Her hands pressed against her cheeks. 'Don't go down – don't let him in.'

'No, of course not.' As May moved away from the window, the bell rang again, several rapid, impatient buzzes. Pam flinched, her face chalk white.

For several seconds, nothing happened. Both women stood still, waiting. May wondered suddenly if the back door was open. No, Carmel would surely have left it locked, and May hadn't gone near it.

She thought of her phone, sitting on the kitchen table downstairs. Left there while she made tea for herself and Pam. She couldn't risk getting it – if he looked through the letterbox as she went down the stairs, he'd see her.

She peered out the window again. The car was still there. What was he doing? Why was it so quiet?

And suddenly there he was, striding quickly towards the car. Blue jeans, check shirt. Wrenching open the door, slamming it shut. A second later, it roared away.

May turned back to Pam. 'It's OK, he's gone.'

Tears were running silently down Pam's face, trailing across the hands she still pressed to her cheeks. Now she started to sob, but quietly, burying her face in her hands.

May crossed the room and put her arms around her. 'Oh Pam, you poor thing. You poor thing.'

What was to be done? Watching him just now, May had sensed the anger in him, had seen it in the rigid way he'd held himself as he'd marched back towards the car. And he'd already proven he was capable of violence. Was he going to get away with it?

But Pam didn't want to report him, and who was May to tell her that she should? How could she understand what went on between a husband and wife? How could she know what private history there was between them?

A little later, they went downstairs and started to

paint, after May had made sure the windows and doors were locked. It was all they could think of to do.

And it never once occurred to May, not that day or the two days that followed it, to wonder if Jack Treacy had noticed her blue bike, locked onto the side gate.

Shaun

'Coffee break.' He opened the shop door and walked in, holding a cardboard tray with two paper cups, and a brown paper bag. 'Oh good, no customers.'

'Actually, no customers isn't good.' Bernard looked sternly at him. 'At least you're not trying to sneak up on me this morning.'

'It'll never happen again, I swear. And you're not entirely blameless anyway – you should have told me about that letter when I called you.'

'Funnily enough, I didn't want to worry you – and then you end up nearly giving me a heart attack.' Bernard opened the bag and slid the biscotti pieces on to a plate. 'I hope these are white chocolate chip.'

'Of course.' Shaun handed him a coffee, then touched the back of his neck gingerly. 'Ow, by the way.'

'Still stinging?' Bernard sipped from the cup, not looking in the least sympathetic.

'Can't believe I forgot the sunblock . . . So anyhow, the cops have the letter now, right?'

Bernard nodded, broke off a chunk of biscotti. 'They're looking into it, whatever that means.'

'And the CCTV?'

'Two o'clock, they said.'

'Good. I'll drop by at closing time.'

'No need. With the cameras going up—'

Shaun ignored him. 'I'll drop by at closing time, and we'll go to O'Meara's first for two half-decent screwballs each, then on to the Kasbah, because that's where I've booked the table.' He looked enquiringly at Bernard. 'OK?'

Bernard smiled – 'If I must' – and Shaun knew he was forgiven.

Francesca

'. . . . so we won't be needing your services any more.' She clicked the suitcase closed and turned back towards Marietta. 'You may stay here for the next two weeks, during which time I expect you to get sorted with another job. I'm sure Paul won't object to having someone around to cook his meals and wash his socks.'

Marietta nodded. Francesca wondered how much of what she was saying the other woman understood, and then decided she didn't care.

Lucia came trotting into the bedroom. 'Mamma, can I take Gregor on the plane?' She held up a giant gorilla, at least three-quarters her own size.

Francesca shook her head. 'No room, *cara*. But we'll send for him, I promise, as soon as we get home, and Paul will make sure he follows us.'

Marietta was still standing in front of her, studying

the floor. 'Was there anything else?' Francesca said. 'Because I have a lot to do here.'

Marietta brought her gaze up to settle on Francesca's left shoulder. 'I make something to eat before you leave?'

'No need.' Francesca turned and walked towards her dressing table. 'We'll get something at the airport.' She began to pile cosmetics into a shiny turquoise cylinder.

Marietta stayed where she was. 'Should I prepare dinner for Mr Ryan?'

Francesca turned back, her face expressionless. 'I don't care what you do for him.' She stood and waited until Marietta had walked quietly from the room, then picked up her phone from the dressing table and found the local taxi firm's number.

May

Philip looked up in surprise and lowered his paper as May came in. 'You're home early.'

She nodded. 'That's because I had help with the painting – Pam's staying at Carmel's for a while.' She paused. 'Dad, I'm afraid she won't be coming back to work here.'

She braced herself for an outraged outburst but, to her amazement, Philip just nodded grimly. 'I thought something funny was going on there.'

'You did? Why?'

'That husband of hers called around earlier.' Philip frowned. 'Got me out of bed, kept ringing the blasted bell till I answered it, and not a word of apology. Wanted to know if Pam was here.'

Jack had called here, to May's house. Had stood on the doorstep until Philip had struggled out of bed and all the way downstairs – must have been at least ten minutes. 'What did you tell him?'

Philip looked at May as if she was half-witted. 'What do you think I told him? I told him she wasn't here, of course.' He lifted the paper again. 'They must have had some kind of a row, that's what I think. We're as well off without her, if that's the kind they are.'

May hesitated, then said, 'Actually, there's a bit more to it than that.'

Carmel

She was getting into her car when she remembered that Pam was in her house – and May was there too, painting. The last thing she wanted now was to have to make small-talk with anyone. Bad enough having to sit through the last-day-of-the-school-year lunchtime, with sandwiches brought in from that new deli and a few bottles of fizzy grape juice. Carmel had picked the corner off a sandwich, nodding politely at whatever the people around her were saying, watching the clock for when she could decently leave.

Wishing everyone would shut up about their hangovers from the night before, or where they were going on their holidays – as if Carmel gave a shit about any of that.

When people finally began to move, she'd gone back to her hot classroom to clear up the debris and organise it somehow for next year's crop of four-year-olds. She'd taken down the paintings, drawings and posters that were on display around the room, stored the reusable ones in her chart press and binned the rest.

She'd cleared the nature table of the shells and falling-apart bird's nest, the feathers, leaves, bits of twig and stones, and she'd stacked the library books in neat piles. She'd washed the paint pots and brushes and left them on the draining board to dry. She'd thrown the old crayons and pencils into the bin, wiped the blackboard and tidied her table.

And as she worked, her mind kept wandering back to the horrible little scene at the classroom door. How she'd got through the rest of the morning after Francesca had left . . . the children somehow sensing her mood when she'd walked back into the classroom, the way they'd looked warily at her flaming face . . . *I'd rather find a teacher who doesn't fuck around* – God almighty, there was nothing you could say to that.

And of course Robbie, the bould Robbie, piping up: 'She said the F word.' Be all over town in no time that Lucia's mother was effing and blinding at the classroom door.

What was killing Carmel, though, was that she still hadn't heard from Paul. Did he even know that Francesca had found out about them? Maybe Francesca had just tried it on with her, trying to scare her off

Paul. Maybe she'd said nothing to him, hoping it would blow over.

But even if Paul did know, so what? He might be angry with Carmel for a bit, but surely he'd enjoy the added thrill this would bring to their affair, knowing that Francesca had her suspicions.

Because that was all they were – she hadn't a shred of evidence. That text proved nothing. And Carmel had admitted nothing. Blushing wasn't proof of anything.

And Paul was mad about Carmel, it was obvious. Called her his little girl – couldn't get enough of her whenever he came around to see her. And that weekend in Italy had been fantastic, even if he'd had to go to some stupid conference all day Saturday. They'd made up for it at night – he'd been like an animal. He'd hardly have taken her away for a whole weekend if he didn't care about her, would he? Or given her that necklace.

She turned right as she drove out through the school gates. She'd go and see him, go to his workplace. She had nothing to lose – what could be worse than this morning's confrontation? And surely he'd admire her for her brazenness. Paul liked a woman with a bit of fire in her.

She glanced at the dashboard clock – half past three. She might even persuade him to leave work early and take her to a hotel room, since her house was out of bounds as long as Pam was there. She could show him how sorry she was, what a foolish little girl she'd been . . .

He was walking towards his car as she drove into the factory grounds. When he saw her he stopped dead, waited until she'd parked and walked over to him.

Looked at her with narrowed eyes. 'What are you doing here?'

He didn't look too pleased to see her – Francesca had obviously been talking to him. Carmel put her head to one side, a finger to her mouth. 'Oh dear, I think I'm in the black books.' He could never resist that childish voice. 'I've been a bold little girl, haven't I? I think I need a good spanking.'

He said nothing. His face was like thunder. She was definitely in trouble.

Carmel changed tack, put a hand up to touch his face, spoke in her normal voice. 'Darling, I know I made a—'

He grabbed her wrist. 'Now listen to me, you stupid bitch.' He spoke quietly and deliberately. 'If you ever try to contact me again, I'll have you arrested. Do you understand?' He flung her wrist away from him and walked quickly towards his car.

Carmel stood motionless, long after his car had disappeared. Long after the feel of his fingers pressed into her wrist had faded.

In the end, she got back into her car and drove home very carefully.

Iseult

What time was it? Half four – he should be home by now. She dialled Paddy's number and listened to one, two, three rings, her hand pressed against her temple. *Please let him be there.*

'Hello?'

She winced. 'Not so loud. Have you milk?' Her voice was husky; she sounded like a frog.

'Sorry, who is this?'

Iseult closed her eyes and spoke slowly. 'Don't – I'm dying. I've got the hangover to beat all hangovers and I've run out of milk, and there's no way I can make it to the shop, and if I don't get a gallon of tea into me in the next ten minutes . . . ' She stopped, out of energy.

'OK, OK.' Paddy sounded amused. 'I'll be right over. Have you painkillers?'

She nodded, then winced again. 'Yes. Just milk.'

It was the last drink that had done it – it was always the last drink. Just after the one that should have been the last, before someone – some evil demon from the Senior School – had put another in front of her, and it seemed like the best idea in the world to knock it back.

She groaned, pressing her hands to the sides of her head. How she'd got through the morning without murdering, or at least seriously injuring, one of her senior infants was completely beyond her. The oniony smell of their crisps at break, every high-pitched sentence was torture – and the clammy heat of the day hadn't helped.

And Carmel had looked no better, even though she hadn't even been out with them last night. Iseult hadn't spoken to her – she'd been sitting at the opposite end of the staffroom table at lunch – but she certainly looked rough. Must have had a good night somewhere else.

Carmel . . . there was something she was forgetting.

The peal of the doorbell went through her like a spear. She opened the door with a finger to her lips. 'Shh. Gimme.' She reached for the carton of milk and walked gingerly into the kitchen. 'God, never again.'

Paddy propped himself against the doorjamb and watched her making the tea, amused. 'Did you not drink a gallon of water when you got home?'

'Can't remember.' She wore a black lace tunic over a lime green dress that skimmed the top of her blue ankle boots. 'It was Gavin Murphy in the Senior School's fault. He kept buying me drink.'

'Maybe he fancies you.'

Iseult made a face. 'Let's hope nobody tells his wife.' Her hair poked through what looked like a striped tea cosy. She poured tea into two cups, added milk to one and sipped. 'Ah.' She handed the other cup to Paddy and picked up the open box of Panadol that sat on the worktop. 'Sit down and I'll fill you in on the bits I can remember.'

It wasn't until he was leaving, several cups of tea later, that Paddy spotted something on the phone table in the hall. He stopped and picked it up. 'Where'd you get this?'

Iseult looked at the necklace. '*Shit*, I knew there was something I forgot. It belongs to Carmel. She lost it and I found it, and I was going to give it back to her today.

Shit – now I'll have to call around to her house. I'll do it tomorrow, when I'm human again.'

'Hang on.' Paddy looked from the necklace to Iseult. 'Where did Carmel get it?'

Iseult shrugged. 'Some child gave it to her as an end-of-year present – why?'

'Because,' Paddy trailed the chain across the back of his hand, 'I happen to know this necklace. Actually,' he looked up at Iseult again, 'I got it made.'

'Huh?' Iseult frowned, then shook her head cautiously. 'No, you couldn't have. I told you, Carmel got it as a present. You must be mixing it up with another one.'

'Hang on.' Paddy fingered the tiny shell, and held it up in front of her. 'Remember how I used to collect shells like this, when I was small?'

'Yeah, but—'

'Just listen. Remember my room was full of them – they used to drive Mam mad when she was trying to clean in there? Remember?'

Iseult folded her arms and leaned against the wall. 'Yeah, yeah, I remember, but—'

'And then I got rid of them all when I was thirteen or fourteen.'

She smiled. 'Yeah – when you discovered Karen O'Toole.'

Paddy grinned. 'Round about then, right. But I kept a few of my favourites, and this,' he dangled the shell in front of her face, 'this was the smallest. I'd know it anywhere.'

A flicker of doubt crossed Iseult's face, but then she frowned again. 'I still don't see how Carmel could have ended up with it. You must be mixing it up, Pad.'

He shook his head firmly. 'No, I'm not. I got a jeweller to put the chain on it and . . . ' now he hesitated '. . . and then I . . . gave it to someone earlier this year.'

Iseult's eyebrows shot up. 'You gave it to someone? Who?'

Paddy let the shell and chain drop into his cupped palm. 'I'm not sure I can tell you – she doesn't know herself.'

'What?' Iseult looked sceptical. 'You gave this necklace to someone, and she doesn't know she got it?'

'Of course she knows she got it – but she doesn't know I sent it. Anonymously.' He smiled, reddening. 'On Valentine's Day, actually.'

'Right.' Iseult nodded slowly. 'So you're telling me you sent this necklace – you're quite positive it was this one—'

He nodded.

'—to some mystery woman, and somehow Carmel ended up with it?' Her voice was full of disbelief.

Paddy shrugged. 'I know it sounds weird, and I've no idea how that happened . . . ' He paused. ' . . . unless the person I gave it to lost it, and then whoever found it gave it to Carmel. You said you found it, didn't you? So Carmel lost it after she was given it?'

'Yeah – the day she got it, actually.' Iseult looked down at the necklace. 'It must have fallen off her.'

Paddy peered at the tiny fitting. 'The clasp does seem a bit loose.' He looked at Iseult. 'So it probably did fall off.'

'Right – hey, it's pretty amazing that it ends up back with you, the person who had it made in the first place. Poor Carmel, though. But Pad,' Iseult looked up at him pleadingly 'you have to tell me who she is.'

Paddy smiled. 'Do I now?'

She moved smoothly between him and the door. 'If you want to get out of here alive.'

'Actually, the funny thing is,' he was still smiling, 'you gave her to me.'

'*Gave* her to you?' Iseult frowned. 'What the heck are you—'

'Izzy, it's May. I gave the necklace to May O'Callaghan. And you gave her to me for my birthday, remember?'

Iseult looked blankly at him. 'May, who did your garden? That May?'

'That May.'

'Oh. My. God.' A slow smile spread over her face. 'I don't believe it. I can hardly remember what she looks like. And there you are, sending her necklaces.'

Paddy smiled. 'Just the one, actually.'

'Oh my God, my little brother is so romantic.' Iseult put her arm through his. 'Do you know something? I think my hangover's lifting. Come in and we'll make more tea. So you sent her the necklace, and then what?'

'Well, there's not much else to tell.' Paddy allowed himself to be dragged back into the kitchen. 'I can't drink any more tea. Have you anything else?'

Iseult opened the fridge and peered in. 'I have Lucozade and tequila. But I've no lemons. Oh, and there's some After Eights left.' She pulled out the box.

Paddy looked at it without interest. 'You'd think you'd have a decent bottle of wine in there at least.'

'Stop changing the subject.' She pulled an After Eight from its wrapper. 'I think I might manage one of these . . . so, what do you mean, there's not much else to tell? Valentine's Day was . . . ' she thought, '. . . four months ago. What have you done since then to win May O'Callaghan's heart?'

Paddy leaned against the table and folded his arms. 'Chicken stir-fry.'

'Pardon?' Iseult stared at him. 'You made her chicken stir-fry?'

'That's what I'm having for dinner, not After Eights, and I'm going home to cook it now. If you want to hear more, you can come to my house. I'll be twenty minutes.'

Iseult considered. 'Will there be wine?'

'There will, yes.'

'That's supposed to be good for a hangover.'

'So they say.'

After he'd gone, Iseult walked slowly back into the kitchen. May O'Callaghan – after all her attempts to find him a woman. But she *had* found him one in the end – so what if it had been by accident?

Maybe she should take up matchmaking professionally – didn't they earn a fortune? Maybe she could try to find someone for Carmel next – *she* could do with a bit of a fling, she hadn't gone out with anyone for ages. And now she wasn't even getting her necklace back.

Iseult went off to have a shower, whistling between her teeth. At least dinner would be good tonight. And a small glass of wine would do her no harm at all.

Pam

She dialled her mother's number, six miles away, and listened to the ringing.

'Hello?'

'Mam, it's me.'

'Pammy love, where are you? I've been out of my mind.'

Pam pressed her eyes shut. 'Sorry, Mam. I told Conor to tell you I'm OK. I'm at a friend's house – I can't say where, but I'm OK. Did . . . ' she could hardly say his name. 'Was Jack in touch since?'

'Only the phone call last evening – what's going on, lovie? Have you two fallen out?' Her mother sounded bewildered. 'Is it serious?'

'Yeah – it's serious.' Pam hesitated. 'I'm . . . I'm going—' She bit her lip, hard. Then she took a deep breath and tried again. 'Mam, I'm leaving him.'

'Oh God, Pammy, you're not. Can't you sort it out? Can't you talk to him about it? It can't be—'

'Mam, he hurt me.' There it was. 'He hit me.'

She heard her mother's gasp. 'Oh Jesus – are you alright?'

'I'm OK now. Look Mam, I have to go away because he might come back and find me, and it could be— It's just for a while, OK? And then if . . . he comes asking for me, you can tell him, quite honestly, that you don't know where I am.'

'Oh, Pammy—'

'Look, I'll be out to see you on Sunday. I'll get Carmel to drive me, or Conor can come in or something, OK? We can talk more then.' By Sunday she should be safe – surely he'd have got tired of looking for her by then, assumed she'd left town somehow. 'I'll ring again tomorrow night, and we can arrange something.' Then she remembered. 'Oh, and Mam, there's another thing. I'll need to borrow some money, just for a bit – say, a couple of hundred euro?'

'Of course, love. I'll get Conor to take it out from the machine in town tomorrow. As long as you're safe, Pammy, that's all that matters.'

'I'm safe now. Talk to you soon.' As Pam hung up, as she struggled not to burst into tears for the umpteenth time that day, she heard Carmel's key in the door. She pasted a smile on her face and walked downstairs to meet her. She couldn't bawl her eyes out to Carmel two days in a row.

But as soon as Carmel saw Pam, she broke into loud, wailing sobs.

Shaun

He typed a few words in a burst, looked at the screen for a few seconds, then deleted them. It just wasn't happening today. His dialogue was wooden, sounded horribly false when he played it back in his head. And his neck felt stiff although, thank Christ, the yoghurt had stopped the stinging.

Just as well they were heading out on the town tonight – he could do with a break. Maybe it was the heat – unbelievable for Ireland, even in the middle of summer. Must be in the eighties today.

A rhythmic clipping sound drifted in through the wide-open window. May sure had a lot of energy on a day like this.

He lifted his watch from the table and read the time, then immediately pressed *save* and stood up hastily, pulling his T-shirt over his head as he walked quickly towards the bathroom. He'd be a couple of minutes late, but Bernard wouldn't mind – no way could Shaun skip a shower in this heat.

May

She sliced through the last overgrown bit of the hedge, which tumbled to her feet as she wiped her forehead with her sleeve. It certainly was hot this afternoon. Wait till Philip discovered they were having cold meat for dinner, after the cheese salad she'd left in the fridge for his lunch earlier. He'd have something to say, no doubt.

She got the brush from the shed and swept the clippings into a bundle. Just as she'd stuffed the last of them into her green garden bag, Shaun came hurrying from the house next door.

'You look as if you're late for something.'

He didn't stop. 'Bernard – we're out on the town

tonight.' He raised a hand as he sped down the road. 'Have a good one.'

'You too.' Now there was a couple with a social life. She hauled the bag of clippings around to the back, then went inside to arrange the cold ham on two plates.

Maybe they'd really live dangerously, have some pickles with it.

Bernard

Ten to six, finally. He emptied the till, bagged the coins, folded the notes together and put the money into his leather briefcase. Then he went outside for another look at the two new cameras. Pity they spoiled the look of the shop front, sticking out like that, but he supposed it was unavoidable.

He waved at Mrs Dooley across the road, coming out of the bakery with bags of groceries, then brought in the buckets with the unsold flowers and wheeled the display units inside the door. No sign of Shaun yet. Still so hot . . . incredible, really.

He took a last look around – must order more gypsophila tomorrow. He was walking towards the door to change the sign from *Come in, we're open* to *Sorry, we're closed* when it was pushed in.

'You still open?' A smell of alcohol as the words came out.

Bernard nodded. 'Yes, of course – you're just in time.' He turned around to put his briefcase on the counter. 'What can I—'

And that was all he got to say before something cold and hard smashed into the back of his head.

Shaun

He half walked, half ran down the street. Two blocks to go and ten minutes late – and almost as sweaty again as he'd been before his shower. He glanced up at the sky: leaden-looking clouds were gathering. Maybe a storm tonight, clear the air.

Two teenage girls came walking quickly towards him, the bigger one brushing against him roughly as she passed, not bothering to apologise. Teens could be pretty obnoxious, the world over.

At the beginning of Bernard's block he spotted the new cameras, jutting out clearly. Great. Bernard would hate them, of course, spoiling the look of the lovely old wooden frontage that apparently hadn't changed since his parents had opened the shop, more than forty years ago. But at least he'd be secure.

The units were in, all the buckets gone. The gently swinging sign on the door said *Come in, we're open.* Not like Bernard to forget that.

The door was ajar. He pushed it in. 'Hello?'

He saw, in this order, the overturned buckets, the scattered flowers, the skewed trestle tables. It took a little longer to spot the thin finger of red liquid that snaked lazily across the vinyl floor towards him from Bernard's unmoving body.

Paul

His phone rang and he whipped it out, read, *John M calling*, and switched it off. Work – that could wait. Then, when he was stopped at the next traffic lights, he pressed Francesca's name, and listened again to her voicemail.

He dreaded getting home: he was afraid of what faced him there. Was Francesca really going to leave him? Had she gone already, taken her daughter and walked out?

What if he never saw her again?

The thought was suddenly unbearable. Never to press his mouth against the warm sweat on her skin, to run his hands over the hot, voluptuous nakedness of her—

No, he couldn't think like that. It wasn't over – it couldn't be over. She wouldn't leave him, not after one mistake. And she hadn't meant what she'd said about Luca. That wasn't true. Francesca loved him. She didn't need to say it for him to know. She wouldn't have got so upset over Carmel if she hadn't loved him, would she?

She hadn't answered his calls, though he'd tried all afternoon, after he'd finally managed to get rid of bloody Bill Hurley, who'd enjoyed the little scene enormously. Who'd gaped at Francesca as she stormed out, then turned back to Paul, trying hard not to smirk. He was probably spreading it all around the place now, getting a great kick out of it – Paul Ryan got caught playing away, got his comeuppance from his Italian bombshell. Paul Ryan and his tiny penis.

And that stupid little *tart*, turning up at his work like that, acting as if nothing had happened, as if what she'd done had been nothing more than a prank gone wrong. If he hadn't been late for his meeting, he'd have told her exactly what he thought of her. Stupid cow, letting the cat out of the bag like that. Ruining everything.

The scream of an ambulance cut through his thoughts. He watched it race past the car, siren flashing, and it reminded him of yesterday, and his own dash to the hospital. Francesca throwing herself into his arms when he arrived, sobbing out what had happened.

As he drove, he scanned the streets automatically for a dark-haired woman and a little curly-headed girl. Had it been only four years ago, just four years since he'd wandered into the family restaurant on one of Perola's back streets and seen Francesca Tuttoro for the first time?

It had been one of those blazingly hot August days, everything still and heavy with heat, that made Paul long for the cool wetness of Ireland, that filled him with nostalgia for the fresh summery showers he associated with home.

Not that he regretted leaving his job in London the year before, not after all that awkwardness, with Sarah turning nasty like that, making out he'd forced her into the abortion, which was utter nonsense. It had been a joint decision – of course it had.

And if Sarah hadn't been the niece of one of the

managing directors, that would have been the end of it. She'd have ranted at him for a bit, and then they'd have gone their separate ways, end of story. There might have been a bit of awkwardness for a while at work, but they'd have been able to avoid each other easily enough, with all the travelling Paul did.

But Sarah had had other ideas. Paul was summoned to her aunt's office a few days after their break-up and urged strongly to apply for another job, preferably outside London. Sarah's name wasn't mentioned, of course, but the aunt's tone was cold, and Paul was left in no doubt as to why he was being invited to leave.

He was tempted to brazen it out – there was no law against having an affair with a colleague, even one as young as Sarah. Wasn't she over the age of consent, by a few years? She was certainly old enough to have more gold credit cards than Paul.

But while he was mulling over what he should do, he heard about a rapidly growing computer company in Italy that was recruiting experienced personnel, and just for the laugh – certainly not because he felt he had to move – Paul sent along his CV.

When he was offered an interview, he hunted for Perola on a map of Italy, and was pleasantly surprised to find it perched on the Adriatic coast, just across the way from Rome. Not exactly in the middle of nowhere, then – and warmer than London in the middle of a particularly harsh January.

By April he'd relocated, settling into the modern apartment his new employers had provided until he found his feet. He was charmed with Perola's mix of ancient cobbled streets lined with small, family-run boutiques, bars and restaurants, and the new bustling industrial district, mercifully free of tearful young women accusing him of ruining their lives.

He'd walked to work along sunny, tree-lined streets, remembering the crowded, silent tubes of London, the snarl of rainy-day rush-hour traffic, and he'd swum in the clear blue sea at weekends, eyeing the elegant caramel-skinned Italian sunbathers.

For the first few months he avoided the social outings organised by various members of the largely Italian workforce. Not because he wasn't included – his colleagues were refreshingly friendly and made a point of inviting him along – but because he wasn't about to jeopardise this new and so far very enjoyable situation with another Sarah.

He'd made up his mind never again to get involved with a work colleague, and it hadn't taken him long to identify at least two potential temptations. Better steer clear – when it came to resisting women, his will power hadn't exactly proved reliable in the past. So he concentrated on his work, and made excuses whenever invitations were issued, and found enough distractions among the lonely female tourists who found their way to Perola.

One evening, when he'd been living in Perola for just over four months, and after a particularly satisfying week at work, he'd showered, shaved and dressed in a grey silk shirt with loose black linen trousers. The day was still heavy – by the time he reached the little bar where he often had a drink in the evenings, the back of his shirt was patched with sweat.

He ordered Scotch on the rocks and sat two stools away from a trio of twenty-something females in strappy tops, mini-skirts and frighteningly high heels, who glanced at him as he sat down, then ignored him.

From the other end of the bar, a dyed blonde woman of about Paul's age caught his eye and smiled tentatively. He raised his glass and held her gaze. He was about to get up and make his way towards her when a slender man who looked young enough to be her son walked into the bar and joined her. She kissed him on both cheeks, and he signalled to the barman as he sat down.

Paul sipped his drink and listened to the chatter of the girls beside him, giggling about some film star or another. He was getting the hang of the language, starting to make sense of the expressive gestures and flowing streams of words.

After two Scotches, he decided it wasn't going to be a lucky night for him. He'd moved from his stool to a little table beside a dark-haired woman of about thirty, who'd politely refused his offer of a drink and left shortly afterwards. Then he'd had a short conversation with a young American tourist who turned out to be waiting for her fiancé. No, not a lucky night.

He'd left the bar and wandered through the straggle of little side streets in the old neighbourhood in search of dinner. After rejecting a few restaurants that he knew were geared to the many tourists who descended on Perola in the summer, he eventually found himself in front of one he hadn't spotted before.

The outside wasn't impressive, with peeling wooden shutters and windows that could have done with a shine, but it smelled wonderful, and he could hear the babble of Italian inside – had to be a good sign. He decided to take a chance, and pushed open the door.

He saw Francesca straight away. She was bent over a table not three feet from him, bundling plates together. She wore a red gypsy skirt and a black low-cut blouse. He saw long dark hair, interesting cleavage, full hips before she straightened and noticed him.

He marvelled at how wonderfully black her eyes were, and how incredibly creamy her skin, as she asked him in a low voice if he wanted a table for one. He followed her as she sashayed to a small table in the corner, and all through his meal he watched her. She looked to be in her late twenties, a fair few years younger than him but still quite a bit older than the women he was normally attracted to.

For some reason, he couldn't take his eyes off her.

He ate scallops in a creamy, cheesy sauce and perfectly cooked penne with pine nuts and fresh sardines, and he drank ice-cold local wine, and glass after glass of bottled water.

She fascinated him. She never smiled. She was beautiful.

When he'd finished, she brought him a little glass of grappa on the house, and a plateful of pink watermelon chunks. He smiled his thanks, and indicated the empty chair opposite him. 'Please, join me.' The restaurant had emptied while he ate – now only three other tables were occupied.

She shook her head solemnly – 'I am working' – and walked away, into the back. She didn't reappear, although he ordered a second glass of grappa from the older, less striking waitress.

The following night he went back, and every night after that for a week. She was perfectly courteous, but refused his offer of a drink, turned down his invitation to dinner, denied him everything except her first name. She didn't give him any reason, just shook her head with the briefest of smiles and walked away.

Far from putting him off, her aloofness tantalised him. He became determined to win her.

One September night, about three weeks after he had first set eyes on Francesca, he waited in the shadows after leaving the restaurant. He watched the last customers going home just after half past one, and a few minutes later he saw the older waitress come out and walk away. He went over what he planned to say to Francesca when she eventually appeared – surely she couldn't keep refusing him for much longer – but when the lights went out a little later, and there was still no sign of her, he went home.

The following day, Saturday, he saw her walking out of a supermarket. She was pushing a baby in a buggy. Without thinking, he went over to her.

'Hello there.'

She looked at Paul, startled. When she recognised him, the same brief smile he'd seen before flashed across her face. 'Hello.' It vanished as quickly as it had appeared. She wore a short deep pink sundress in T-shirt material, which crossed over her breasts and flared at her hips. He smelled flowers.

'Is this your baby?'

She glanced down, and nodded. As she went to move away, something made him say, 'Are you married?' He had no idea where the question had come from – it was suddenly there, hanging in the air between them. And as soon as it was said, as soon as he saw her reaction, he regretted it.

Her eyes filled with tears. She turned on her heel and practically ran away from him, pushing the buggy ahead of her. He cursed himself for the rest of the day, and avoided the restaurant that evening and the next.

On Monday night, she acted as if nothing had happened. She served him solemnly and politely. He ate goat's cheese and rocket bruschetta, and mussels in a white wine sauce. In the past three weeks he'd gained five pounds.

When his plates were empty, Francesca cleared them away and brought his glass of grappa and plate of melon. Then she pulled out the chair opposite him and sat down.

He didn't dare say anything. For a minute they looked at each other across the table. Then she said, 'I am sorry

I ran away the last day.' Up to now, she'd spoken to him in Italian. Her English was heavily accented.

Paul shook his head. 'Serves me right for being nosy.'

The tiny smile flashed across her face. She bent her head. He saw minuscule red sparks in her dark hair – some kind of jewellery.

'My husband died seven months ago.' She lifted her head and looked straight into his eyes. He saw tears glittering in hers. 'He was a fisherman, and he drowned.' She stood up abruptly and left the table. He didn't see her again that night.

He waited three more days before he went back. As soon as he walked in, Francesca came over to him. He said quickly, 'If you'd rather I left you alone, you'd better tell me now.'

He rejoiced when she didn't answer, simply walked ahead of him to what had become his usual table.

Even after she eventually agreed to go for a drink with him, two months after they had first met, it took all his ingenuity, every ounce of patience he possessed, to win her. She was like some timid forest creature, shying away if he came too close. Tensing when he touched her hand, if his body made any kind of contact with hers.

It was three more weeks before he attempted to kiss her, after one too many Cognacs on the way back to the restaurant that turned out to belong to her parents, and where she and Lucia had returned to live after Luca had died.

She rarely mentioned her dead husband, and Paul

never asked. But that night they'd been talking about Italian food, and the different styles of cooking in the various parts of the country, and Francesca said suddenly, 'Luca came from the north. He was a good cook.'

Paul hesitated. Should he pass over it, change the subject? Or was it better to let her talk about Luca? He decided to wait and see.

Francesca drained her glass, and Paul raised his hand to the barman. After two more Cognacs had arrived, Francesca sat back and began, in a low voice, to tell Paul about her husband. How they'd met, when Luca had come to work on his uncle's fishing boat, down the coast. The wedding in Perola that had gone on for three days and nights. Lucia's birth ten months afterwards.

The freak storm that had claimed the lives of two fishermen from Francesca's home town, and Luca.

She didn't cry. Her voice was steady, and heavy with sorrow. When she finished speaking, Paul reached over and took her hand. For the first time, she didn't try to pull away.

It was enough for him to turn her quickly towards him on the way back to the restaurant. Her mouth tasted of brandy. Her scent made him dizzy. It took all his self-possession not to try anything more.

They continued to meet whenever Francesca could get away from the restaurant. Sometimes on her nights off they went out to dinner. Other times they met for an hour, between Paul finishing work and Francesca starting in the evening. Occasionally they took Lucia to the beach on Saturdays, or drove into the country and walked among the vineyards on dry, sun-baked lanes.

He still ate at the restaurant several times a week. He'd watch her serving other customers, bending over the menu with them and taking their orders, and he'd wonder how much longer she'd keep him waiting.

He tried to remember the last time a woman had resisted his bed for more than a fortnight, and failed. But Francesca was different. The longer she refused to visit his apartment – the more she pulled away if his kisses got too urgent – the more he wanted her, and the more determined he was to have her, however long it took.

And then one Saturday in April, more than six months since they'd first gone out, after a lunch of warm bread, olives and cheese in a village inn, Francesca turned to him and said, 'I will come tonight, after work.'

Paul dipped the last of his bread into the little bowl of dark yellow olive oil on the table. Lucia sat on her mother's lap and sucked loudly at a wedge of orange. The elderly woman behind the counter flicked a cloth at a fly that was hovering around the suspended cylinders of knobbly sausage. In the distance, a tractor puttered.

Paul said, 'Good,' then found himself completely unable to eat the bread.

She cried when they made love. He held her and told her he adored her. When he woke in the morning she was gone, leaving a pillow that smelled of her scent.

From then on, she spent at least one night a week in his apartment.

The following October, more than a year and a half after Paul had joined the company, his boss called him into his office and commended him on his performance. In fact, he continued, Paul had made such an impression on the board of directors that they had decided to offer him the opportunity of setting up a new branch the following year. In Ireland.

In Ireland?

In Ireland. It had been on the cards for some time, and with Paul having proven himself to be so competent and efficient – and, of course, in view of the fact that he was Irish – he seemed like the perfect choice to head up the venture.

Paul wondered aloud what kind of effect such a move would have on his salary, bearing in mind the higher cost of living in Ireland.

His boss smiled and assured him that he would be well taken care of in that respect, that the financial director would draw up a rewarding package to reflect Paul's new position. Would he think about it?

He would. He certainly would.

Paul decided not to remind his boss that he hadn't worked in Ireland for almost twenty years – at least until after he'd spoken with the financial director. Back at his desk, he began to imagine moving home. And the more he thought about it, the more the notion appealed to him.

Perola was fine in the spring, and mostly in the

autumn and winter too, but it was bloody murder in the middle of summer. The heat was unbearable without air conditioning, which was sadly lacking in many of the town's shops and restaurants.

By five o'clock he'd made up his mind. If the package he was offered was good enough – and he suspected it would be – he'd take it. It needn't be forever: if the new branch went well, he could negotiate another move in a few years. He was the golden boy, apparently.

And he'd be the golden boy back home too, having proven himself abroad. He wondered where the company was thinking of basing the new plant. Hopefully not around Dublin – he'd had enough of big cities to last him a lifetime. Maybe he could suggest somewhere in the west, somewhere fairly close to Shannon Airport, for ease of travel back and forth to Italy.

Somewhere like Kilpatrick, maybe. But first, of course, he'd have to persuade Francesca to come with him. The thought didn't worry him: his powers of persuasion had rarely let him down in the past.

He waited until they were in bed the following Saturday night. Until after he'd satisfied her, until after he'd claimed his reward.

'Ireland? For how long?' Her dark eyes gave nothing away. He might as well have told her that it had just begun to rain.

He shrugged. 'A year, maybe a little more. Just long enough to get the new plant up and running.' It wasn't a lie − nothing had been settled yet. It might easily happen that he'd end up back here again. Who knew? 'You will come, won't you?' He stroked her arm lightly. 'I couldn't bear it without you.'

'Ireland . . . ' He watched Francesca's face, saw indecision. *Don't push.*

He leaned across and brushed her lips. 'Just think about it, that's all. Promise you'll think about it.'

And of course, she said, 'I promise.' He smiled to himself. It was just a matter of time.

After that, things moved fast. Paul's half-joking suggestion of Kilpatrick as the location for the new plant was taken seriously, and the site was found and purchased within weeks. He found a house to rent over the internet, making sure there was plenty of room for the three of them, still convinced that Francesca would agree.

And he was right. They travelled to Ireland in the middle of January, going from a cold, dry Perola to a grey, squally Shannon Airport. Driving to Kilpatrick in the unfamiliar rented car, wipers flicking noisily, trying to remember to keep to the left, Francesca sitting silently beside him, Lucia sleeping at last in the back, Paul felt the first stirrings of unease. What if she hated it?

He needn't have worried. She took to the translating jobs he found for her straight away. Lucia was young enough to settle easily into her new surroundings. The house he'd found was comfortable and well situated, and little by little, as the weeks went by, Francesca looked as if she was finally beginning to put the past behind her.

And of course, Paul was happy. What man in his right mind would object to the affections of a woman like Francesca? Lying beside her at night, he felt perfectly happy, absolutely content. For the first time in his life, he had everything he wanted.

Marriage had never come up between them – he'd always sensed that Francesca would shy away from that kind of commitment with another man. And Paul had never hankered for the tie of matrimony. Weren't they fine as they were?

And then, a year and a half later, Lucia had started school and he'd met Carmel Gannon, who offered Paul her little-girl body with her eyes. He tried to resist. He did his best to ignore the brazen stares, the braless nipples that pushed at her stretch T-shirts, but in the end he simply had to take what was so blatantly available.

And the excitement of exploring Carmel's childish body, her eagerness to please him by doing anything – *anything* – he wanted, was gratifying. Apart from Francesca, he'd always liked them young.

He told himself it was harmless, just a bit of fun. Nobody need ever find out – and anyway, wasn't everyone at it?

How could he have been so stupid? How could he have jeopardised what he had with Francesca for some skinny little tart who meant nothing, *nothing* to him?

He pulled into the driveway, his heart jumping when he saw the little red Punto he'd bought for Francesca.

So she hadn't gone after all. She'd said what she'd said in the heat of the moment, and then she'd gone home and cooled down.

There'd be a row. Francesca would probably scream at him – she might throw a few things. Paul would apologise and promise never to see Carmel again. They'd have sensational sex to make up, and that would be the end of it.

As he walked towards the front door Marietta opened it, and one look at her face told him how wrong he was.

Paddy

He dried his hands and hung the towel back on its hook. Then he switched off the kitchen light and walked into the living room with the remains of his coffee. Tomorrow he'd get the gold chain repaired – hopefully he could persuade them to do it on Saturday, it only needed a new clasp – and on Sunday evening he'd take a chance that she'd be at home and bring it round in person to May. No big drama, no intrigue this time.

He picked up the remote control, pressed *on*, and watched someone talking earnestly in a studio somewhere about somebody else's book: '. . . *she writes with a detached air, and a precise eye for detail. Take the character of Timothy, who . . .* '

He lowered the volume. But what would he say to May when she opened the door? And, more to the point, what would she say to him? How would she react when she knew who he was?

Paddy O'Brien, whose garden she'd worked in every Thursday for the past several months.

Maybe she'd be annoyed that he hadn't introduced himself earlier – especially when they saw each other at least a couple of times a week. But he'd never managed to find a way to bring it up, their meetings were always so brief. Maybe he should have, though.

And he'd never had any sign from her that she had the slightest interest in him. Oh, she was friendly when they met – but she was probably like that with everyone. And now here he was, planning to turn up on her doorstep, a man whose name she'd recognise the minute he said it, and present her with a necklace, just like that.

Iseult didn't see his problem. 'I'd be delighted if someone called around and revealed himself as my secret admirer. And really, what's the worst that can happen? You hardly think she'll throw it back at you?'

Paddy tried to imagine May throwing the necklace back at him, and failed. Of course she wouldn't do that. She'd probably . . . what? He had no idea what she'd probably do.

Well, only one way to find out, he supposed. He drank his coffee and changed the channel.

*

May

Rebecca looked towards the window. 'I'd say the heat wave isn't going to last much longer.' As she spoke, they heard a distant rumble of thunder. 'Hey, I couldn't have timed that better.'

After a minute, May said, 'By the way, I'd better warn you that I may be cooking Sunday's dinner on my own.'

Rebecca added milk to her coffee, frowning. 'I thought Pam was helping you out.'

'Well, she was going to, but brace yourself – there've been big changes there.' May gave a brief version of Pam's story to Rebecca, who narrowed her eyes when she heard about Jack's violence.

'Didn't I meet him at your house? Good-looking guy?'

'Yes – and I always found him very nice. A bit quiet, maybe, but friendly too, you know?'

Rebecca sipped. 'Has Pam reported him?'

May shook her head. 'She doesn't want to. She can't bear the thought of doing that to him.' She twirled a spoon slowly through her coffee. 'I suppose . . . well, maybe it feels a bit like a betrayal.'

Rebecca stared. 'So she'd rather wait till he beats her to a pulp some fine day?'

'Well, she *has* left him – and she's leaving Kilpatrick on Monday, moving back to Cork. She's staying at her friend's till then – the place I'm painting at the moment, actually.' May told her about Jack's earlier visit to Carmel's house. 'Pam was terrified – and, to tell the truth, I was a bit nervous myself.'

Rebecca was still looking at her in disbelief. 'And she won't get the guards on him? She'd rather let him run her out of town?' She lifted her mug. 'I can't understand that mentality.'

May thought. 'Maybe it's hard to admit that the man you loved enough to marry, the man you chose to spend the rest of your life with, could turn around and hurt you. Maybe it's just too embarrassing.'

Rebecca gave her a sceptical look. 'So you'd rather be battered than embarrassed?'

May grimaced. 'Well, when you put it that way . . . '

Suddenly there was a flash, and for a second the kitchen lit up brilliantly.

'Hey.' Rebecca grinned. 'Looks like we're in for a big one – I'll run you home, you can't cycle in this.' Raising her voice, she added, 'Hope poor Brian isn't scared of the storm.'

From the sitting room, a voice said patiently, 'Shut up, Ma,' and May laughed.

'You have that poor boy tormented. It's a wonder he's as well balanced as he is.'

Rebecca grinned, her whole face softening. 'I know – he's great, isn't he?' She cradled her half-empty mug for a minute, then said, 'May?'

'Mmm?'

'I have something to tell you that you're not going to like.' Rebecca put down her coffee on the table and looked May in the eye. 'It's about the postman.'

May's heart fluttered. 'What about him?'

Rebecca drummed her fingers on the table. 'Bloody hell . . . I hate to be the one to tell you, but . . . '

May waited.

'Look, I saw him earlier.' She paused. 'And, May, he wasn't alone. He was with a woman. He had his arm around her.'

'Oh.' May nodded slowly. 'Oh, right.' She lifted her mug and drank. 'Right.'

That was that, so. She should have known. Of course he was attached, of course he was only being friendly when they met, nothing more. She tried to push away the heaviness that had come out of nowhere.

'May, I'm so sorry.'

Rebecca's concerned face was almost comical. May might have laughed at it if she'd felt remotely like laughing.

Instead she made a face. 'Don't be daft – it's not as if I was serious about him. It was a bit of fun, that was all.'

And now it was over, end of story. No harm done, no heart broken this time. She pushed her mug towards Rebecca's battered coffee pot. 'A drop for the road.'

As Rebecca poured, another flash lit the kitchen, and this time both women ignored it.

Shaun

His hands trembled so much that the cardboard cup was in great danger of falling and spilling all over the green hospital tiles. Not that he could drink the pale brown liquid that was masquerading as coffee inside it. But he needed something to hold, or try to hold, to stop him biting at the skin around his fingers – two were already bleeding, but the pain wasn't the distraction he'd hoped for.

Bernard lay unmoving in the bed beside Shaun's chair. The top of his head was completely bandaged, the white cloth patched with red. His nose was broken, badly. Several teeth were missing. One of his cheeks had a row of black stitches in it. Two of the fingers of his right hand, which he'd probably put up to protect himself, were broken. There was a tube going up his nose and another going into the back of his left hand.

He had broken ribs, and extensive bruising on his shoulders.

And since the attack, more than four hours ago, he hadn't woken up. And until – unless? – he did, they wouldn't be able to tell if he was brain-damaged.

Shaun kept getting the overpowering urge to wail, to open his mouth and roar like some prehistoric creature. To rid himself of the rage he was afraid would kill him otherwise. But because there was a chance it would get him thrown out of Bernard's room, because of the uniformed guard – too late, too fucking late – stationed outside the door, he managed to channel it into occasional choking sobs.

And of course, there was also the question of Bernard's parents, sitting silently on the other side of their son's bed. Shaun had called them, once he'd found their number in Bernard's phone. The father had answered, had listened without comment as Shaun had stammered out the news. Then, tersely: 'How is he?'

'They don't know yet – he's in intensive care, still unconscious.' Shaun's hand was white, gripping Bernard's phone.

'Right.' Bernard's father had hung up before Shaun had a chance to say any more.

They had made no attempt to shake hands when they arrived, just nodded at him when Shaun stood up and introduced himself. He knew how they felt about him, of course, was reminded of it every time Bernard went to dinner at their house without him.

But just now Shaun couldn't have cared less how they felt about him. They could hate him all they wanted, resent his presence at their son's bedside till hell froze over. He was there, and he was staying.

He was staying until Bernard got better. And then he was taking him home.

Francesca

She watched the jagged forks of lighting criss-crossing the night sky for a few minutes, then pulled down the little white plastic blind. Thank goodness the weather had only delayed the flight, not caused it to be cancelled. Now that they were finally on their way, Francesca was impatient for Italy. The flight was due into Rome at eight thirty in the morning, then a bus from the airport to the railway station. They should be in Perola by around eleven, all going well. Just in time to help her mother prepare lunch. She thought of freshly baked focaccia, sweet, juicy tomatoes drizzled with oil and scattered with torn basil, creamy goat's cheese . . .

Lucia stirred beside her, curled in a thin blanket, her feet in Francesca's lap. One thumb was in her mouth, her small fingers curled around her nose. Above the dull roar of the plane's engines, Francesca could hear the little moist sounds she made. They reminded her of Lucia as a tiny baby, sucking greedily at her nipples.

Luca had loved to watch her breast-feeding. After he died, Francesca's milk had dried up.

She lifted her arm and pressed the button for assistance. When the stewardess arrived, Francesca whispered that she would like a Cognac, *per favore*.

Saturday

A mild day, with little sunshine and moderate south-westerly winds. Rain spreading from the west, reaching all areas by nightfall. Highs of 15 to 19 degrees.

Philip

He spooned up some more of the tasteless cereal that May had brought him this morning – like cardboard, it was, and he didn't trust those red bits – and lifted it carefully to his mouth. Outside his bedroom window the morning was calm, the sky a washed-out blue after the wildness of last night.

Such a storm there'd been, he'd thought he'd never get to sleep. All that thunder and lightning, then the downpour that went on for what seemed like hours. They hadn't had a storm like that in a long time.

A thrush sang, not far from his barely opened window. He'd always loved birds, loved to look at them coming to perch sideways on Aideen's nut-feeder that swung from the overhanging roof just above the sitting room window. Sparrows, robins, goldfinches, blue tits – he'd sit and watch them when he got in from work, while Aideen got the dinner ready and the children looked at TV, or did their homework.

Where had that nut-feeder gone? He hadn't seen it in years.

He chewed the cereal and lifted his cup to take some tea. Saturday today. No work for May – she'd be around the house, or the garden, more like, if the rain held off. Good job she'd mown the lawn yesterday before all that rain. In fairness, the gardens, front and back, were a credit to her. She had a gift, no doubt about it. Knew what would look well together, what should be moved and when to prune.

He supposed he should be glad for her, being able to make a living doing something she enjoyed. But cleaning other people's houses, washing their windows – he drew the line at that, definitely. Taking dogs out walking, now that was just plain daft.

He heard the theme tune for the news and turned up the little radio on his locker. More talks about the north – would there never be an end to that? Another drugs seizure in Dublin, more bombs in the Middle East. And then he heard 'Kilpatrick', and listened more closely.

' . . . the serious assault on a local shopkeeper yesterday evening. Bernard Macey, forty-five, was left fighting for his life following a vicious attack in his florist's shop around six o'clock. According to local shop owners, Mr Macey's premises had been regularly vandalised over the past few weeks. Gardaí are appealing to anyone who was in the area at the time to come forward . . . '

Bernard – wasn't that the name of the fellow next door? And he had a flower shop. It had to be him. Vicious attack – had they said he was fighting for his life? He wouldn't wish that on anyone, even—

There was a tap on the door and May put her head in. 'Are you finished?'

Philip blinked at her. 'I've just heard on the radio – you didn't hear the news, did you?'

'No.'

'Well, it sounds like it's the man next door, some kind of assault.'

'What – which man? Who was assaulted?' May walked quickly to the window and looked towards the next-door garden. 'What did they say?'

'That Bernard fellow, the one with the shop, they said he was attacked. Sounded bad.'

'Oh my God, is he OK?' And before Philip had a chance to answer, she was halfway down the stairs, leaving him trapped under the breakfast tray.

May

Nobody there. No sound inside, no answer. How was she going to find out?

Rebecca. May called her as soon as she got back into the house.

'Yeah, it's terrible. Unprovoked, by the sound of it.

They're interviewing staff in the nearby shops, but nobody seems to have seen anything. It was just around closing time, about six.'

'How's Bernard?'

'Bad, apparently – critical, they said.'

'Oh my God . . . who would do something like that?' Bernard, with his ridiculous ties, his shy, crooked smile and his big, generous heart. Taking in Lonesome George when May had had to find another home for him, telling her that the cat was just what he and Shaun needed, another demanding male around the place. Presenting her with a beautiful soft leather belt when he got back from a week in Portugal a few years ago, because she'd watered his house plants a couple of times and put out his bin. Calling to her over the hedge, offering her bunches of freesia, little pots of cyclamen that hadn't sold. Inviting her next door for a glass of champagne when Shaun turned thirty-five in April.

'Who would do a thing like that?' May repeated.

Rebecca sighed. 'May, unfortunately there are plenty of sick individuals out there who can't cope with the fact that we're not all heterosexual.'

'You think it was because Bernard's gay?'

'Probably. Apparently he'd had some trouble before, graffiti and stuff.'

'Yes, he mentioned it. You think whoever did it will be caught?'

Another sigh. 'Maybe, if there's any justice in the world.'

Pam

She turned on the radio, softly in case Carmel was still asleep. Poured boiling water over the teabag in her cup – Carmel didn't bother with a teapot – put a slice of brown bread into the toaster and pushed down the lever.

As soon as Carmel got up, Pam would talk to her. Poor Carmel had enough on her plate right now, with all that had happened to her in the past couple of days. It wasn't fair of Pam to be staying. So, instead of waiting until tomorrow, she'd pack up her stuff after breakfast and call Conor to come and collect her this afternoon, when he'd finished the morning's jobs. She could stay out at Ma's till Monday. She'd be as safe out there as she was in here – safer, probably, with Conor around the farm all day. And Carmel wouldn't have to be making an effort, for Pam's sake.

Poor thing, she'd been devastated when she arrived home yesterday, barely able to tell Pam what had happened, what Paul had said to her. Looked like that was definitely the end of it. Maybe she'd be luckier next time, find a man who was unattached.

Or maybe she'd decide, like Pam, never to touch another man with a barge-pole as long as she lived.

Pam wondered, couldn't help wondering, how Jack had taken her departure. Had he been angry? Was he still mad at her for leaving him? Did he feel any bit guilty for having hit her the night before?

Was he at home now, hoping she'd get in touch – or

was he out looking for her, driving around in his car, waiting for her to show up?

She shuddered, thinking of how her heart had plummeted when she'd turned around in the pub and seen him standing there. How she'd sat nervously beside him in the car on the way home, listening as he told her how he'd followed Carmel from school, then sat in the car, waiting for Pam to turn up. The way he'd almost bragged about it to her.

'I knew you were lying this morning.' His voice, so calm. So matter of fact.

'No, Jack, I just wasn't sure—' She could feel her heart racing, feel it thudding in her chest. 'Carmel phoned later—'

'Oh, you were sure alright.' He signalled to turn on to their road. 'Oh, you lied to me alright. Make no mistake about that.'

The fear, the icy feeling in the pit of her stomach. His face, giving nothing away. His hand on her arm, leading her up to the front door.

And then, as soon as they'd got home, as soon as he had her inside, his hand swinging back and—

He was sick, he had to be. His mind wasn't right, to do something like that. He probably saw nothing wrong in what he'd done, probably blamed Pam for everything that had happened.

Did he know she'd miscarried, that he'd frightened her so much he'd made her lose his baby?

The toast popped up, and she spread it with Carmel's butter and Carmel's fine-cut marmalade. As she forced herself to bite into it, the news came on Carmel's little radio, and she listened to a calm male voice telling her what had happened to May's next-door neighbour.

She couldn't believe it. Bernard, violently assaulted in his shop. It didn't sound possible, in the middle of Kilpatrick, still broad daylight at six o'clock on a summer evening.

Pam hadn't met Bernard as often as Shaun — he was always gone to work by the time she arrived at May's — but once when he'd been home for some reason, Shaun had introduced him to Pam over the hedge, and she'd been into his shop a few times too. He was nice and friendly, just like Shaun.

Had Bernard been attacked just because he was gay? She remembered how angry Jack had been the day Shaun had given her the lift home, the sneer on his face when he'd called Shaun a homo. She hated that blind prejudice, hated the—

Then she stopped, struck by a thought so terrible . . . No, she must be mad even to . . . Surely there was no way *Jack* could be responsible for this? No matter how angry he felt right now, he'd never do a thing like that . . . would he?

No, it was crazy even to think it.

But . . . couldn't he have discovered somehow that Bernard was Shaun's partner? So easy, with Bernard's white van parked outside the house next to May's, Flower Power written in big blue letters on the side. And couldn't Jack have gone to Bernard's shop at closing time yesterday, and done this?

Couldn't he have hurt Bernard, such an easy target, simply because he lived with Shaun, who'd been too nice to Jack's wife? Had she made him so angry by leaving that he'd had to lash out at somebody – anybody – when he couldn't find her? Was he twisted enough, sick enough, to have done that? Or was Pam hallucinating from stress and lack of sleep? She prayed she was.

Her phone rang, making her start violently – Jesus, she was going to have a breakdown if this went on much longer. She checked the name, and pressed *answer* when she saw it was May. 'Hello, May.'

'Pam, how are you?'

No way could she say out loud what was in her head. No way could she voice that particular thought. 'Fine, just finishing breakfast.'

'You're still at Carmel's, aren't you?'

'Yes, but I'll go home today, I think. I'm going to phone for Conor to come and collect me. I may as well be out there as here.'

'Right . . . Did you hear about Bernard?'

Pam closed her eyes. 'I did. I heard it on the news just now. It's terrible.' She paused. 'Do you know any more? Have you met Shaun?'

'No – he must be at the hospital. I'll call around there this afternoon if he doesn't show up here in the meantime.'

'Let me know when you find out . . . how Bernard is.'

'I will. Are you sure you're OK?'

'Yes.' She wondered if she'd ever be OK again.

'And you're still planning to leave on Monday?'

Pam sighed. 'Yes, for a while anyway. I know it's like I'm running away, but . . . just for a while. Oh and May, I haven't forgotten about your father's dinner tomorrow night.'

'Ah no, don't worry about that. You've enough to—'

Pam broke in. 'Actually, May, it would give me something to do – I've thought it all out. Conor can run me to your house around four and collect me later. He's very obliging, so I know he won't mind, and he's free on Sundays.'

What could possibly happen, with Conor driving her there and back, and lots of other people around? And going to May's would take her mind off things for a while – look what having too much time to brood was doing to her. Imagine thinking for a second that Jack could have been responsible for assaulting Bernard.

Of course he couldn't – the idea was preposterous.

Hilda

She slid the soft-poached duck egg onto the slice of toast. Such laziness, nearly midday and still in her dressing-gown, breakfast on the table when she should have been getting ready for lunch.

Ah, who cared? Who was there to see her, an elderly woman sitting in her own kitchen on a Saturday morning? She picked up her fork and poked it into the egg, watched the dark orange yolk slither slowly over the toast. Such luxury, not to have to rush anywhere. She reached for the salt cellar.

Terrible news earlier, listening to the radio in bed, half dozing until she heard 'Kilpatrick'. What was the world coming to? She wondered if May or Philip knew that poor man. Really, it was hardly safe for May to be out at night on her own any more, even if she had a few dogs with her. Little poodles, probably, or those—

The bell rang. Hilda looked towards the hall door in mild annoyance. Now who could that be? Not Betty – she was on duty in the charity shop this morning. Hopefully it was nobody she knew. Her breakfast would get cold if she had to stand talking to anyone. She put down the salt and went out through the hall.

Her daughter Terri and her daughter's husband stood on the doorstep, both holding bags, both smiling broadly at her.

Jack

His mouth was bone dry. The bedroom stank of his stale breath – and he could smell his unwashed body when he turned over. Thank Christ it was the weekend and he could stay in bed all he wanted, wouldn't have to pretend to be too sick to go to work again.

It wasn't the lies he minded – it was having to talk to Janice, the bimbo of a receptionist, who shoved her tits in your face any chance she got. Barely covered with frilly little tops, they were. Janice probably knew well he was putting it on, but she insisted on telling him to stay in bed and get well soon. Probably wished she was there with him.

He wouldn't mind getting Janice on her own some night – tearing the frilly little top off her, shoving her up against a wall. She could take it, he'd be willing to bet she'd love it. Love someone to push her around, would Janice, show her who was boss. Most women liked that kind of thing, that rough stuff, even if they said they didn't.

His head felt itchy, and he put up a hand to scratch it. Saw the graze on his knuckles, the dried blood on the back of his hand. Must have fallen last night, or banged into something. He rubbed his face, feeling the rasp of his stubble. What time was it? He turned towards the clock radio, wincing at the pain that shot through his head.

Half twelve, just after – Jesus, so late. He hadn't slept as late as that since he was a teenager. What time had he gone to bed? He had no idea, vaguely remembered staggering home from the pub and – shit, cracking open the bottle of wine he'd found in the fridge . . .

He groaned. No wonder he felt like crap. Shouldn't have started drinking so early, around four o'clock, and on an empty stomach too. Asking for trouble. Hopefully he hadn't done anything too stupid.

This was what Pam had brought him to, walking out on him like that. Messing with his head, driving him to drink, when all he'd ever wanted to do was look after her, keep her safe.

Knowing what men were like, knowing that, given half a chance, any man would steal her away from him.

So maybe he'd overreacted now and again – was that a crime? Saw threats, maybe, where none were intended. Anyone could make a mistake, couldn't they?

Giving her that slap the other night, that had been a mistake. But she'd lied to him, told him she was meeting Carmel in a coffee shop. He'd known, by her voice, that she was lying – Pam couldn't lie to save her life. So he'd skipped off work early, told them he had a toothache, and waited outside the school till Carmel drove out. He followed her to the pub and he'd sat in his car till Pam had shown up.

What did she expect, when she lied to him like that? What was he supposed to think? And her jumper off in the pub, that T-shirt stretched across her chest, you could see the shape of her underwear . . . and lipstick, which he'd deliberately asked her not to wear.

It was the lipstick that did it, that made him want to grab her by the hair, haul her back home and teach her a lesson. He didn't know how he'd managed to sit and talk to the two of them like nothing was wrong – well, talk to Carmel mostly. Pam hadn't said very much, knew she was in trouble the minute she saw him.

But collapsing on the floor, after one little slap, frightening him like that, for fuck's sake. There was no need for it. And then grabbing her stomach, making such a fuss – wasn't it just her period? Couldn't have been as painful as she made out, surely.

Still, he'd decided to keep his distance for the rest of the night, cleaned up the carpet as best he could, made himself beans on toast. Wondered briefly if he should bring some up to her, then decided to leave her alone – if she was hungry she'd come down. But she hadn't.

In the morning, he hadn't wanted to go to work, was nervous of leaving her in case she did anything stupid, and then he'd thought of taking her money and cards. He wasn't going to keep them – of course not. It was just a safety measure, in case she got any ideas, that was all. If he came home and found her still in bed, he'd put them back and she'd be none the wiser.

But, of course, she hadn't been in bed. She was gone, without a cent to her name. And he'd searched for her yesterday – everywhere he could think of – and he hadn't found a sign of her. Nobody had seen her, nobody had heard from her.

Yeah, right. His mouth twisted in a sneer. They expected him to believe that, did they? Her mother, her best friend, her employer, no word from her to any of them? Jesus, they must think he'd come down in the last shower.

Of course he'd find her and bring her home, eventually. She belonged here, didn't she? They were meant to be together, anyone could see that.

He'd have to punish her, though, for going off like that – she'd have to be made to see how wrong that had been, running away from someone who loved her so much. It wasn't something he looked forward to, but it would have to be done, if he was ever to trust her again.

And then, when she understood, things would be fine.

But he'd have to be careful. What if Pam had told people about his mistakes? He wouldn't want anyone to go calling the guards, nothing like that. He'd have to convince them he'd meant no harm, that he was sorry, so sorry, for anything that might have happened in the heat of the moment, that all he wanted was to have his wife back.

He'd call to May first – she'd be easy enough to get around. He'd start with May, see what she could tell him. And then he'd take it from there.

He pushed back the duvet and got himself gingerly out of bed. Then he lurched towards the bathroom. Better tidy himself up a bit, if he wanted to make a good impression.

May

Water, salmon, lemons, spinach – it seemed heartless somehow to be going on with her normal day after what had happened to Bernard. But what else could she do? The dinner was going ahead tomorrow night; everyone was still coming.

She must remember to put an ad into the local paper next week to find a replacement for Pam. Such a pity she wouldn't be working for them any more – Philip had got used to her, even if he did moan about her now and again, and she had such patience with him.

May supposed there was little hope of Pam's marriage surviving after this, not after Jack treating her the way he had. It didn't bear thinking about. Whatever Gerry

Scanlon had done to May, at least he hadn't abused her physically. She couldn't imagine how that might feel.

She hoped Hilda was happy about Terri's news, now that she'd had time for it to sink in. And would the pregnancy change things? Would Terri and Gerry decide they'd rather raise a child in Ireland?

They'd been back here, she presumed, since they'd finished travelling. They must have come to visit Hilda now and again. But May had never asked, and Hilda had never said, and she'd never seen a sign of them in Kilpatrick, even though Gerry's parents still lived here, not too far from May. She saw his mother sometimes, out walking.

It had been a long time before she was able to pass the butcher's shop without looking up at the two windows of the flat above it. Without remembering the nights they'd spent there together . . .

She often imagined meeting Gerry again. How would it be now, seeing him after so long? She tried to picture him with a tiny baby in his arms.

She shifted her rucksack – the bottles of water were heavy – and glanced across the road at the few people standing outside Bernard's shop, looking towards the windows. Relishing the excitement, probably. Dying for another bit of scandal about the gay man. Some people had no scruples.

Then she shook her head. Why should she assume that? Maybe they were as shocked as she was, trying to get their heads around the fact that an innocent man had been viciously attacked.

She was in bad form this morning. She was – she forced herself to admit it – disappointed about the postman, whom she'd thought might be interested . . .

She walked on towards the bakery. She'd collect the cake, drop everything home, then get some kind of lunch together for herself and Philip, and check next door to see if Lonesome George needed feeding. Later on she'd cycle to the hospital if there was still no sign of Shaun.

She'd keep busy. She'd forget about him.

Paddy

He tucked the newly repaired chain into the pocket of his shirt and strolled past the shops on Kilpatrick's main street, nodding to the faces he recognised. A little chillier today, the fierce heat of yesterday well and truly gone. He enjoyed Saturday mornings, stocking up in Kilpatrick's farmer's market, a lunchtime pint and *The Irish Times* at O'Meara's—

Something happening up ahead. A small crowd gathered on the path, in front of – which shop? Looked like the florist, Bernard Macey's place. Closed up, some kind of yellow tape across the door. A thin, tired-looking woman whose face Paddy vaguely recognised on the edge of the crowd: he thought she worked in a shop – one of the supermarkets, maybe. He could see her in a dark green overall.

And there was Mrs Dooley from Glenmorris Avenue, whom he knew quite well – whom he'd be trying to avoid if he was running late, she talked so much. As Paddy approached, she turned and spotted him. 'Oh Paddy, isn't it awful? I was telling Ann that I passed right by here yesterday. I was over there' – she pointed across the road – 'coming out of the bakery and poor Bernard waved at me.' She shuddered. 'Must have been right before it happened.'

'Before what happened?'

Mrs Dooley looked at him in disbelief. 'You didn't hear? Bernard was attacked, badly beaten, right there in his shop. He's critical in hospital, they said on the news.' She shook her head. 'Poor Bernard, he was as nice a man as you could meet, wasn't he, Ann?' Turning to her friend, who agreed that, oh God, he was, he certainly was.

Bernard Macey, living next door to May. Always a friendly word when Paddy would meet him. 'Do they know who did it?'

Mrs Dooley pursed her lips. 'Not a clue. Probably somebody high on drugs, if you ask me.' She looked around and lowered her voice. 'Could be anyone, if you ask me. Sure, they're all at it now, aren't they, Ann?'

Ann agreed that, oh God, they were, all at it. And then they both looked at Paddy, who felt obliged to nod in agreement.

Walking home, he wondered if he had met whoever was responsible. Somebody living in Kilpatrick, most likely, so Paddy might well have come across them. He knew so many people through his job, knew their names and their faces, from the various streets and avenues and housing estates of Kilpatrick.

He hoped Bernard would be OK. He hoped whoever had done it would be found. He hoped he didn't know them.

Shaun

Frenzied, that was what the police were calling it. A frenzied attack. And random too, no motive that anyone could see, because there was no earthly reason to attack Bernard, unless you chose to be offended by the fact that he lived with another man.

The policeman who spoke to them told them that they were following up a few leads. The weapon, a heavy brass candlestick, had been left at the scene, for one. And then there was the anonymous letter – 'Letter?' Bernard's father had asked, looking from the policeman to Shaun. 'What letter?' – and the CCTV cameras were also being examined for evidence. They'd put out an appeal on the radio for witnesses to come forward, which often threw up something. It was a busy time of the day, shops closing, people heading home from town. Chances were, someone had seen something that might help.

Shaun tried to think if *he'd* seen anything, on the way to the shop. There had been people about, the usual Friday-evening bustle, but he hadn't noticed anything unusual. Nothing that stood out, nobody acting suspiciously at all that he could remember. People just rushing past, bumping into him, some of them . . .

The shop door had been left ajar – but it hadn't

struck him as out of the ordinary, since Bernard had been expecting him. Of course, now he knew it hadn't been Bernard who'd left it ajar.

Bernard's mother had disappeared earlier, after a whispered conversation with her husband. Shaun had looked across the bed after she'd left, wondering if the older man would feel more inclined to talk when it was just the two of them, but Bernard's father had continued to ignore him until the policeman had appeared at the door and motioned them both outside to tell them about the leads they were following up.

And still Bernard didn't wake. Still the machine by his bed breathed for him, still his white face remained motionless, his eyes closed, his hand limp in Shaun's.

The only prayer Shaun knew was 'The Lord is my Shepherd', which his Polish-born Catholic mother had taught him as a boy. He said it now, surprised at how easily the words came back to him –

The Lord is my shepherd, I shall not want.
He maketh me to lie down in green pastures:
He leadeth me beside the still waters . . .

– wishing he could concentrate on them, instead of seeing, every time he closed his eyes, a heavy brass candlestick smashing into Bernard's head.

May

Still no sign of life when she rang the bell next door. She remembered Shaun rushing out the evening before, on his way to meet Bernard. Had it happened by then? What if Shaun hadn't got to the shop when he had – or what if he'd arrived a few minutes earlier? She tried to push away the useless thoughts.

'Here, puss, come on, George.' She banged his grey dish on the patio – that always used to bring him running from wherever he'd been. And here he came, not running any more, too grown-up for that now. Walking sedately towards her from under the hedge, tail raised – pleased to see her, at least.

'Hi there. You hungry?' But he only sniffed at the little brown pellets, then wound his way around her crouched body, purring. 'Too well fed, that's what you are.' May stroked his ginger fur. 'Pampered puss.' He pressed his body against her calves, butted his head into her hand, making her wish again that she didn't have to do without him at home. Still, he was close enough here.

She straightened up and looked around Bernard's patio. What could she do, to help out? Clothes on the line: she could bring them in and iron them – good job they'd left the spare key with her. And the lawn could do with a cut; she'd bring the mower over later.

But first, a quick cycle to the shop to pick up the milk she hadn't noticed they needed this morning. She was wheeling her bike down the path towards the gate when she saw a dark blue car pull up outside.

A dark blue Mazda 626. Jack and Pam's car, she was sure.

May's grip tightened on the handlebars. He was looking for Pam. May would tell him she hadn't seen her, and he'd go away again. It was the middle of the day, broad daylight.

But there was nobody else around. And Bernard had been attacked in broad daylight.

Stop it. May stood her ground as Jack opened the gate, held on tightly to the handlebars. Why would he want to attack May? He was only looking for his wife.

He nodded at her. 'Hello.'

May nodded back at him, unsmiling. 'Jack.'

He looked sick, and tired. His eyes were bloodshot, and he was deathly pale. 'May, I've come to have a word.' His voice was subdued. She smelled musky aftershave.

'I – I don't know how much Pam has told you . . . ' He stopped, and looked enquiringly at May, who looked steadily back at him in silence. He sighed. 'Look, I don't blame you if you – don't feel like talking to me. The truth is, I've behaved abominably, I admit it. I understand why Pam left . . . but, look, I really need to talk to her.' He shifted his feet, put a hand up to rub his face. 'I haven't slept a wink since she left. I don't know what to do. I just – I really want to meet her, and tell her how sorry I am.'

He stopped again and looked beseechingly at May. 'Won't you help me?'

May thought of Pam's terrified face, the tears running down her cheeks. The baby he might as well have punched out of her. He must be mad if he thought she was going to help him. She shook her head. 'I'm sorry, Jack, but I don't know where Pam is. All she said when she phoned was that she was leaving Kilpatrick, and she wouldn't be coming back to work.' She made herself keep looking at him, right into his eyes.

'You haven't met her since Wednesday? She hasn't been back here since then?'

'No. Just a phone call.'

'When did she phone?'

May pretended to consider. 'Thursday.'

'And did she say where she was then?'

'No.'

'Right . . . ' He nodded slowly. 'Right. Well,' turning away from her, 'that's that.' He got into his car without another word and drove off.

May waited until he was out of sight. Then she pulled out her phone and found Pam's name.

Bernard

His mother's voice, telling him to wake up. Another voice – he didn't recognise it, some man, calling his name. Asking if he could hear him. *Open your eyes, Bernard.*

Something beeping, something gasping like bellows, lots of noises.

And Shaun – Shaun was there. Holding his hand, whispering to him to *Hold on, don't go.*

Bernard wanted to go. He wanted to turn off all the noises, all the voices. All the pain. He wanted it all to stop and leave him in peace.

Jack

Bitch. Fucking bitch. Looking at him like he was a bit of dirt under her shoe. What poison had Pam been spreading about him? He gunned the engine as he turned on to Carmel's road. Better luck here, maybe, with the teacher. He should have tried her first – the teacher was gagging for it. Giving him the glad eye whenever she thought Pam wasn't looking.

He pulled up outside the house and took three deep breaths. *Calm down, now. Get yourself together.* His head was still thumping with the hangover.

He needn't have bothered calming down. Nobody answered the front door. There was no car in the driveway, no sign of life around the back.

And half an hour later, at Pam's mother's house, his brother-in-law told him no, they hadn't seen Pam in over a week. Yes, as far as they knew, she'd left Kilpatrick. No, they had no idea where she'd gone. All delivered in a flat voice, Conor looking at a spot over Jack's shoulder, the shotgun held casually by his side.

No sign of Jack's mother-in-law, who'd usually have come straight out to say hello.

And no sign of Pam. Maybe she *had* left town.

He drove back down the lane, gritting his teeth every time he bumped over a pothole. Drove back past Carmel's house – still no car there.

Stopped at the off-licence on the way home, opened the whiskey as soon as he got back inside the house. Hair of the dog, that was what he needed.

And it was somewhere around his fifth glass, going back over his earlier conversation with May O'Callaghan, that he remembered where he'd seen her blue bike recently. It had been propped against the side of Carmel's house yesterday when he'd called around – he'd swear to it. Same basket on the front. He remembered noticing it.

Which meant, didn't it, that May had been there, and she hadn't answered the door when he rang the bell?

He frowned, trying to clear the buzzing in his head, trying to figure it out. Now, why would she not answer the door? What possible reason could she have had for not opening it unless she was trying to hide something from him?

Something, or someone.

Pam had been in there with her, he was certain of that now. The two of them had been inside, listening as he rang the bell. Watching him, maybe, as he walked away. Laughing at him, maybe, at how they'd fooled him.

He could feel the rage build up inside him. They were all in it, those three bitches, all in cahoots, running rings around him. Telling him lies, trying to confuse him. Thinking they had him fooled.

He sloshed more whiskey into his glass. Pam was still in Kilpatrick – she hadn't gone away. That was just a line to throw him off the scent.

Well, he was going nowhere today, he'd done enough running around already, and he was bloody tired.

Tomorrow he'd find her.

Pam

She watched him walking back to the car. He wore the green check shirt she loved, and his oldest blue jeans. The stubble that always caught up with him at this time of the day was shading his chin. His hair was dark and thick and tousled. If she saw him coming towards her as a stranger in the street, she'd think, *He's not a bad bit of rough.* She'd always gone for the dangerous-looking ones.

As the car pulled away, she heard Conor walking back into the kitchen. She heard him say, 'He's gone.' She knew that the shotgun he'd been carrying when he was talking to Jack wasn't loaded. He never left it loaded.

She heard her mother saying, 'Thank God. Call Pammy in, will you?' She heard Conor walking across the kitchen floor and opening the door into the hall, and when he said, 'Pam?' she called, 'I'll be down in a minute.'

She looked into the bathroom mirror. Her face was empty. She thought of all the times Jack had driven her here, all the Sunday lunches. She remembered him telling her mother he'd never eaten apple crumble like hers. She remembered him going fishing with Conor, just two weeks ago the last time.

And they hadn't a clue, either of them. How could they have, when Pam hadn't admitted it to anyone, even to herself?

Her mother's tears when she'd told her about losing the baby that should have been Mam's first grandchild . . . Was she mad to go running off to Cork, as if she was the guilty one? Was Mam right? Should she get the guards involved?

No, she couldn't. She couldn't do that to him. He was Jack, whom she'd promised to love and honour till the day she died. She couldn't do that.

She wiped her eyes and walked downstairs, and halfway down she smelled rashers, and realised she was starving.

May

The woman behind the reception desk told her that she wouldn't be allowed into intensive care, but that if she rang the bell beside the door, someone would see if Shaun was in there.

He looked wretched when he came out. Pale, red-eyed, clenching and unclenching his hands as he told her, shakily, that Bernard was still unconscious. 'They can't tell me yet if – if he'll make it . . . ' He put a hand up and pressed it to his mouth. 'He has to wake up before . . .' He stopped, and drew a shuddering breath.

'Shaun, I'm so sorry – is there anything at all I can do?' May knew he'd shake his head, knew there was nothing he could think about now except Bernard. She held out a tinfoil packet, pressed it into his hand. 'Here, I made a few sandwiches – they're only ham and cheese.'

Shaun's eyes filled with tears. 'Thank you.'

'Will I get coffee? You'll need something to drink.'

But he was already turning away, easing his hand from hers. 'Thanks, May – I must get back now, in case . . . ' He trailed away from her, holding the silver package that she doubted would ever get opened, back to his bedside vigil.

In case Bernard woke up.

May's heart ached for him. There was nothing she could do – nothing anybody could do now until Bernard opened his eyes.

If that ever happened again. She turned and walked slowly towards the lift, pressed the arrow that pointed downwards. Such a tragedy. Weren't the first twenty-four hours the most crucial? Hadn't she heard that somewhere? And Bernard had already—

'May?'

She turned, and there he was. His hair was longer, brushing his shoulders now. Same reddish-brown colour.

He'd put on weight, his face was fuller.

She felt hers flushing. 'Gerry.' And then she couldn't think of another thing to say to him.

'How are you?'

He wore a thin gold ring on his left hand. They'd been going to buy their wedding rings the day after he'd told her about Terri. The thought thudded into her head. 'I'm fine, and you?' Like they were acquaintances, like they hardly knew each other. Like the most contact they'd ever had was a scattering of polite phrases bounced off each other, instead of—

He cleared his throat. His hair was too long, really: it looked dated. And those trousers – she'd never seen him in anything except jeans, apart from the awful brown suit he'd worn when he'd met her parents for the first time. She remembered how she'd laughed at that suit, how he'd pretended to be offended.

'So . . . I'm here to see my mother. She's had a hysterectomy.'

'Oh. Is she alright?' May had always liked Dolores Scanlon. She'd be delighted with the news about the baby.

'Fine, yeah.' He ran a hand through his hair. Funny, how sexy May used to think that was, once upon a time. 'And you? Your parents are well?'

May looked steadily at him. 'My mother died eighteen months ago. She got cancer.'

'Oh God, I'm sorry – I never heard'

But of course he'd heard, from his parents, who'd been at the funeral. Or from his wife, who hadn't been there to see her aunt buried. He'd forgotten, that was all. He'd forgotten because May O'Callaghan was nobody to him now, just someone from his past. Her mother's death meant nothing to him.

The lift door opened and he waited for her to get in, but May turned. 'Actually, I think I'll take the stairs. Goodbye, Gerry.'

Goodbye, Gerry. She didn't look back. She heard the lift doors sliding shut as she walked towards the stairwell.

She probably should have mentioned the baby. That had been a bit mean.

Marjorie

She stood at the bottom of the stairs. 'Jude? Are you there?'

No response. Jude might well be still asleep at five o'clock in the afternoon. And even if she wasn't, she'd answer her mother's call only if she felt like it.

Marjorie lowered her heavy bags until they touched the floor, easing the handles from her cramped fingers. The few groceries seemed to get heavier every week. She took off her summer jacket and hung it on the hallstand, then lifted the shopping again and hauled it into the kitchen. Thank God for the shorter shift every third Saturday – they were always so busy at the weekend that Marjorie was exhausted when four o'clock came around.

As she was stowing the dented cans – half price, and still a good date on them – her daughter walked into the kitchen. Without a word to her mother, she took a box of Frosties from one of the presses. She wore grubby pink pyjamas, rumpled from the bed, and a pair of thin grey ankle socks. Her hair was tousled, and one cheek was blotchy.

Marjorie passed a carton of milk to her from the fridge. 'Don't eat much now – dinner in an hour.'

Jude took a bowl from the draining board and filled it with Frosties. She poured milk from the carton, splashing it carelessly. Out of the corner of her eye Marjorie watched some snaking towards the edge of the table, knew it would be ignored too. She finished putting the groceries away and looked at Jude. 'I'll make your bed, love, will I?'

Jude shrugged, didn't look up. Marjorie plodded up the stairs and pushed open the door of her daughter's bedroom, wrinkling her nose at the strong smell of alcohol.

She hated that Jude drank like that, hated that she came home the worse for wear nearly every time she went out, but what could Marjorie do? Jude was eighteen, legally entitled – not that being underage stopped the kids now, of course. They could get it so easily, and not only drink. Marjorie didn't like to think about what else Jude might be taking when she and that Kathleen Farrell went out.

She sat down heavily on the bed. She knew it was daft, the way she ran around after Jude. Making her dinner, cleaning her room, never saying a word to her about her behaviour, never asking her to help out around the house. Marjorie knew it was all wrong, the way things were.

It was daft, that was what it was, to be so unnerved by your own child that you spent your life tiptoeing around her, afraid to open your mouth for fear of what she might say, or do.

Because somewhere along the way, sometime in the middle of her growing up, Jude had gone wrong. There was something not normal in her, a kind of mean streak – a hardness that shook Marjorie every time she got a glimpse of it.

From early on, Jude had been a handful. She had bullied in primary school, was often in trouble for terrorising other children. She was a sturdily built girl, taller than most of her classmates and bulky with it. She had the perfect body for a bully, and she'd made the most of it.

Hardly a fortnight had gone by without Marjorie being called into the school to talk about Jude's behaviour – and once a youngish couple had arrived at the house, demanding that Marjorie keep Jude away from their daughter, who was wetting the bed every night.

What could Marjorie do? What could anyone do with a child like Jude, who snarled at you if you opened your mouth to correct her, who told you to eff off as soon as she'd look at you? Who was bigger than you when she was thirteen, and a lot stronger. Giving out to her was useless: she'd stare back at you as if she hated you, turn on her heel as soon as you stopped talking.

She'd been caught shoplifting once, in her teens. Marjorie had got a phone call at work to come and bring her home – thank God the shop hadn't pressed charges. On the bus, on the way home, Marjorie had begged Jude not to do it again, and Jude had sullenly agreed, and the very next week Marjorie had seen her wearing a new and obviously expensive watch. She'd said nothing, because what good would it have done?

And then there was the little cat, which Marjorie could hardly bear to think about, even now. The cat at Hallowe'en, hardly more than a kitten really, that had to be put to sleep after fourteen-year-old Jude and her friend Kathleen Farrell had finished with it. How could anyone torture a helpless animal for fun? There had to be something wrong with anyone who'd do that.

Maybe if Tony had stayed around, things might have been different. But he'd disappeared when Jude was still a toddler, run off with some teenager he'd met at the nightclub where he worked as a bouncer. No loss to Marjorie really, except that he might have been able to handle Jude – at least he'd have been big enough to make her listen to him.

If Jude would only look for a job, have something to do with her days, instead of staying in bed till all hours, then mooching around the house till evening, when she caked herself in make-up and dressed in what Marjorie privately considered to be extremely vulgar clothing, and headed out, night after night.

The streets were no place for young girls after dark, look at that poor man beaten up in his own shop yesterday, and that was in broad daylight. What if Jude ran into the kind of characters who'd do a thing like that, some night she was out? God knows what they'd do to a young girl, big and all as Jude was.

Surely she wouldn't go out so much if she had a job, something to get up for in the mornings. But ever since she'd failed her Junior Cert and flatly refused to go back to school, Jude had had a total of four jobs. The longest one, in a chip shop, lasted six weeks, until she came home and told Marjorie that she'd been sacked for eating a battered sausage.

When Marjorie went in to complain, the owner told her that Jude had been caught taking money from the till. Jude denied it, of course – got angry with Marjorie for butting in, told her to keep her effing nose out of other people's affairs.

These days, Jude took money from her mother's handbag whenever Marjorie forgot to keep an eye on it. Nothing was ever said about these thefts, no confrontations ever took place. Marjorie managed without the ten or twenty euro, came home with more dented tins for a while, worked an extra shift at the supermarket, coped as best she could until payday came around again. Anything for peace.

Marjorie had done what she could for Jude, had gone to Mr Mitchell in the supermarket when Jude had made it clear that she wasn't going back to school. Mr Mitchell agreed to try her out part-time, twenty hours a week, see how she got on. Marjorie had thanked him, gone home and told Jude they were looking for staff at the supermarket: would she think about applying?

And Jude had sneered at the thought of working

alongside her mother. Told Marjorie she was living in Cloud Cuckoo Land if she thought Jude was going near that dive, and that was the end of that. Marjorie went back and told Mr Mitchell that Jude was thinking about doing a secretarial course instead.

And still she tried. Oh, she tried with Jude. Brought home little treats that were barely past their sell-by date, those macaroons Jude liked, or a few buns that hadn't sold. That nice little necklace someone had handed in the other night, very like the one May had.

Marjorie knew it was wrong to take it home, of course she should have left it for someone to claim – she felt bad when some woman *did* come in the next day looking for it – but she'd thought it might soften Jude, a nice bit of jewellery like that. Take the hardness out of her for a while.

And Jude had taken it and put it on, and seemed pleased enough with it – not that she'd said much, least of all 'thank you'. But Marjorie hadn't seen it on her since, and the very next day Jude was back to her usual grumpy self – even grumpier, after her visit to the dentist.

Marjorie sighed heavily, looking around the small, messy room. Jude's clothes thrown anywhere. A jumble under the chair – for the wash, probably. Wastepaper basket overflowing, a bundled-up newspaper sticking out at the top.

Newspaper? Jude never read a paper, never read anything, not even the out-of-date magazines Marjorie brought home from work sometimes.

She reached down and pulled out the paper. As she opened it, little pieces fluttered to the ground. Wednesday's *Sun*, it was. Marjorie looked in puzzlement at the gaps in the headlines, some of the letters missing. What was Jude at, cutting up the paper?

Then she shrugged, pushed the whole lot back into the basket. No point in asking her, Marjorie would be told to mind her own effing business. She made the bed and picked up the wastepaper basket. As she reached down for the bundle of dirty clothes, something poking out from under the bed caught her eye.

A sleeve of a sweatshirt; probably could do with a wash too. Marjorie pulled it out. What was all that, spattered on the front? Paint, was it? Had Jude been— And then she saw it wasn't paint, and she dropped the sweatshirt onto the floor and put a hand up to her mouth, to stop the scream coming out.

Hilda

Terri sat back and yawned. 'God, I never knew being pregnant made you so tired. I could sleep for a week.'

Hilda smiled. 'Wait until it arrives – then you'll know all about wanting to sleep for a week.'

Terri made a face. 'Was I awful? Did you get any sleep at all?'

Hilda considered. 'The first month or so was pretty bad, but you settled a bit then.' She could have said, *You weren't as bad as Maisie, keeping her mother up all night for the first six months*, but she didn't.

'And you didn't have my father to help you out, when I was growing up.' Terri picked a bit of ham from the corner of her sandwich. 'I couldn't imagine bringing up a child on my own.'

Her face was filling out already – Hilda remembered how hers had blown up like a balloon when she was pregnant. It was strange, the thought of your own child becoming a mother. Made you think about things you normally left alone, things that could make you nervous sometimes, like mortality and eternity.

But Terri looked happy today, and that was all that mattered. As long as the baby was healthy, and Terri was happy, that was all Hilda cared about.

'So what d'you want to be called then? Granny? Gran? Nana?'

Hilda laughed. 'God, they all make me sound a million years old – I think I'll have to come up with a more flattering one. Now, any tea left in that pot, or will I make more?'

It was lovely, just the two of them chatting in the kitchen, like old times. Selfishly, she hoped Gerry wouldn't be back for ages. Surely he'd have to spend a decent amount of time with his mother in the hospital, especially with the news about the baby. And then he was going to call around to his father, to see how he was managing on his own at home. Gerry might stay and cook dinner for him, or take him out, even. They mightn't see him again till late.

And he and Terri were leaving tomorrow afternoon, both needing to be back for work on Monday morning.

With any luck, Hilda wouldn't have to be on her own with her son-in-law at all.

Because no matter how many grandchildren he provided Hilda with, no matter how happy he made her daughter, they would never have anything to say to each other.

Carmel

She lay in the bath, letting the tears flow down her cheeks and drip into the steaming water. Everything was going wrong, everything. She reached for her glass of wine – the end of the bottle she'd opened on Thursday, when everything had been perfect.

And now, just two days later . . . She took a gulp. Paul's face yesterday when he'd said those terrible things – as if he hated her. Less than twenty-four hours after she'd sat on his lap, after he'd had his hands all over her, teasing her. She drank again, trying to ignore the desire that ran through her. How could he have changed so quickly after she'd made one little mistake? How could his feelings vanish like that?

And then Pam arriving with her problems at the worst possible time. Carmel felt guilty about Pam moving back home, guilty about the relief she'd felt when Pam had told her this morning. But it was for the best – Pam had her mother, who'd be much more able to comfort her than Carmel could right now. Pam understood.

And then the bloody car packing in. She'd been on

her way back from dropping Pam home – having felt obliged to insist on doing that, at least – and out of the blue the car had stalled. Just what she bloody needed.

At least it had happened within half a mile of a garage, at least she hadn't been in the middle of nowhere. But now she was without a car, till after the weekend, they'd said. Monday evening at the earliest. And she'd got oil on her good jacket from the mechanic's car as he was driving her home. Just what she *fucking* well needed.

She sighed and reached for the almost-empty glass. The only thing she could think of to console her was that nothing else could possibly go wrong now.

Sunday

Sunshine and showers from early on, becoming more settled as the day progresses. A clear, mild night everywhere. Highs of 17 to 20 degrees.

Marjorie

It hurt to blink, like sandpaper rubbing against her eyes. Her hands were cold. She curled her fingers into her palms in an effort to warm them. Not seven o'clock yet, the day only beginning, and it felt like an eternity since she'd watched the sun come up at twenty past five. It was raining now, one of those light summery showers that you can hardly see, tiny drops floating out of the sky, making no sound when they landed.

She might be wrong; she kept coming back to that. She could have got the wrong end of the stick completely. It might have been a joke. You could cut letters out of a newspaper for any number of reasons, couldn't you? It might have been for fun, just to have a laugh with someone. It needn't have been something so awful that your mind wouldn't even let you think it.

And the blood: there might be an innocent explanation for that too. A cut finger, maybe. You could bleed an awful lot from a little cut. Remember when she'd sliced into the base of her thumb, when she was chopping up that turnip a few weeks ago? She'd thought she needed a stitch, it had bled so much. Kept coming through the plasters. And you'd hardly see the mark now.

So it might be anything. It might be totally innocent.

She hadn't said a word to Jude. She'd shoved the sweatshirt back under the bed, gone downstairs, put on the sausages and opened the spaghetti hoops as if nothing was wrong. Even chatted a bit as they ate – well, Marjorie chatted. Jude grunted or nodded. But that was normal.

And then Jude had gone upstairs and Marjorie had heard the shower going, and half an hour later Jude came down all made up, and told Marjorie she was going out. And at eleven o'clock Marjorie turned off the telly, having successfully avoided the nine o'clock news, and went up to bed. And just after half three, Jude had come in, thumping her way upstairs. And at five o'clock, Marjorie stopped trying to think of innocent reasons why you'd want to cut letters out of a newspaper, and got up.

She stirred her cold tea and waited, with dread, for what the day might bring.

*

Philip

Eighty years old, and he felt every bit of it. Golden years, my foot. Good for nothing, a burden to your family – that's all you were at eighty. Ready for the grave.

May's light tap broke into his thoughts. 'Come in.' He didn't want a fuss – the last thing he wanted was a fuss.

'Happy birthday.' May put the tray on the table by the window and opened the curtains while Philip pulled himself awkwardly into a sitting position. Then she plumped up his pillows, laid the tray on his lap, and waited for him to notice the cream envelope.

He picked it up and glanced at her before he slid his finger under the flap. 'Thanks, May.' He pulled it out and read the greeting. 'Thank you, that's nice.'

Just a card – was that all he was getting? You'd think she'd have got him something small, at least.

He cut crossly into a piece of dried-up white pudding. It wasn't every day you turned eighty. Some would say it was quite a milestone. Look at all the ones who didn't make it that far.

'Have you everything you need?'

He nodded without looking up. *Everything except a birthday present from my only daughter*, he felt like saying. *Everything except a breakfast I could look forward to.*

Happy birthday, my foot.

*

Shaun

He stood under the too-hot water, welcomed the stinging pain as he scrubbed himself clean. Later, standing in the kitchen, he wolfed a hunk of cheese and two apples, washing them down with what was left in Bernard's carton of cranberry juice.

May met him as he was leaving the house, came hurrying out of her garden towards him. 'Shaun, I was just— What's the news?'

'No change.' He wondered how long he'd have to go on saying that. 'He's still unconscious.'

'Is there anything at all I can do?'

Shaun looked wearily at her. 'Thanks, May, if you could keep an eye on things around here. I'll let you know if there's any change.' He walked towards the van, fishing the keys from his pocket.

The CCTV cameras had picked up two grainy figures leaving the shop less than a minute before Shaun had arrived. Huddling together, hoods of their sweatshirts up. One taller than the other. Probably young, from the way they moved swiftly out of the camera's range.

Impossible to identify, the guard had admitted. Useless as evidence, without something to back it up.

And nobody else, not one other shop on Kilpatrick's main street, had CCTV cameras. Bernard had been the first to have them installed, three hours before he was attacked.

*

Paul

Something happening next door. The American chap arriving home early this morning – must have stayed somewhere else last night. Hurrying into the house, looking like death warmed up. No sign of the other one, the one with the shop. Maybe they'd split up too.

Not that Paul was too bothered about what was going on next door. He had enough to concern him without worrying about the neighbours.

Francesca hadn't brought her mobile phone with her. Just left it sitting on the bed – Paul had heard it ringing as he was trying again to call her. Why would she leave a mobile phone unless she'd thought she'd never need it again?

He'd bought the phone for her when she came over. She hadn't had a mobile in Italy, didn't believe in them. Hardly ever used the one he'd given her, except to answer his calls.

Lucia's ridiculous gorilla, which Paul's parents had given her at Christmas – they'd left that behind too, sprawled across Lucia's narrow bed. And the Punto, of course, because Francesca couldn't take that on a plane. He'd checked her laptop – his laptop, he'd bought it – and found the Ryanair booking for Francesca and Lucia Tuttoro.

He'd opened her wardrobe and buried his face in the few tops and skirts she'd left behind, still with long, dark hairs clinging to one or two of them, still full of her smell. He'd slid open her underwear drawer and looked at the red basque and matching thong he'd got her on her last birthday. He remembered how she'd looked in it.

He'd filled the big bath, poured in the oil she'd left behind and taken off his clothes. But the thought of stepping in, by himself, had made him pull out the plug and listen to the scented water gurgling away.

No doubt Marietta would be leaving soon, when she got fixed up somewhere else, and then he would be left completely alone. He looked around the big, airy, empty kitchen and remembered it filled with the others. Remembered sitting around the table, listening to Lucia's chatter. Remembered how Francesca would smile at him over the top of her daughter's head.

He remembered how she hated rhubarb, loved asparagus, smothered in butter. How she would eat spare ribs, licking her fingers slowly, one by one.

And he realised, much too late, what he had thrown away.

Jack

No car again today. Was the teacher out of town? It was – what? He checked his watch. Half eleven. He debated going to the door and ringing the bell, and then he thought, *What's the point*? If she was there, her car would be too.

And if Pam was alone in the house, no way would she open the door to him.

The more he thought about Pam being at Carmel's,

the more sense it made. Of course she'd have come here when she walked out on him – women always stuck together, and she and Carmel were thick as thieves. Or at least they used to be, until he'd managed to pull them apart a little. But Carmel was still Pam's best friend – of course she'd have come straight here. And he was willing to bet she was still here, hoping he'd soon get tired of trying to find her, and give up.

Well, he could wait. He had nothing else to do all day. Someone had to come in or go out at some stage, and he'd be there when they did. He walked back to his car, half a block down on the other side of the road. Close enough for him to see any activity, far enough away not to be spotted easily.

He settled himself behind the steering wheel and peeled the foil from a strip of Juicy Fruit. Sooner or later something would happen.

Rebecca

'It's me. Are you all set for this evening?'

'All set. Pam's coming – her brother's driving her over – so dinner will be edible after all.'

'Pam's coming? I thought she wasn't going to show her face in case Psycho Man was on the lookout.'

'Well, actually, he did call around here yesterday, looking for her, but I told him I hadn't seen her. He acted all upset, said he just wanted to see her to say sorry.'

Rebecca said quickly, 'May, if he comes around

again, don't entertain him. Call the station, or call me. I really don't think Pam should be going to your house.'

'Ah no, why would he come back here? I told him Pam was leaving Kilpatrick, and I'm pretty sure he believed me.'

Rebecca was insistent. 'There's no knowing what he'll do. Promise you'll call if you see any sign of him – and keep Pam indoors. Don't let her out.'

May laughed lightly. 'God, you've such a suspicious mind. What time are you going in to work?'

'Now. I'll see you around six. And *call* me if you see any sign of him, d'you hear?'

She heard the smile still in May's voice. 'Yes, I hear and I obey.'

She hung up, frowning.

Pam

'I don't like it, Pammy. It's looking for trouble.' Her mother cut into a tomato and sprinkled it with salt. 'What if you meet him?'

Pam speared a little cube of cheese. 'Ma, Conor's driving me straight to May's house, and I won't stir outside until he comes back to collect me. And May's two brothers will be there – I'll be perfectly safe.'

'Still . . . ' Her mother looked over at Conor. 'You'll keep a good eye out for him?'

Conor nodded. 'And you lock yourself in here when we leave, and don't open the door to anyone till I get back.'

Listen to them. Listen to what he's turned them into. The sooner she was out of here, the sooner they could get back to normal. Pam was beginning to regret having promised May she'd help out – she hadn't thought Mam would be so worried about it – but she couldn't let May down now, not at this short notice.

And really, what could happen to her in broad daylight?

Carmel

She flicked through the TV guide, found Sunday. Half past three, what was on? Sport – no thanks. Nature, a documentary about the Second World War, God, so much rubbish . . . and then she saw *Poirot*, starting in twenty minutes on BBC. That'd have to do.

Her stomach rumbled, and she remembered that she hadn't had lunch. She thought about what was in the fridge – yoghurt, cucumber, cheese, pâté – and she wasn't tempted. She didn't want lunch, she wanted junk. She needed a treat after the week she'd had.

Chocolate – that was what she wanted. A big bar of Fruit and Nut, or a giant Aero – and a tube of Pringles Sour Cream with Chives. Pig out, why not? Who cared what kind of rubbish she ate now? And a bottle of wine, although the selection in the corner shop was dismal. Still, beggars couldn't be choosers.

She hauled herself up from the couch and plodded upstairs, peeling off her dressing-gown. She'd throw on a pair of jeans and a T-shirt; hopefully she'd meet nobody from here to the shop.

The fresh air was welcome after the stuffiness of the house. A nice little breeze – sky looked a bit grey, though, rain on the way. Thankfully, no sign of anyone on the street. She walked quickly in the direction of the shop.

She was unlocking the door on her way back, her purchases cradled awkwardly in her arm, when she heard, 'Hello, Carmel,' behind her.

She whirled around, almost dropping everything – she hadn't heard him come up the path behind her. 'God, Jack, you gave me a fright.' She grasped the bottle more firmly, hoped he wouldn't notice the crisps and chocolate wedged behind it.

'Sorry – didn't mean to scare you.' He looked very pale, and subdued. 'I just wanted to . . . talk to you for a minute, if you don't mind.' His glance rested for a second on the key, still stuck in the lock, then flickered to the bottle in her arms.

God, what must he think? She must look like a right wino. 'No, I don't mind, but if you're after Pam, she's not here.' She remembered, as she said the words, about all that trouble. About Pam out at her mother's house, hiding from him.

'Is she not?' His expression didn't change. 'I was hoping she was.'

'No, not any more.' Carmel thought quickly. 'She did stay here, a couple of nights, but she left yesterday.'

'Left town?' He seemed so defeated, not at all

threatening. Hard to imagine him being violent towards Pam at all. 'She really left?'

What should Carmel say? 'No – I mean, yes. Left on the bus, at about, er, six o'clock, I think it was.' God, she sounded pathetic. No way was he going to swallow that.

'Did she say where she was going?' He held his hands loosely at his sides, watching her face closely. 'Because I really need to know, Carmel. I really need to see her, and tell her how sorry I am for . . . treating her badly.' He dropped his eyes – she noticed how long his lashes were. 'I've behaved . . . very badly, but you probably know all that.'

Should she tell him? He really did seem genuine, really sounded desperately sorry . . . and he'd had plenty of time to think about what he'd done, to see the error of his ways. Didn't he deserve a second chance? Shouldn't she at least let him meet Pam and put his case to her?

As she tried to decide what was best, Jack suddenly dropped his head into his hands, and his shoulders began to shake. Jesus, was he crying?

Carmel shifted her load from one arm to the other. 'Look, I'm not sure if I should . . . '

His voice was muffled. 'I don't blame you for not trusting me – I've behaved abominably, I just wanted a chance to apologise to Pam, that's all.' He began to turn away, head still bowed. 'Thanks anyway.'

'No, hang on.' Carmel took a step towards him, still reluctant to give too much away. 'Look, Pam told me what happened between you – she's very upset.'

He nodded, keeping his eyes lowered. 'I know – I acted like a right shit, and I hate myself for it, I swear.' He lifted his head, looking pleadingly at her. His eyes glistened and he swiped a sleeve across them. 'If I could turn the clock back, believe me, Carmel, I would. I'd give anything to change what happened, honest to God.'

She bit her lip. Should she tell him? He did sound sincere – surely he deserved another chance? She shifted the bottle slightly; it was getting heavy. 'I don't know. I'm not sure if Pam would want me to tell you.'

'Oh please, Carmel.' He stepped closer then, speaking rapidly. 'Please let me know. I need to see her. I need to tell her how sorry I am. Please, you can trust me, you know you can. I just made a mistake. It'll never happen again, I swear to God.' His jaw was dark with stubble. He was almost touching her, his face was inches from hers. His eyes darted to the key again.

Carmel's mouth felt suddenly dry. She became aware of her heart thumping against her chest. He was bigger than her, and very strong. Look at those broad shoulders; he could easily force the information out of her – who was around to stop him? She had to tell him, to get rid of him. She could call Pam straight after he'd gone and let her know.

She spoke in a rush. 'Look, Pam hasn't left town yet – although she is planning to go tomorrow. She's at home, I mean at her mother's house, but she's going to May's later, there's a dinner. You'll find her there.'

The change in Jack's expression was startling. He

smiled widely, still standing too close to her. No sign of the remorse he'd been full of seconds before. No trace of tears now. 'Thanks, Carmel. You've been a big help.'

Then, before she knew what was happening, he lunged towards her and kissed her full on the mouth, hard, pushing her back against the door. The wine bottle dug into her chest. She tasted mint, felt his stubble rasping against her cheek, felt his tongue begin to – and then he stepped back.

'Enjoy your wine, and thanks again. You're great.' Then he turned and walked rapidly down the path.

Carmel stood reeling, her lips smarting. That was a bit weird, to kiss her like that. Right on the lips, almost sexual . . . her friend's husband, for God's sake. She wondered if she'd made a big mistake, telling him. Better get on to Pam right away.

But she only got Pam's voicemail, and May's phone was engaged. Carmel left messages on both and then stood uncertainly, her phone still in her hand. Was she misjudging him? Maybe he genuinely wanted to apologise to Pam. Maybe she was overreacting, letting her imagination run away with her. And really, what harm was there in a little kiss? He just acted on impulse probably, because he was so grateful to her for letting him know where Pam was.

Whatever happened now, Carmel had done all she could. Pam would get the message and be ready for him – and what could he possibly do anyway, with all those other people around? No, there was nothing to worry about. She settled down on the couch and tore the bronze-coloured paper from her Aero. As she picked up the remote control, she ran a finger over her lips.

Bet he'd be dynamite in bed.

May

Pam handed May's phone back to her. 'Sorry about that, May – she's worried about me.'

Her mother had rung, making sure that Pam had arrived safely at May's house. Calling May's phone because Pam had left hers at home.

'No problem.' May hauled the bag of potatoes from the fridge. Jack's name hadn't been mentioned by either of them. 'Conor should have come in, to say hello. I'd have liked to meet him.'

Pam smiled. 'He's so shy, I'd have had to drag him in by the hair. But anyway, he was anxious to get back to Ma.'

Her smile faded, and May said quickly, 'Is that a new top? It's gorgeous.'

Lavender edged with pale grey lace, stretched slightly over the curve of her breasts and falling softly to just below her waist. Pam shook her head. 'I've had it for ages – I just . . . haven't worn it much, that's all.'

'Suits you – shows off your figure. You usually wear looser stuff.'

A grimace flashed across Pam's face, so quickly May wasn't sure she'd really seen it. 'Not any more.' Then she opened the cutlery drawer and took out two knives.

'Right, better get started. D'you want to peel or chop?'

Marjorie

It wasn't until she missed the candlestick. If she hadn't noticed it gone, she'd have done nothing, just waited and hoped and prayed that whatever Jude might have done, whatever she might have got herself involved in, wouldn't come back to torment them.

But then Marjorie had gone in to open the sitting room curtains, and whatever look she gave to the mantelpiece when she turned around, she saw that one of the candlesticks was gone. One of the two brass candlesticks she'd been given when Granny Kilbane died was missing from the mantelpiece.

And normally Marjorie wouldn't be too bothered if she missed something, she'd just assume she'd moved it when she was cleaning, and forgotten – and anyway, what was the loss of a thing that stood useless on the mantelpiece? What call did they ever have for candles?

Except that it was one more thing Marjorie didn't understand, one more odd happening she couldn't explain.

And what had come creeping into her mind, since she had discovered its loss, was the awful, unvoiced notion that you could do terrible damage with a heavy brass candlestick. You could certainly draw blood with it. You could bash somebody's brains out with it.

By the time Jude finally got up, well after four o'clock, Marjorie knew what she had to do. She went upstairs when Jude was having her Frosties and she pulled the grey sweatshirt out from under the bed and she shoved it into a plastic bag, trying not to touch the front of it, dried and matted now.

Then she went back downstairs and out the back to the bin, and she found the newspaper with the letters cut from it, and she pushed that into the bag too. Knowing that Jude wouldn't take a blind bit of notice of her, as usual.

And when she had done that, she left the bag sitting in the hall, and she walked into the kitchen.

Jude glanced up from her cereal, and down again. A few Frosties were scattered across the table.

And her heart hammering in her ribs, Marjorie said gently, 'Jude, love, is everything alright?'

Because even now, even when she was sickeningly sure that something was terribly wrong, she was ready to help her daughter, if only Jude would ask. If only, for once in her life, she'd talk to her mother as if she was someone who mattered. If only she'd look up at Marjorie with something other than disgust in her eyes, and say, 'Ma, I've done something bad, and I need your help.'

Marjorie would help her. She'd break the law, lie under oath and go to prison for her daughter. All she wanted was to be asked.

But Jude looked up, scowling, and said, 'Course it is. Why wouldn't it be?'

And now Marjorie O'Dea walked through the doors of the Kilpatrick garda station and up to the big wooden desk, and she told the guard who sat behind it that she needed to talk to someone about her daughter. As she spoke, her voice cracked.

And the guard, whose name was Rebecca Donegan, came out from behind the desk and saw the blood-spattered sweatshirt poking from the plastic bag, and she steered Marjorie gently towards an inner room.

May

'Your father still has no idea?' Pam pulled the cauliflower apart and dropped the florets into the steamer.

'Not a clue. I gave him a card this morning and as far as he knows, that's all he's getting. I think he was a bit put out that there was no sign of a present, even though he kept insisting he wanted no fuss.'

May put the last knife beside the last plate on the table – it'd be a pretty tight squeeze but they'd manage – and then she checked her watch. 'Right, we've got about ten minutes before they start arriving. I'm going to run up and change, and you're going to make yourself a cuppa while you have a chance.'

The kitchen was filling with the smell of dinner. In the oven, the potato wedges were crisping up nicely and the pastry on the salmon and spinach pies was turning a beautiful pale gold. Pam's cheese sauce bubbled softly on the cooker, waiting to be poured over the cauliflower just before serving.

The white wine was chilling, the cutlery sparkled on the table. And Philip sat behind the closed door of the sitting room, reading his paper, completely unaware of Pam's presence.

May ran lightly up the stairs. It was all going to go fine.

Jack

He parked a block away, just to be on the safe side, and strolled unhurriedly towards May's house. A casual walker, out for a saunter on a Sunday afternoon. He smiled when he thought how easy it had been with Carmel. How she'd swallowed his sob story, just like that.

And that kiss was a stroke of genius. It had just come to him on the spur of the moment. He'd felt such a stab of triumph when she'd told him where to find Pam, he just went for it. What a laugh. Probably made her day, the sad bitch. Getting tiddly all by herself with a bottle of wine.

Of course, she probably called Pam as soon as he was gone, to tell her he was on the way, but that was OK – he knew how to handle his wife. All he needed was to get her on her own, without that other biddy poking her nose in. And the old man, he wouldn't be a problem.

As he approached the house, he slowed down. Two cars outside, parked half up on the path, right in front of the privet hedge. Visitors – just what he didn't need. He crossed to the other side of the road and leaned against a wall, pretending to adjust his watch, keeping the house in his line of vision. What now?

Pam was in there, he was sure of it. But if the house was full of other people, he needed to be careful. He'd go and get a paper, park the car a bit nearer and sit in it, wait for whoever was visiting to get lost.

It was a delay, that was all.

Philip

He should have been annoyed. Keeping it from him like that, springing it on him at the last minute, everyone arriving in on top of him, just when he was in the middle of the sports section. The boys and their wives, then Hilda waltzing in the door not ten minutes later.

The noise of them, all talking together, thrusting presents at him. Laughing at his surprised expression, William telling him he didn't look a day over seventy-nine. Gaby putting the baby on his lap.

The baby, looking up at him with those enormous blue eyes. Not a bit put out at having to sit on an old man's lap. Reaching out for Philip's finger – which looked like a giant's in his fat little fist – pulling it into his mouth, making them all laugh again.

He'd forgotten how babies felt, the powdery smell of them. How new they looked, just starting off. The fresh little whites of their eyes.

And they'd named this one Phil, after himself. Another Philip O'Callaghan. He'd have to teach it to say 'Granddad' – or maybe 'Gramps'. He'd have to think about what he wanted to be called.

He couldn't remember how old they had to get

before they'd listen to a story. He lifted a knee slightly, gave a couple of exploratory little bounces, and the baby took Philip's finger out of his mouth and his face broke into a gummy smile. And Philip smiled back, and bounced his knee again and said, 'Ride a cock horse to Banbury Cross.'

And the presents – from Cathal and Gaby, a thing for all the world like a giant furry boot that heated up when you plugged it in. Then you put your feet in, apparently, both of them, and it kept them warm. He'd never heard of such a thing, often wished for some magical solution for his chilly feet. He'd try it out the minute they were gone.

And the grey cardigan he'd got from William and Dolly, with the zip going up the front, a nice chunky end to it that he'd have no bother managing. The right size too, he'd known by looking at it.

And Hilda had given him a jigsaw, a photo of Clifden cut into five hundred pieces. Not a thing he'd ever have thought of doing, a jigsaw, but it might be good to pass the time when he was finished with the paper, and there was nothing on the telly, as usual.

Clifden, where he and Aideen had gone on honeymoon, where they'd taken the kids every summer for years, renting the same little bungalow on the coast road . . . Maybe Hilda and himself could take a drive over there some time, he might suggest it soon.

And wasn't it funny, May giving him that nut-feeder, after him thinking only the other day about the one they used to have years ago? She was going to hang it outside the sitting room window, where Philip sat with the paper every day, and he could watch the birds through the pair of binoculars May had got him too.

And then Pam appearing out of nowhere, with a tray of drinks, presenting him with a disposable camera and a little album to stick the photos into when they were developed. Already they'd taken six of big Philip and little Philip together.

And really, for something that had been sprung on him without so much as a by-your-leave, he had to admit that this whole affair was turning out pretty well.

He wondered what was cooking for dinner. Whatever it was, it smelled wonderful. He took another sip of Powers and smiled around at everyone.

Paddy

Ridiculous, how nervous he felt – like a sixteen-year-old on the way to his first date. He was thirty-five, a grown man. Mature enough to deal with whatever reaction he got from May.

Except that if it turned out badly, and she had no interest in him, he'd still have to see her every week. That wasn't something he looked forward to dealing with.

Ah well, faint heart never won fair lady, apparently. He patted the breast pocket of his shirt, heard the crinkle of the little brown envelope the jeweller had given him.

As he turned on to May's road, a man got out of a dark blue car and crossed the street ahead of him.

Pam

She squeezed around the table, pouring coffee, making sure there was enough cream in the two little jugs. At the far end, May was gathering plates. They met at the sink.

'It's gone really well – thanks a million, Pam. I'd never have pulled it off without you. I can tell you now, I was panicking at the thought of having to do it on my own.' May's face was flushed, probably from the wine. She wore a pale blue top that suited her colouring, and a rust-coloured skirt. Her hair was pinned up on one side with a slide that sparkled when the watery sun caught it.

Pam scooped more coffee into the cafetière. 'No problem, May, I enjoyed it. And I think your father's having the time of his life.'

They both looked at Philip, laughing over something with Hilda. Laughing. 'Mmm. Pity Rebecca's missing it, though. She must have been delayed at work.' She took the scoop from Pam. 'Now, will you please sit down and have some coffee? You've done more than enough running around.'

At that moment, a face appeared at the window. May tapped at it. 'Oh, poor Lonesome George – Shaun must still be at the hospital.'

Pam watched the cat mouthing a mew. 'Any more news of Bernard?'

'Nothing since this morning.' May reached under the sink and pulled out the bag of dried cat food. 'I'll just run next door and feed George – he's probably starving.'

Pam put out a hand. 'Here, give it to me. You stay and talk to the others. Where's his bowl?'

'On the patio round the back . . . ' May hesitated. 'But Pam, maybe it's better if I go – maybe you should stay inside.'

Still no mention of Jack.

Pam shook her head, craving a breath of fresh air after the overheated kitchen. 'Ah, I'll be fine, it's only next door.' She took the bag from May and opened the back door. 'Back in a sec.'

It was drizzling slightly, half sun, half rain. Pam called 'Puss, come on,' and walked ahead of Lonesome George to the front of May's house. Glanced quickly around as she opened the gate – no sign of anyone.

She walked down next door's driveway and around to the patio. Shook a scattering of pellets into the empty bowl and stood for a moment, breathing in the fresh, damp air and watching Lonesome George crunching his food. Then she came back out to the front.

And as she reached the path, she saw him. Standing by May's gate, waiting for her.

Her heart leapt at the sight of him, then pulsed steadily and painfully in her throat. The bag of cat food thumped to the ground, scattering pellets across the path.

'Pam.' He hadn't shaved. He was pale. He looked calm. She found her voice. 'What are you doing here?'

'I've come to bring you home.' One of his hands rested lightly on May's gate. She'd have to push past him to get in.

She began to shake her head slowly. 'You know I'm not coming.' The others were in the kitchen, around the back. No way would they hear if she shouted, not with all the chatter.

'Ah Pam, don't be like that.' He took a step towards her. 'You know we belong together.' Another step, while she stood frozen, watching him. 'We're made for each other, you and me.'

And then, just behind Pam, a man's voice said, 'Is everything alright?'

Paddy

As he'd got nearer, he'd realised that the man was heading into May's house. Or, at least, he had his hand on the gate – looked like he was about to go in. But now he was talking to the woman who'd appeared from the next-door garden. Maybe he was asking her for directions.

Hang on, though. She dropped something, a bag of some stuff that spilled all over the path. And neither she nor the man, who'd started walking towards her, made any effort to pick it up.

And then, as Paddy got within earshot, the man said, 'We're made for each other, you and me.' And Paddy realised, with a sinking feeling, that this was nothing as innocent as someone looking for the right house.

Bloody hell, what could he do? It looked like some kind of a scene – he'd have to intervene. He stopped just behind the woman and said, 'Is everything alright?' Hoping to God she'd look around and say yes, or even snap at him to mind his own business – that would be fine too.

But instead she turned – and Paddy recognised her face, he knew her – and she said quickly, 'No, please help me. This man is trying to force me to go with him.'

And the man, whom Paddy didn't recognise, kept his eyes on the woman's face and said, 'Look, this has nothing to do with you. Just move on, OK?' His expression didn't change, but there was an edge in his voice now.

Paddy stood his ground – what choice had he? 'Look, I don't mean to butt in, but—'

The man swung his head towards Paddy then and glared at him. 'So get lost, OK? This is between me and my wife – we'll sort it out.' He grabbed the woman's arm. 'Come on, let's go.'

She shook her head, looking frightened. 'No – I told you, I'm not going with you.' She was trying to back away from him, trying to wrest her arm from his grip.

Paddy stepped in closer, heart suddenly thumping, trying to get between them. Why was nobody else around? The little pellets crunched under his feet. He put a cautious hand on the man's arm. 'Look, she doesn't want—'

The man shoved at Paddy, making him lose his grip and stagger sideways off the path. 'Fuck off, you – this has nothing to do with you.' His face was dark with rage now, his lips curled into a snarl.

Paddy steadied himself, feeling unreal. Could this actually be happening in the middle of a quiet street on a Sunday evening? What the hell could he do? Now the woman was being dragged along the path, shouting at the man to leave her alone, let her go, shouting for Paddy to help her.

Paddy's heart was racing. He'd never in his life been involved in violence, had never found himself in a situation where he was called upon to confront anyone physically. He was absolutely terrified. But he had to do something – and it had to be fast, before he had a chance to think about the awfulness of what was happening.

Jesus Christ, I'm going to have to hit him. He strode over to the man, closing both of his hands into fists. He yelled, 'Let her go!' as he shot out with his right hand, praying that by some miracle he'd hit the man hard enough to slow him down, at least.

His punch was clumsy – it landed just under the man's armpit, barely connecting with him. But as the man struggled to hold onto the woman, she pulled away suddenly to the side, and Paddy quickly shoved his other fist straight towards the man's exposed belly, putting all his weight behind it.

The man's breath escaped with a loud whoosh, and he bent double with a groan. The woman, freed from his grasp, half ran, half fell towards May's gate, whimpering.

Paddy's fist was throbbing; he shook it to take the sting away, keeping his eyes on the man, who was still crouched on the ground, wheezing loudly. He didn't look like he'd be doing too much more of anything for a while. Paddy turned shakily towards May's gate.

He was only halfway there when the man launched himself on him – 'Fuck you, bastard!' – and grabbed Paddy by the shoulders and flung him against a parked car with a solid *whump*.

Paddy's cheek slammed into the side window, his hip connected with the door handle. He thought, as pain hammered in the side of his face, *I'm in trouble now*.

Just as the man grabbed him again by the hair, as he forced Paddy's head backwards, there was a screech of brakes – *thank Christ* – and Paddy heard rather than saw somebody *erupting* from a car and striding towards the man, and in the confusion that followed, and because of his own dazed state, Paddy couldn't be sure what caused the man to collapse on the path a moment later with a bellow of pain.

So it was with some considerable surprise that he gradually realised it was a woman who was sitting squarely on the man's back, pinning one of his arms securely against his body, tucking a phone back into her pocket and telling the man in no uncertain terms, and in far from ladylike language, what would happen if he tried to move.

*

Shaun

And just around the time that Paddy had been making contact with the parked car, at roughly the same instant that the tiny pink shell was being smashed to smithereens with the impact, Shaun woke from the light doze he'd fallen into, in the chair he'd hardly left since Friday night, and he lifted his exhausted, tear-stained face and looked straight into Bernard's opened eyes.

May

She hadn't enough chairs for everyone, even after William had brought down the two canvas ones from the bedrooms, but there was plenty of birthday cake, and lots of coffee to go round – and Pam's brother Conor seemed quite happy to be half sitting on the radiator as he ate cake and talked to May's father about fishing.

Shaun wasn't eating cake – he was still making his way through the plate of hastily reheated potato chunks smothered in cheesy cauliflower that May had put in front of him.

He hadn't planned to stay – had just called in on his way home from the hospital to tell May the good news – but it hadn't been hard to persuade him to come in and let her feed him before getting the few hours' sleep he could allow himself at last.

He had an elbow on the table, head propped up as

he forked heaps of cheesy potato into his mouth, half asleep already – or he would have been if Hilda, on her third gin, hadn't been reminiscing about her trip to Boston with a friend ten years before. Shaun was smiling tiredly at her, and even nodding every now and again, but May was willing to bet that his thoughts were far from Boston.

Bernard had regained consciousness earlier, and was breathing on his own, and didn't appear to be brain-damaged. His injuries, while still serious, were no longer considered life-threatening. Barring any new complications, he was officially out of danger. And Shaun was smiling at Hilda, and at anyone else whose eye he caught.

Rebecca wasn't listening to Hilda's holiday memories – she was too busy cooing over Phil, and telling Pam's sisters-in-law about her grandfather's seventy-fifth birthday party, six months before. 'The caterers were an hour and a half late – they got a puncture on the way. My mother nearly had a seizure, waiting for them. By the time they arrived, my grandfather was singing "She Moved Through the Fair"'

Hard to believe, listening to the happy chatter around the table now, that less than an hour ago Pam had burst into the kitchen, half crying, hardly able to talk – *hurry, please, call the police, May, he's out there* – and when they'd all rushed outside, they'd found Rebecca looking totally unfazed, with a knee planted solidly in Jack Treacy's back as he lay on the path.

'Hello everyone, everything's under control now.

I've just called for back-up, they should be along any minute.' She jerked her head to the side. 'Someone might look after that man there – he probably needs some ice.'

Only then did they notice the blond-haired man who was half sitting on the bonnet of Hilda's car, feeling his cheek gingerly and looking sheepish. A dark pink streak ran down the left side of his face.

It was him. It was the postman. May's hand flew to her mouth, as Pam, who had followed them all outside, stepped forward and spoke quietly: 'What happened?'

He tried to grin, then thought better of it. 'Er, I whacked my face against the car just now – don't think it's too serious, but it's stinging a bit.'

Pam pressed his cheek gently. 'Come into the house, I'm a nurse. I'll take a better look at it inside.' She kept her face turned from the scene on the path.

Rebecca spoke again as they walked away. 'Go on in with them, May – there's nothing more to be done out here.' And May must have imagined the wink. Rebecca couldn't possibly have winked at a time like that.

Even as she spoke, a police car turned into the road and stopped outside the house. As soon as the two male guards got out, Rebecca released her hold on Jack. They pulled him to his feet and bundled him into the car.

Back in the kitchen, they put ice on the postman's cheek, which Pam pronounced not to be broken. 'You'll probably have a bit of bruising for a few days,' she told him.

He held the ice-filled tea towel to his cheek with one hand and cradled the brandy that Rebecca had insisted on pouring for him in the other, and as the kitchen filled up again, and everyone found a place to sit, May tried hard not to eavesdrop when he began to chat to her brothers. She did her best not to listen as he told them about the woodworking classes he'd been taking for nearly a year now, then described the bird table he'd recently put together, his most ambitious project to date.

Bird table? May shook her head. Something wasn't making sense.

'He was great,' Pam told May as they stood together at the sink. 'You could see he hadn't a clue what to do, but he really tried to help me. So chivalry's still alive and well in Kilpatrick.' She looked across at Paddy. 'I was very lucky he came along when he did.'

'Mmm.' May was trying hard not to keep glancing towards him – he'd already caught her at least twice.

'His name is Paddy,' Pam said.

'Right.' May heard William laughing at something the postman had said, and wished she knew what it was.

'Paddy O'Brien,' Pam said. 'I knew his sister Iseult years ago – we met in Irish colleges a few times. He used to come and visit her at weekends. Funny, him turning out to be our postman years later.'

May turned slowly towards her. 'What?'

'Iseult. I met her—'

'No – I mean, what's his name?'

Pam looked at May strangely. 'Paddy. Paddy O'Brien.'

And slowly, May began to piece it all together. Paddy O'Brien, whose garden she'd been tending for months now. Who she'd been sure must be a carpenter, or a woodworker of some kind, because of the wood and the tools around the place, and because of the beautiful bird table that had appeared in the garden. Clearly hand made – and who else but a carpenter could put together something like that?

But he wasn't a carpenter at all, she'd been wrong about that. He was a postman who played with wood in his spare time.

Suddenly she remembered Rebecca saying that she'd seen the postman – seen Paddy, across the table – with another woman, with his arm around someone, just a few days ago. But Paddy O'Brien, whose garden she tended, clearly lived on his own . . . so it sounded like he and this woman Rebecca had seen weren't married. Maybe they weren't even serious about each other, maybe it was just a casual thing. May wished she knew, wished he'd get up and come over to her and explain.

And soon after that Shaun had arrived, and everyone had more coffee or wine to go with the story of Bernard, and for once, Philip was perfectly civil to Shaun, telling him he'd been sorry to hear about Bernard.

And half an hour after that, Pam had stood and reached for her coat. 'I think I'm getting a signal from Conor. Time to get moving.'

May walked out with them to the car, her arm through Pam's. 'Are you alright?'

Pam nodded. 'I will be.'

'What do you think you'll do now?'

Now that Jack is safely bundled away. She knew the same thought was flashing through Pam's head.

Pam paused, her hand on the car door. 'I don't know, May. I just don't know what's going to happen.' She watched as Conor walked around to the driver's door. 'I haven't a clue.'

May hugged her. 'Don't think about it tonight. I'll call you tomorrow evening, and we can have a chat. You need to have a long sleep now.' *And then maybe you'll be ready to consider my idea.*

Pam nodded. Then, as she got into the car, she looked back up at May. 'Enjoy the rest of the night now, alright?'

In the darkness, May couldn't be sure whether she was smiling.

She watched the car pulling away. *Enjoy the rest of the night.* She turned to go back indoors, and Shaun was there.

'May, I'm off.' He was shrugging into his jacket. 'I'll be back in the hospital tomorrow, but when I get home again you're gonna tell me why that handsome postman has been sitting in your kitchen making eyes at you all evening. Has it something to do with the bruise on his cheek? Did he declare undying love, and did you slap his face for being cheeky?'

May laughed. 'Nothing like that, I'm afraid.

Tell Bernard I'll see him when he's up to it. Sleep well.'

Making eyes at her? That was just Shaun's usual teasing. Wasn't it?

Back in the kitchen, May's sisters-in-law were putting on their coats and bundling Phil into a tiny puffy jacket, and Rebecca was filling two hot water bottles, and Hilda was looking distractedly for her handbag, while she organised some kind of trip with Philip. 'Next Saturday, if the weather is fine. We'll talk about it in the morning.'

And Paddy O'Brien would probably have felt obliged to leave too, out of politeness, if Rebecca Donegan hadn't poured him a fresh cup of coffee without asking him if he wanted it – and adding a generous dollop of brandy to it without clearing that with him either – so he was still sitting at the table, watching everyone else making a move.

When they'd all driven off, and Hilda had made her way upstairs to the tiny spare room, Rebecca turned to Philip. 'Now Mr O'Callaghan, you mustn't dream of doing the washing up – you look exhausted. I'm going to walk you and your hot water bottle upstairs to bed, and then the rest of us' – winking at Paddy and May – 'will tidy up down here. It won't take us half an hour.'

And Philip, who hadn't had the least notion of doing the washing up, left his chair as hastily as his eighty years would allow, and walked out of the kitchen on Rebecca's arm.

And as soon as the door closed behind them, Paddy,

whose left eye was now swelling impressively, and who was starting to feel the effect of the brandy, pulled a little brown envelope from his shirt pocket and emptied the broken chain and bits of pink shell into his hand, and looked across the table at May O'Callaghan and said, 'I believe you lost this.'

Marjorie

She took two pairs of clean pyjamas from the chest of drawers and added them to the bag that already held Jude's dressing-gown, slippers and clean underwear. If she didn't think about it, she'd be alright. Keep busy, that was what she had to do.

She took T-shirts and jeans from another drawer and put them on top of what was already packed, and then she filled her pink toilet bag with Jude's toothbrush, hairbrush and moisturiser, and a new bar of soap and the half-empty tube of toothpaste that they never remembered to squeeze from the bottom.

It would take three-quarters of an hour to walk back to the police station. She'd hand the bag to whoever was behind the desk and tell them it was for Jude O'Dea, who'd been brought in earlier, and then she'd turn around and walk home again. It would keep her busy, the walk. She might even come the long way home, not get back here till it was nearly time for bed.

And she was on the early shift tomorrow, so that was good. She'd go to Mr Mitchell at her break and ask him if she could have extra shifts, as many as he had. As long as she kept busy, that was the main thing.

Because if she had a chance at all to think about what her daughter had done, there was a strong possibility that Marjorie O'Dea would bring home a bottle of vodka from the supermarket and use it to wash down the almost-full bottle of sleeping pills that she kept in the small white locker by her bed.

Pam

Her mother's hands twisted and untwisted the tea towel. 'I still can't believe he was there, at May's house. Oh God, Pam.'

Pam caught her hands and held them. 'Mam, I keep telling you – he didn't lay a finger on me. I'm only letting you know now because it's all over – he's been taken into custody. It's finished.'

'But how do you know he—'

'Mam, look at me.' Pam waited. 'Look. I'm fine, I'm not hurt. Jack wasn't able to hurt me. He'll never hurt me again.' She paused, her mother's hands still held tightly. 'And you know what else? May asked me tonight what I was going to do now, and I told her I didn't know.' She looked down at their clasped hands, and then up again. 'But Mam, I know one thing – I'm not leaving Kilpatrick. My life is here, and I'm staying.'

'And if he's let out, and if he—'

'I'll be fine, Mam, honest. Whatever hold he had

over me is gone. Whatever happened tonight, I know he can't hurt me any more.' Pam shook her mother's hands gently for emphasis. 'I'll be fine. Believe me.'

And looking into Pam's steady gaze, her mother believed her.

Paddy

'Lord God almighty.' Iseult's hands flew to her face. 'What happened to you?'

Paddy smiled, feeling the dull tug of an ache, and not caring at all. 'It looks worse than it is – doesn't really hurt unless I touch it.' Already that side of his face was darkening. By morning, as Pam had predicted, he'd have a very definite black eye.

But well worth it, all things considered.

Iseult was still staring at him. 'You either walked into a door or someone thumped you – and yet you look like the cat that got the cream. Are you going to tell me what happened or do I have to beat it out of you?'

'I'm going to tell you what happened.' Paddy put an arm around her shoulders and steered her back inside. 'I've had enough beating for one night.'

Iseult wrapped her arm around his waist as they walked. 'Is there a happy ending?'

Paddy's smile widened, his cheek aching in protest. 'Oh, indeed there is.'

Yes, all things considered, it had been very well worth it.

May

'So he's under arrest?'

'Not yet – just cooling off in a cell overnight. We'll see what he has to say for himself in the morning. If he's still moaning about police brutality, we'll hit him with disturbing the peace. That should hold him for a while. But we need Pam to press charges – I told her that tonight.'

'I think she will now, after what happened.'

'Good. That fellow needs locking up.'

'Actually, I had a bit of an idea about Pam, over the past couple of days . . . I'm wondering if she'd like to come and work for me.'

'I thought she already did.'

'No, I mean helping me with my own work, painting and stuff. I have more enquiries than I can cope with – and really, it would be so much easier if I had transport. Pam can drive, we could get a second-hand van – and she'd be great at all that stuff. She's a hard worker and so capable. We painted Carmel's room together on Friday, and we flew through it.'

'Well, you seem to have it all worked out – but who'd look after Father O'Callaghan?'

'I don't know – I'd have to find someone else, I suppose. I could ask the au pair at Paul and Francesca's tomorrow morning, when I go round there. She might have a friend she could recommend.'

'Worth a try, I suppose.'

'Mmm . . . and isn't it great about Bernard? Shaun looked so happy tonight.'

'Yeah – oh, I couldn't say anything earlier, but we've got a lead on that too.'

'You have? You know who did it?'

'We've got a pretty good idea, yes. We brought two into custody, and get this – they're females.'

'What?'

'Teenagers, but hard as nails. I was there when they brought them in – two right tough cases, one of them as big as any man. Her mother gave us the information – you should have seen her, such a worn-down little creature.'

'Poor thing.' May wondered if Rebecca was ever going to ask. She counted to three in her head.

'So anyway…the night was a success?'

May smiled. 'Great. They all seemed to enjoy it, didn't they?'

'May O'Callaghan, you know very well I'm not talking about your father's birthday party. I'm asking how the night went after I took your father up to bed – in a manner of speaking.'

'Yes – and never reappeared. I might have known you'd do a runner.'

'Well, I figured if anything was going to happen with that nice young postman you've been panting over forever, and who you kept staring at all night, I'd better make myself scarce.'

'Oh God – was it that obvious?'

'Only to me, who sees everything. And he was staring at you just as much. So clearly I got it wrong about the other woman.'

'You did – he's unattached. I'm guessing it was his sister Iseult you saw. She lives a few doors up from him.'

'Funny-looking, wild hair? Weird clothes?'

May laughed. 'That's Iseult. And I know her. I met her before – remember? She's the one who contacted me in the first place to ask me if I'd do his garden.'

'What do you mean, do his garden? You were working in the postman's garden and you didn't know it?'

'Well, we never met, so I never knew it was him. I thought it was a completely different man who owned that house – you know, the one I go to on Thursdays.'

'Good God, you couldn't make it up. So tell me, what did he have to say for himself?'

So May, giggling, told Rebecca about the necklace.

'He was the one who gave it to you? So you've got it back now?'

'Well . . . kind of. It's all there, but I won't be wearing it any more.'

She heard Rebecca's deep sigh at the other end of the phone line. 'I've had at least two brandies too many, and I have work at eight in the morning. I would appreciate not having to drag this episode out of you, word by word.'

After she'd hung up, May filled her rucksack with what she needed for the morning's work, then went upstairs to bed, where of course she didn't sleep.

'What is it?' She asked him, unable, at first, to make sense of the squiggle of gold and pink that had tumbled into his palm. And then, before he'd had a chance to answer, she said, 'Oh,' and picked a tiny piece of pink shell from his palm. 'Oh, it's—' And she looked up at his face again, and he had the loveliest expression, all shy and hopeful and nervous. She reached across and took his hand and tipped all the pieces of the necklace into hers, and said, 'Thank you. I love it. I was wondering what happened to it.'

She threw back the duvet, got out of bed and rummaged in the chest of drawers for the envelope. *Mai*, it said, he'd written *Mai*. Not *May*, which suddenly seemed terribly old-fashioned. May was the person whose heart Gerry Scanlon had broken. It was May who'd cried herself to sleep for weeks, months, even. Who'd been far too afraid after that to look at anyone else.

Until she'd begun to notice the postman, and to wonder if she'd ever dare . . . And tonight, as Paddy O'Brien reached across the table and took her hand for the first time, as he told her about all the times he'd wanted to talk to her, to ask her out, she realised that her second chance had finally come.

His kiss, on the doorstep, was the sweetest thing. His hand, cradling her head, twining his fingers in her hair.

May was gone. From now on she'd be *Mai*. Ready, at last, to begin again.

She tucked away the envelope, slid the drawer closed and got back into bed.

And So It Goes

And as Sunday evening passes slowly into memory, the time has come to leave Kilpatrick, and the scattering of its inhabitants who criss-crossed through the days of the past eventful week.

Time to leave Pam Treacy, sitting dry-eyed in a blue dressing-gown at her old bedroom window, a cooling, skin-topped mug of Ovaltine by her elbow on the sill.

And time to leave Carmel Gannon, sleepless and headachy from the wine earlier, deciding never, ever to look at another man. Although that mechanic was quite attractive, if you could ignore the missing tooth.

Time to let Paul Ryan alone with his regrets, with his doomed plan to follow Francesca back to Italy. Little realising, but soon to find out, how her family feels about his infidelity.

Time to tiptoe away from Shaun, deeply, happily asleep, and Bernard, lying unmoving in his hospital bed, morphine dripping steadily into his arm, trying to make sense of the confusion that had surrounded him since he'd woken up.

And Marjorie O'Dea, tossing through the sleep that three pills and warm milk finally brought, who'll wake with wet eyes before the alarm goes off and wonder why, in the instant before she remembers.

Just as well she can't hear her daughter now, kicking the door of her little barred room, shouting obscenities at the guards outside. Poor Marjorie.

And Rebecca? Sleeping the untroubled sleep of the truly good, as always. Snoring loudly – happily just out of earshot of her son across the landing.

And time to leave Paddy O'Brien with his battered face, lying awake in his bed, too full of May to close his eyes. Too happy to care. And Iseult, three doors down, buried under her summer duvet, dreaming of something that makes her chuckle suddenly in the dark.

Philip O'Callaghan, eighty years and a few hours old, isn't dreaming. But he's asleep, which is enough to keep him happy, these days. On the floor by the bed is the foot-warmer, which he tried out earlier, closing his eyes as the heat stole gently around his toes.

And Hilda in the little room next door, nudged into sleep by three of May's generous gin and tonics. What's a little headache the next morning when you've closed your eyes for a whole eight and a half hours?

And time now to leave May – *Mai* – falling into sleep and falling into love, and who's to say but that love will last this time around?

Let's hope so.

Permission Acknowledgements

'Let It Grow' by Eric Clapton. Featured on *461 Ocean Boulevard*, published by Polydor (1974).

Despite our best efforts, the publisher was unable to contact all copyright holders prior to the publication of *The Last Week of May*. The publisher will make the usual arrangements with any copyright holders who make contact after publication.